YOUR RESTING PLACE

David Towsey

Jo Fletcher
BOOKS

First published in Great Britain in 2015 by Jo Fletcher Books
This edition published in 2017 by

Jo Fletcher Books
an imprint of
Quercus Publishing Ltd
Carmelite House
50 Victoria Embankment
London EC4Y 0DZ

An Hachette UK company

A CIP catalogue record for this book is available
from the British Library

PB ISBN 978 1 78206 443 5
EBOOK ISBN 978 1 78429 040 5

10 9 8 7 6 5 4 3 2 1

Typeset by Jouve (UK), Milton Keynes
Printed and bound in Great Britain by Clays Ltd, St Ives plc

For Grandpa, *i.m.*,
who never understood where I got
such 'bloody strange ideas'

PROLOGUE

Walter had five bodies on the bed of his wagon. Judging by the clean holes through their heads, they'd stay that way. He liked that: one less thing to worry about. They weren't bleeding much, either. The boards of his wagon were stained plenty already; the rusty smell was a constant, as were the specks. But it was important to keep the bed clean. He had a reputation to think of.

He waited on the edge of Pine Ridge until dawn, and then waited some more. Law-Man Miller was not an early riser. Walter couldn't fault him for that – Pine's trouble kept late hours. He licked his lips at the memory of whiskey and took a slug from his water-skin, then grimaced; he didn't have the imagination to fool his mouth. Collect from the Law-Man first, then see to Patches and the wagon, and then a soft bed and a soft body. He rubbed the base of his back. He'd earned a little respite. He glanced at the bodies in the wagon. A canvas sheet covered all but their feet.

'I too have earned it!'

They stayed silent.

He rubbed his nose and was shocked at the chill of his finger. He'd waited long enough. The first flick of the reins had no effect. He leaned over to find Patches asleep. The shaggie's talent for sleeping standing up rankled him and he slapped the reins harder. He was pleased with the resulting snort as Patches lurched forward, the wheels creaking their own protest. They were all idle – he was the only one in this outfit who understood hard work. As he rolled into Pine Ridge, he figured he might be the only one in the whole county.

The streets were empty: not just the main thoroughfare, but the side streets and alleyways. He was relieved to see a mouser scratching at the side of a tanner's shop – he was starting to worry that this was a dream. Dreaming of coming to town with a full wagon wasn't new to Walter, and it was after those dreams that he generally thought seriously about his line of work. He waved to the mouser. Its contempt was real.

He pulled up outside the Law-Man's building, one of the smaller places on the thoroughfare. It was just a single storey; the windows were barred and the door was reinforced with heavy studs. He eased himself down from the seat, his cold joints popping with the first few steps, and knocked on the door with the side of his hand, hitting one of the studs. He cursed under his breath.

'He's not in yet.'

The face at the window had a rough red beard with plenty of knots and what looked like bits of food tangled in the hair. That and his nose were all that poked through the bars.

'Many of you in there?' Walter said.

'Just me and two old-timers. If they're still breathing.'

'Will you shut it?' a voice came from inside.

'Drink, was it?' Walter said.

'Don't remember. S'ppose he'll tell me.'

Walter sat down on the narrow porch, shifting until his back was comfortable against the wall. Miller shouldn't be too late if last night's duties were limited to three scruffy drunks.

'Full load, I see,' the bearded man said.

'For once.'

'What'd they do this time?'

'Does it matter?' Walter said.

'Don't you wonder?'

'I just collect. The things I wonder about happen after that.'

The man spat through the bars. 'Bet you don't even find out their names, do you?'

Walter noticed a streak of dried mud on his boot. He took out his pistol and scraped away the flakes.

'Do you?' the man shouted.

'Quit your noise, Robson,' someone said, and Walter looked up to see Law-Man Miller coming round the corner of the building. His deputy, a large lad with small eyes, followed close behind.

Miller tipped his hat when he saw Walter. 'Morning,' he said.

'So it is.' Walter stood with some difficulty.

Miller made no offer to help. 'Full wagon today.'

'That's what I said,' Robson squawked.

Walter led the Law-Man and his deputy to the back of the wagon. He pulled back the sheet with a little flourish. Five dead men, eight pistols still in their holsters. Five hats. Ten boots. One or two pockets bulged with who-knew-what. Walter made sure their possessions were easy to see; he wasn't a thief.

'Recognise them?' he said.

'Do you?'

Walter laughed awkwardly, unsure if Miller was joking. "Course I do – every one's on a poster.' He pointed towards the Law-Man's office and the wall that was papered with faces.

The deputy – Lacey or Macey, something like that – went to the side of the wagon and lifted one man's hat to get a better look.

'You working alone these days?' Miller said.

'Henry's off planting crops.'

'And these – all the same gang?'

Walter spread his hands. 'Who can tell, with all their comings and goings?'

'All clean shots,' Macey said – it was definitely Macey. 'One here, one here.' He pointed at his head and then his heart.

Miller glanced up and down the street. 'You'd best come in. Put the bodies in the back, Deputy.'

Macey set to, ignoring the jibes of the bearded prisoner.

Inside the office, Miller put his hat on his desk. 'Sit,' he said.

Walter did as he was told, and Miller put his hands on the desk, palms down, and leaned forward. Walter noticed his greying ponytail was tied tight back today.

'You can stop pissing up my wall now, Walter.'

'Wh—?'

'As in: I know how small the cock is, despite the display. That's not your work out there.'

'I don't follow,' he said.

'Yes, you *do*. You've brought in bodies before with more lead in them than bone.' He turned to the wall of posters, examined them for a moment, then yanked five from their pins. 'And now you bring me half a gang threaded as neatly as needles.'

'Well, there's no need—'

'Walter, if these posters are right, this isn't just a bunch of roughs. You're talking about guns who ride with the Pastor's boy.'

He sighed. 'Does it really matter? They're here . . .'

'That's not what I'm worried about. I'm worried about who *isn't* here, who *isn't* sitting in that chair claiming their bounties.'

'You know already though, don't you?' he said.

'I could take a guess.'

'Is it my fault she don't bring in the bodies?'

Deputy Macey came into the office, his smile so big his eyes were lost completely amongst the wrinkles. 'They say she can't be killed. Not like Walkin' normally can, anyhows,' he said.

Walter had to shift bodily in his chair to confront the deputy. 'And how do you know who we're talking on?'

'Oh, Deputy Macey has made her a special project,' Miller said.

'They say it's because she drowned: so burning her would be like trying to set fire to a wet log.'

Walter shook his head. 'Are you hearing this?' he said to Miller.

'The Drowned Woman – that's what they're calling her.'

'I don't care what she's called, even if it is as stupid a name as that. If she don't want the bounties, then I do.'

'She just leaves the bodies there, out in the sun, ready for the blightbirds?' Miller said.

Macey came over to him and stood real close. 'Have you seen her?'

'From afar,' Walter said, undoing the top button of his shirt. 'And yes, she leaves 'em where they fall.'

'You're not there when it happens?' Miller said.

'No.'

'You don't chase her off?'

'Are you serious?' Walter said.

'I need to hear you say it.'

'No. I just cart 'em to town, is all.'

'Picking over the bones,' Miller said.

'I'm not getting any younger.'

'Come on then.' The Law-Man picked up his hat. 'Let's make sure it's them.'

Macey led the way. He had laid out the bodies under an

overhanging roof. Walter dabbed at his forehead with a handkerchief and then kept it pressed to his face, to mask the too-sweet smell of rot. Funny he'd not noticed it in the wagon.

Law-Man Miller looked at his first piece of paper, then dropped the poster on the chest of one of the men. The resemblance was clear as day. The number at the bottom would buy a drink and some company. Times that by five and it would be a good week. Or a bearable month.

Miller paused at the final body. 'Deputy, you know little Billy Crawford, lives on Upper Lane?' he said.

'My second cousin, Martha, she learns her letters with Billy.'

'Would you fetch him?'

As Macey hustled between the houses and was soon lost to sight, Walter asked, 'Problem, Law-Man?'

'This here is Arthur Crawford, Billy's pa.'

'Oh.' Walter peered at the slack, clean-shaven face. 'Wouldn't Mrs Crawford want to know too?'

'No, I don't reckon she would.'

As they waited in silence for the deputy, Walter edged away from the bodies as much as he could without making it obvious. He couldn't settle on whether it was better to breathe in through the nose or the mouth – more years than he could remember in the job and there was still no getting used to that smell.

Macey returned holding the hand of a skinny, dark-haired boy. Billy was wide-eyed, and Walter could see he was shaking a little.

The Law-Man said, 'You're not in trouble, Billy.'

The boy, so young he couldn't have been into double figures, almost collapsed in relief. When he smiled he was missing most of his teeth – but no one else was smiling and he soon stopped.

'Come here, boy. I want you to see this,' Miller said. The Law-Man put his hands on the boy's shoulders. 'This is your pa, Billy.'

The boy stared dumbly at the body. Macey had closed the eyes, though there was still the matter of the hole in the head. Walter wished he were back at the wagon or, even better, in the saloon – this boy's grief was none of his business – but there weren't any tears. Billy stood there until the deputy came and led him away. The boy didn't even look back.

Walter whistled through his teeth. 'That's left me cold.'

'How so?'

'I hope someone weeps when I go.'

'Don't lose sleep over it,' the Law-Man said. 'Billy never met his pa.'

BOOK ONE

BOOK ONE

1 : 1

The summer sun was hotter than a cornered mouser. Ryan pulled his straw hat down till it almost covered his eyes, though the sun still went on through to most of his neck and shoulders; dead-lies and the seasons had eaten away at it. He chewed on a hay stalk like he'd seen the men do.

Stepping onto the lowest beam of the fence, he looked out across their one field. The hay was getting tall, and no amount of looking would get the harvest done; the army man was late. Crops were being worked all along the low hills. The McGraw fields were already on their second cut. He bounced on the beam, half hoping it would break.

He turned his back on one mess only to face another. Their house squatted at the top of a long slope leading down to the road. Between the road and the house was an old corral that hadn't seen use in years, and a chook house with half the chooks already dead and eaten. They had sold the neats two summers back; fat Simmons, with his sweaty hands and busy eyes, taking pity and paying for what he could've stole.

Ryan headed over to the well, kicking any stones in reach. They rattled across the dry dirt. One hit the back wall of the house and he waited for a shriek, but it didn't come. It wasn't long past noon; she'd still be drunk. At the well he lowered the bucket, rattling it all the way down. It might remind her of what went on outside and piss on her morning.

Despite his racket, today was too peaceful for that. Even the chooks didn't start a fuss when he took them the water. The heat might have slowed their senses, still, he didn't take any chances: they were a malicious bunch. Chooks and mothers were created under the same bad moon – they made soothing sounds, all right, but there was evil in every eye and their claws were knife-sharp. The sickly warm smell of chook shit, old and new, made Ryan gag. He filled up their water bowl with one hand over his nose.

They would need feeding later, a few handfuls of seed from the bag that sagged against the house. It was half seed, half wheatle now, but the chooks weren't worried. Loveless, demon-eyed chooks. He kicked a stone at their house and even that raised nothing more than a warble from them.

'Ryan!' his ma screamed. She was standing in the doorway glaring out at the world. 'What are you doing out here?' She leaned hard on the frame. She was wearing nothing but a nightdress: a string of bones topped by lank black curls.

'Morning, Ma.'

'Don't you sass me. Where's the—?' She belched and spat onto the porch. 'Where's my eggs?'

'I'll see to them d'rectly, Ma.'

'Well then. Don't go waiting for them to hatch, eh?' She stumbled back into the house.

He took the bucket back to the well. Taking off his hat, he scratched the sore on his head. It was dry today. He checked over the field again. Them soldiers had better come soon or he'd have to watch it all rot, as useless as a bucket full of holes. He took two logs from the woodpile, which left a big empty space where the pile should've been. There weren't any trees worth chopping down on the McDermott farm. At least he now had a reason to be away from the house that night; sometimes his ma thought that was important when she had company; other times she didn't seem to care. First he'd steal the axe and then steal the wood – or maybe just steal the wood, depending on where McGraw chained up his rufts.

'I told you not to move that damn chair,' Ma yelled. She could've been bawling right in his ear, the gaps those walls had. There was a crash, likely the chair hitting the table. Even drunk, she had a wiry strength.

Hefting a log in each hand, just in case, he went round to the front of the house and peered in. Ma was sitting, arms crossed, at the small table, which had been shoved up against the wall. The other chair was lying on the floor. One leg was missing.

'That'll need fixing,' she said. She must have eaten the leg; it was nowhere he could see.

The bedroom door was shut. There were marks on the floor where he'd dragged his pallet out. He remembered kicking at it, just to see the dust cloud up – did he move it last night, or was it the night before? Either way, he'd slept by the cooking fire that he'd managed to keep going on hope and ashes, warmed by the embers, trying not to hear. When he needed to, he went and did his business outside, at the far end of the field, then walked back slowly. His ma wasn't so picky.

He'd swept the floor that morning whilst she was sleeping, but now he was bringing it all back in. There was black stuff between the floorboards; who knew what that was? He opened the stove and shoved one of the logs in.

His ma was drumming her fingers on the table. He washed his hands in the bucket while the pan heated up.

'There any bread?' his ma said.

It was four days old, and mould covered half of it. He hacked off the bad bits, then cut the rest into slices that hissed as he dropped them into the pan.

'I don't want it *cooked*,' she said.

'You don't want it like rock neither.'

He had broken one of the yokes as he'd dropped them into the pan; he put that egg on his plate.

'You eat like a mouse – look at you, all elbows and wrists.' She seized his arm with one of her claws. Her nails were bitten to the quick. 'I am cursed with weak men.'

He'd given her three eggs, taken just one for himself.

Ryan wasted the afternoon hours in the shade behind the house, throwing stones and watching any critter that moved, while his ma sobered up. She found him there as the sun started to get red, all colours of angry. She'd had a wash and her cheeks had a little colour. She'd changed into a flowery cotton dress, not her best but it had only one hole, which she had patched over using cloth from an old red blouse so the patch looked like a faded bloodstain. She wasn't smiling, but she wasn't glaring either.

'We got washing to do,' she said, and he got up and followed her into the house.

Ma came out of the bedroom with a bundle of sheets. The broken chair was leaning against the wall. Chances were she couldn't remember lunch. He picked up the table, turned it sideways, and started for the back.

'No, Ryan, put it in the sun.'

She was ready with the soap and a small pruning knife that had rusted near the handle. She shaved three slices of soap into the water and started scrubbing. His job was to drape the clean clothes over the fence. Left out overnight they would be icy-cold by morning, though mostly dry. Both of them knew this was a chore that should be done early, and they both knew why it wasn't.

'My ma used to make me wash my own clothes, all on my own,' she said. 'She was a hard woman – not soft on me, like I am on you.'

He knew better than to disagree. 'Do you miss your ma?'

'Of course.' She wiped her brow. 'We fought plenty, but she's my mother.'

'Will she ever come visit?'

'Someone's coming over tonight,' Ma said eventually. 'An important man.'

That meant his pallet stayed out. If he got back too early from thieving McGraw's wood he'd have to stuff his head under a pillow if he was to get any sleep.

'You'll like him; he rides a big white courser. Deep pockets.'

He didn't want to hear it.

He went to the fence and wrung out a pair of cotton trousers, the cloth straining in his fingers. His stomach was bile and his breath was hotter than coals.

He stood for a while, watching her as she fought with a sheet. She'd tied her hair back, but stray curls kept slipping out. Her face looked rounder and her skin warmer as she worked. Her arms were too skinny and the black marks under her eyes never went away, but maybe she was pretty.

She passed him the sheet. It still smelled of men and their business.

1 : 2

Night dropped slowly onto the hills around the house. The scrapers started their wasteful noise and Ryan was glad for it. He was sitting in front of the stove, making a show of looking after the fire. Ma was at the table. They were both waiting on the dark. She lit a tallow candle, its stink cloying beyond its little bubble of light. He put on his jacket. His skin was pale through the holes.

'Where are you going?'

'We need wood.'

She'd put on her rouge and done her lips, though she didn't go as far as the women in Fort Davis. 'You be careful,' she said.

He stopped by the door and pulled on his wool hat. There was a box of nine or ten little bottles, all empty, waiting to be taken away. They clinked like a handful of coins as he slammed the door behind him.

The air was as clear as spring water and almost as cold. There wasn't a cloud to block out the stars. He nearly turned back into the house, considering his chances against McGraw and his rufts pretty poor in such light. But they needed wood. He picked up the stick he favoured for walking and headed down the track. His feet were slipping around inside his pa's old boots like two drunkards trying their first barn dance. Most of his clothes had been his pa's, left behind like the farm, like his ma and him, before he was old enough to be wearing proper clothes. The man couldn't have been particularly fat or tall, though the clothes still hung loose on the boy's shoulders. The brown woollen trousers were rolled up, the legs each kept in place by a couple of stitches.

As he passed the chooks they gurgled away inside their house. The corral stood quiet as a graveyard; fenceposts were headstones marking where neats had once been. He pulled his hat further over his ears and shivered.

The end of their track bled into the main drag which ran from the foothills to the Fort some miles away. If he followed that meandering trail he would come to the front of McGraw's farm, but quickest was straight through the woodland that blessed that miser's land. The trees would spit him out at the back of the house, right at the woodpile. Which side the rufts were chained to: that was something Fate would decide.

In the woods he thumped his stick on the dry ground as hard as he dared; hushts weren't the only thing needed scaring off. The trees looked thirsty. Some were dry to the bone, as naked as a newborn, and had low branches he could snap right off, but they'd barely be a nibble for the fire. Other trees were covered in needles or sharp leaves and had long branches that clawed at you. He stepped carefully between those old-timers, knowing one might swallow him whole out of spite.

The feebleness of Ryan's situation was not lost on him. The gift of knowing when you were feeble was a McDermott family heirloom. He was walking through a field of wood, all of it waiting to be harvested, to steal another man's labour. The half-mile or so of woodland gave him plenty of time to stoke his shame.

The spectre of McGraw floated between the trees as Ryan thumped along in his oversized boots and with his beat-up stick. His ma's sole comment on the man was: he's a widower from the East. That was all there was to it, to her mind. That he had no wife explained the dirty, matted hair, how bad he smelled, and the mess of a house. But it didn't explain the temper.

To Ryan, the bigger mystery was how McGraw chopped down trees with only one hand. The boys at the Fort figured the other was a hook, somehow surgeoned on, though no one had ever seen it. McGraw wore a long jacket the whole year round.

A watcher hooted somewhere; a big noise for something so small. It cut across the racket of the scrapers. He stopped banging his stick. There was the cabin, all dark.

He stood behind a trunk, ready to run, and surveyed McGraw's estate. The cabin was a miserable-looking shanty. There was an outhouse that leaned heavily; it would've toppled if it weren't for the huntsmen's webs. Unless McGraw did his business in the dark, he was either asleep in the house or drunk at the Fort.

One of his rufts started hollering.

Ryan ducked behind the tree, not sure if the ruft had seen him or just smelled him. It made a hungry sound, full of saliva, that turned to growling. He heard the clinking rattle of a chain. Ryan hoped, his eyelids clenched tight, that McGraw hadn't conjured more chain for the ruft. He was fairly rewarded as it grunted and stopped well short.

The animal was the gritty brown of a farmer's fingernail but had the cleanest set of teeth you'd find this side of the Gregory. She – anything that mean *had* to be a she – hunkered down, making ready to pounce. Eyes and teeth were all Ryan could see properly, but he knew there were claws to match; McGraw's rufts were legendary.

As if rushing might break the spell, he stepped slow and circular towards the woodpile. Big shutters covered the windows; there was no sign of warm, furry candlelight. The ruft inched round with him. Her chain made half the pile hers. She kept biting the air. The wood was stacked waist-high, the logs cut clean and even. All done by that single hand.

'Shut up, damn you!' McGraw's voice boomed and slurred, so close he had to be standing right next to Ryan. McGraw on one side, the ruft on the other. If McGraw were to open that shutter, there'd be nothing for Ryan to do but stare him in the eye and raise his hat. The ruft stopped its barking, happy now to just growl at the boy. When he picked up his first piece of plunder it stopped even that. The ruft was smiling at him, he was sure of it.

Ryan heard the soft sound of paws on dirt the same time as his leg exploded. He fell back, away from the chained animal who spewed hellfire again. A dark mass of teeth was burrowing into his leg, searing the flesh – he was being branded like a neat. Branded a thief. He clamped his lips down so as not to scream and holding the log tightly in his hand, he took a heavy swing at the ruft biting him.

He must have hit something important, an ear maybe, because the animal made a mewling sound. It was cutting to hear, and despite the situation, his heart turned for it. Yelping, dragging its head along the ground, the ruft stumbled off.

Ryan didn't have time to dwell on the blood pooling in his boot for McGraw had struck a light. He grabbed three more logs and stuffed them under his arm, then turned tail. He left behind the stick he favoured for walking; he was running now: a lame courser gait.

Over the sound of barking he heard the shutter swing open. He might have even heard the rifle snap shut. McGraw's aim proved thirty-odd feet off. How did the man fire a rifle with one hand and a hook? Ryan figured the unfortunate tree somewhere in the dark was proof of how.

He kept pushing on, tears running down his face, blood down his leg. It was a long half-mile. Skeleton trees loomed over him, scrapers laughed at him, the logs got heavier and heavier. He hoped nothing hungry could smell the blood.

He was imagining all kinds of fantastical things that might haunt these woods as he took a breath, leaning against a tree. The bark flaked in his hand. There was enough noise around him to drown out an Easter Day parade and he tried to look every which way at once. He didn't stop for long.

When he finally came out from under the trees, he had the idea he'd left his leg a hundred paces back. He couldn't feel anything except the cold; he was shivering all over. He hobbled up their track, but didn't want his ma to see him like this so he aimed for the well.

But candlelight and who knew what else was escaping from their open front door.

1 : 3

He limped towards the house. It was different somehow, its measurements altered or a piece missing, though he couldn't quite recollect what that might be. When he'd catch a stag-bug or bright-lie or anything like that he would cup it in his hands, but he couldn't ever resist peeking, so he'd open up and out the creature would come. The house looked like his empty hands: something had gone.

Soft, so as not to break the silence – and it was silence, the scrapers were either all dead or all spooked or all both – he put McGraw's logs down on the porch. He kept one, feeling its weight and the destruction it might make. The blood on his leg was drying, sticking to his trousers. Dark now, it might have been the stain of soil fat with clay – if it didn't smell so sharp.

He looked round the doorframe. The room was shocking in appearing so normal. The chairs were upright, the table neat, the candles alight and fine in themselves. The box of bottles was gone. A glow came from the fire, pitiful, but still burning. The door to Ma's room was closed.

He readied himself again. He wasn't to open that door; that door was either open or closed and he had no business with it in either state. He listened hard, and heard nothing. If she were asleep, alone or not, he'd just close it again. If she was hurt . . .

The handle felt wrong, hot and cold under his fingers, and heavier than a whole herd of neats. He found the strength, somehow, and eased the door out.

The linens were all messed up: pillows strewn across the room, one of which was lying at his feet. Candles glared at him from each corner. There was a small bloodstain, dead centre of the bed. His ma was sitting against the wall a few feet away. She looked up. She wasn't scared or nothing. Half her face was storm clouds, purple and black and veined in red.

'He didn't like it on him,' she said, staring straight ahead.

Ryan sat down beside her, keeping his bloodied leg to one side. He let the log thump on the floorboards. Tear tracks had carved through her rouge. Her lip paint was smudged. She was breathing steady, and all was calm, despite how she looked.

'Where is he?' Ryan said, his voice thick.

Ma shook her head. 'Long gone.'

But he wasn't. Ryan could still smell him, still feel his hulking frame filling the room, taste his sweat. Gazing at her bruises, he knew she wouldn't tell him who it was.

'What got you?' she said.

'One of McGraw's rufts.'

'That'll need washing,' she said.

He peeled up his trouser leg, wincing as it tugged at his skin. He looked like a piece of gristle, chewed up and spat back out, all teeth marks and dried blood. There were two big holes where the animal had really got hold, though the rest wasn't more than scratches.

Ma didn't even look. He left her sitting there and washed his leg in the other room. The water in the bucket was clean, though it was soon red and soiled with flakes of him.

When he came back she was sitting on the bed. It took up most of the room, leaving only a man's width either side. It was simply made, and solid. A travelling man – it would be too kind to title him a carpenter – on his way west had stopped at the house and made it. For payment, he put his work to good use. Ryan had had to remind him which direction west was.

'Come here,' she said.

He was too big, but he sat on her lap anyways and hugged her as hard as he could. She lifted up his leg and turned it over. He didn't make a noise as she prodded, even though it hurt.

'Would we know ourselves, if it weren't for the bruises?' she said.

That night he slept with her in the bed, but on top of the covers. He was too tired to get into his night-clothes, though he took off his boots and his bloodstained socks. He curled up, and she was asleep before him. He couldn't find peace with the stink of iron and its bitterness, whether it was hers or his.

He was warm and the smell and feel of sleep was a winter blanket that had started as a comfort but was getting too heavy. His mother's arm was around him. The first shots of dawn fired across the bed. He had to be up before her; he would put down all the coin he might ever earn that she'd drink like a summer field that morning.

He eased her arm up and slid to the edge of the bed, then, forgetting himself, he stood. Fire shot up his leg and he bit hard, so as not to yell. He aimed all kinds of silent curses at himself as he hobbled out and pulled the door to.

He cursed himself again: the front door was still wide open, inviting trouble of every shape – but the living room was as he'd left it, which was now twice a miracle. Stepping out onto the porch he sucked hard at the fresh day. The sun was starting early, warm on his face and bright on the farm. The chooks were up, pacing their patch with the majesty of foreign queens until they lunged head-first at the dirt.

Bringing out the bucket, he sat on the porch steps. He took his time wiping the dried blood from his leg, smiling as the red crust came away. It was replaced by the raw pink of his skin. There was a long scab and a lot of bruises that made him wince as he prodded and poked them. 'Would we know ourselves?' she had said. She had that turn in her, where she would start philosophising. Pa hadn't liked it, so she always said, though that wasn't why he left. No, she made it clear that Pa *really* hadn't liked the sight of a swaddled babe; she made it clear all this was Ryan's fault – despite her quick temper and her eyes that swam with more than just tears. Even in those quieter, more contemplative moments he was still ready to duck. Ryan wondered how good his pa had been at ducking.

He heard the courser before he saw it. He waited for the sound of more, but this was a lone rider. He rolled down his trouser leg and eased himself up. Nothing to steal on this farm except chooks. And drink. Part of his calm came from knowing that McGraw rode a wagon not a courser. And this sounded like the hoofbeats of something dainty, not a shaggie.

When they came into view the man was wearing a Northern uniform: a lone Northerner; not the crew the field needed so bad. This one, here he was, riding all the way from the Fort – during the day – and stopping at the end of their track to take off his hat. There just wasn't any earthly way to predict such a thing.

The man dismounted with a soldier's ease and dropped the reins. Fancy war coursers, they stood stock-still so as to look lifeless without their rider. Ryan didn't have a hat to take off, or he would have done so.

The man was ropey, without an ounce of spare fat to him. His face was all bearded, except for a spiteful scar that ran down one cheek. His short hair and his beard were the same mud brown and his skin wasn't much lighter. His uniform was clean but used and he had stripes.

'You lost your crew, Bryn?' Ryan said.

'Not in the way you mean, son.'

'Got the wrong time of day then, haven't you.' Ryan wasn't asking, he was telling.

'Ryan, you know I don't come here for that.' He said each word carefully, so each came out whole, like he was blowing bubbles.

'And you don't come here alone, neither.'

The soldier smiled at something. He was looking over Ryan's head and without turning, Ryan knew his ma was at the door. The sun caught the soldier's smile and it glittered with gold.

'You got some guts,' Ryan said. 'Coming back after—'

'That wasn't me. But I have something for your ma,' he said. He undid a saddlebag and, as if he was handing over a newborn, lifted out a bunch of flowers. They were a little squashed, though he saw to that. Most were regular plains types: pale colours and small petals that came in twos or threes. But the one in the middle – Ryan had never seen that before. It didn't grow around here, sure as chooks had claws and fire was hot. It was such a deep blue as almost to be black. Bryn had dropped a gem amongst pebbles. It looked expensive.

He handed them over, still staring up at the house. He then got on his courser and raised his Northern hat before putting it back on. Ryan watched the soldier go.

The house door was closed when he turned around.

*

The following day Bryn showed again. Punctual as the sun, he rode right to the house this time and got off his cold-eyed animal. Ryan stood at the front door, watching with his mouth wide enough to catch specks. Ma hadn't as much as sniffed at yesterday's blossom and here was another. The Northerner took off his hat and brushed it against his leg. He headed on up the porch stairs.

His uniform looked smarter than the day before – his morning ride hadn't left a mark, as if he'd been borne on the wings of angels. Or devils. He smiled at Ryan, which made Ryan ball his fists tight.

'I need a word with your ma.'

'She don't need a word with you.' She hadn't said as much – she hadn't said a thing about Bryn – but that was the impression Ryan got. He had half a mind to advise the man that his mother wasn't the kind of woman to be moved by flowers.

'I told you I wasn't the man who raised a hand to her,' he said, putting back his hat. 'And she'll be wanting to know there's boys in the field.' The soldier gestured to a wagon rolling up their track: a small flatbed pulled by two white-haired shaggies. Poor things looked hot. One of the so-called 'boys' was driving; another few were in the back and there were four or five trailing behind on coursers. They were all uniformed and carrying rifles as casual as their beards. If they hadn't looked so bored, Ryan would have worried they were there to raid the farm.

Ma came out of her room. She'd made no effort to cover

her bruising, but her hair was brushed. She glared at the Northerner.

'These are for you,' Bryn said, holding out the flowers. To his credit, he'd put an expensive one in this bunch too. She tossed them onto the table with the others.

'Come to admire my colouring?' she said, so flat that Ryan swallowed down his breath. There were a lot of rifles on their land.

'It's the same as every year: you've got a field of corn ready for harvest. I've got an empty store, and a purse to fill it. Any objection?'

She went to the window. 'They don't come in the house. Not this time.'

'Of course,' Bryn said.

'And we can't feed them.'

'Oh, they brought a fine picnic.'

She went back to her room. She wasn't quiet about closing the door.

1 : 4

They drove the wagon up to the field. The shaggies were taken out of the traces and then hitched to the fence, the coursers trusted to stay by their dropped reins.

With nothing more exciting than clearing the chook house to fill his day, and that done, Ryan settled in to watch the men at work. They wouldn't take any help from him, though he ran buckets of water over to them when they had a thirst.

To begin, they all slung their rifles in the wagon and drew out hand sickles. Some of the blades were older than Ryan. With one sharpening stone between them it was a while before they got going.

Ryan was sitting in the shade of the house and Bryn perched his wiry self on the fence. The boys took to the field in a regimented way to begin with. Bryn barked orders that weren't needed – the boys had been farm-hands; Ryan could tell by their smooth cutting. Fat Simmons and his gang could do no better.

As morning wore on shirts were undone and then taken

off and draped on the fence. Tongues loosened and a banter began. Despite looking the same in their uniforms and bushy faces, they had come from all over the North. County names rang out in their jibes: strange names that didn't sound like they'd have farms or farm-hands: 'Westwick boys have the strength of ten girls.' Sniggers, then, 'If they were Burnton girls, those boys must fell trees with their bare hands.'

It was good to hear the voices and laughter of men on the farm again.

When they stopped for food, Ryan drew a fresh bucket from the well and dragged it over. The boys were sitting apart from the officer. They stopped their talking as Ryan got near, and more than one wouldn't meet his eye. He left them the bucket and pulled himself up on the fence with Bryn.

The man was looking out over the field, smiling to himself as if he'd done the work. He had some meat wrapped in brown paper; smelled like hog dried and salted.

'You can have some if you stop staring,' Bryn said.

Ryan took the offered share. It was tough, chewy and caked in salt, and it was good.

'Don't take no notice of the boys,' he said. 'They're grateful they aren't mucking out shaggies or washing linen.'

'Shouldn't you be out chasing off Southerners?'

'In case you were thinking on a stint in the army, I'll tell you what it is: boredom. The majority of your days are spent sitting idle. That isn't a problem for most men: most men *are* idle. But the army has rules against the obvious ways to relieve a boredom.'

'Rules against hitting a woman?' Ryan said. It was bold, and he was ready to duck a swinging fist.

Instead, Bryn sighed. 'Shouldn't need a rule for that. Sometimes men do things when their blood is up and they left sense on their pillow that morning. If she'd hear it, I'd say how sorry I was it happened.' The man showed his age; his cheeks sagged and his eyes clouded over.

Ryan finished his strip of meat. 'Most men don't cut our corn the next day.'

'She doesn't like flowers, does she?' he said.

'Not one bit.'

1 : 5

Ryan stood by the gate as the soldiers left. There was still light in the day, and the ride to Fort Davis would take the rest of it. The boys in the back of the wagon raised their hats to him and he waved. They were older, but not old – eighteen maybe. They made him feel younger than he did with his ma or Bryn.

The door to the house was closed. Ryan pushed it open quietly, poked his head inside and then drew back. She was sitting at the table. He'd caught the shine of bottles. She was singing something – he couldn't make out the words but they were soft and tired. The tune was familiar, she sang it often when she thought he couldn't hear. He inched the door open further and a bottle hit the wall next to him, shattering into angry pieces that hit the floor like hail. He pulled the door shut and sat on the porch, his back against the house. One less bottle she had to fill. She started singing again.

He enjoyed the sunset. They snoozed together, him out-side, her inside, until the sun was well below McGraw's trees and he started to get cold. He couldn't hear his mother singing so he risked the door again, ready for another explosion of glass.

She was asleep, her chin resting on her chest, arms crossed like she was done waiting for him. Years ago, when he was little more than a baby, she must have waited like this for his pa.

'He never came back,' he said. She didn't stir, and they both knew that fact. More important: there weren't going to be any men, of any kind, for her that night.

At the table he took some care righting the toppled bottles. There wasn't any liquor to clear up; she'd not spilled a drop. Her bad leg was bleeding through her dress – they had matching bad legs now, though hers was trouble even before he was born. There wasn't a lot of blood, but a line of thick red ran from her thigh down to her ankle where it dripped onto the floor. She must have been scratching at it. He'd deal with the stain later. He took the blanket from his pallet and draped it over her shoulders.

They needed more wood already, so he gathered himself for a run to McGraw's ample pile. He had no stick to scare away hushts and the like – he'd just have to stamp out each step. This time he'd come back with a proper number of logs, so there'd be no need to brave McGraw's rufts every night.

McGraw's cabin was dark, same as the last time. Ryan stood behind a tree and readied himself for the sound of the chain. He stayed ten paces further away this time. The one with the smile should fall well short but he was less sure of the one he'd knocked on the head. Perhaps McGraw didn't even chain it. That was the kind of one-handed logic Ryan expected. But he didn't hear the cold sound of links unravelling. He skipped forward to the next tree – maybe he was too far for the rufts to scent him? Still nothing. He scratched at the bark, which flaked about his boots. Ryan's leg throbbed; for some reason it was bleeding again.

The noise of the scrapers grew around him, coming in waves, and he started to rock back and forth with the juddering rhythm. Moonlight edged the cabin in ghosts. It didn't look like a place for a man to live, more a place to remember him.

Ryan walked towards the woodpile as brazen as day, no rufts to challenge his right to warmth. Had the rufts really ever been there? Or, like other legends, were they all hot air blown by bored mouths? His limp suggested not. They weren't there now and that was good enough. He laid a hand on a log. He could feel its weight before he'd even picked it up. A few hours on the fire and that weight would be gone.

'Come inside, boy.'

Every part of Ryan tensed. He looked at the shutters but they were all closed. Behind him was nothing but trees. His hand was still on the woodpile.

'Don't worry, they won't hurt you any more.' The voice was definitely inside, and it was definitely McGraw, old hook-hand, inviting him in. His feet were betraying him: he was heading round to the front of the house. He couldn't help thinking all those stories about curiosity had the same ending.

The door was open, but the room was dark. McGraw was sitting in a big high-backed chair without a fire going. 'Well, well, well, three holes in the ground,' he said.

Ryan stayed in the doorway. 'What's on your mind, Mr McGraw?'

'A great many things lately. Most recent, how a little grain-thief keeps making away with my wood.'

'I'm no thief,' Ryan said.

'Yes you are. And there's no wrong in that: men take what they can and work for what they can't. Your pa knew that.'

'I meant no disrespect, Mr—'

'Don't worry yourself, Mr McDermott. I haven't much need of firewood these nights, not unless I wanted to start a fire under my own two feet.'

Ryan took a deep breath; he'd been getting by on scraps and his blood was pumping too fast, getting ready to run faster than two rufts.

'My ma and me, we get plenty cold,' Ryan said.

'That's not what I hear,' McGraw said. His laughter was hollow and creaked like the wheels of a wagon.

Ryan balled his fists, his cheeks hot, but McGraw held up a hand. His one hand. 'Easy, boy. We mean no disrespect, remember?'

Ryan took a step into the room. Claws scrabbled against the wooden floor as they moved from the shadows at the far end of the room: the one that smiled and the one that dragged its head along the ground. Eyes and teeth – all he'd ever seen before – but both looked worried somehow.

'They're not so happy with the present state of things,' McGraw said. 'Shoot them, if you want.' McGraw motioned to a rifle that leaned by the door, the one Ryan had run from just the night before.

'What?'

'I'll even load it for you.' The old man stood and came towards Ryan. He was an unhealthy colour; his cheeks were slack, all skin and no flesh, and his forehead was large and stretched. This was age – what it was to grow old, and how it changed a man. Ryan rubbed a fingertip against his thumb, feeling its youthful softness.

As McGraw handed Ryan the gun he could see the bones in the man's fingers. He tried to catch a glimpse of the hook, but McGraw wore a long coat and there was nothing beyond the sleeve.

'You know how to shoot?' McGraw said.

'You know how to ask idiot questions?' Ryan braced the rifle against his shoulder. It was hard to make out the rufts in the darkness. They weren't smiling now. They whimpered, as if they knew what was coming.

'The way the world is going, it would be a mercy,' McGraw said.

'Then why haven't you done it?'

'Couldn't.'

Ryan tried to remember how those teeth had felt on his leg, how heavy the ruft was, and how the other one had watched like she was enjoying it. But those weren't the same animals as the two scared shapes at the other end of the cabin. He lowered the rifle.

'They'll have to fend for themselves,' McGraw said, kicking a battered leather bag against the wall. It was full to bulging. 'No reason for me to stay here now.'

'What about your farm?' Ryan was already figuring the best way to take all the wood.

'I won't need a farm on the Walk.'

Ryan dropped the rifle.

They both stared at it, wondering at its silence.

1 : 6

McGraw watched as Ryan piled the logs high in his arms; he was overly ambitious and the top two fell to the ground, just missing his feet.

'They're not going anywhere,' McGraw said.

'Around here? I give your whole farm a week,' Ryan said, though he left the two logs.

'You might be right.'

'What will you do now?' Ryan said. His arms were starting to ache but he wanted to know.

'I'd have liked to see mountains before I died. I think I'll head west.'

'Did it hurt?'

'I don't remember,' McGraw said. 'I think I was sleeping when it happened.'

'Do you have a hook for a hand?'

'Full of questions aren't you?' McGraw snapped. But he held up his arm until the sleeve rolled down. There was no hook. There was no hand. A rounded stump was all. 'You can tell all your little friends at Fort Davis.'

'They wouldn't believe me.'

'Then maybe I'll pay them a visit.'

Ryan looked away. 'Thank you for the wood.'

He started home. Not long into the trees he wanted to stop and rest his arms. His bad leg was making noise too, but he pushed on. He hummed his mother's song to take his mind off his body: that's why she did it.

It was a relief to see their front door still closed. He opened it awkwardly but managed not to drop the logs until he was kneeling beside the stove. He let them tumble to the floor, then tried to rub life back into his arms. Red marks and scratches ran from his wrists to his shoulders.

He went to open the stove door and the hinges screamed. He held his breath.

The bedroom door opened and she stumbled out. Her nightdress was ripped on one shoulder. 'Spitting bones! I was sleeping.'

The bottle she was holding said otherwise.

'I'm—'

She hit him on the side of the head and his ear rolled with thunder. 'I said I was sleeping.' Her voice was far away. Her hands were closer.

He nodded, but she lashed out at the other side of his head, this time missing the ear. He knew better than to cry, or fall over. She'd take that as a challenge.

'Don't make me come out here again.'

'I won't, Ma,' he mumbled.

'What's that?' She raised a hand again.

'I won't, Ma.'

When she'd shut the door he risked touching his ear. It wasn't bleeding, though it stung enough to chase out all other thoughts. He steadied himself against the table. His eyes were watering but he couldn't risk sobbing; instead, he sniffed the tears back as silently as he could. Taking his time, he piled the logs neatly.

'I'm sorry, Ryan,' she moaned through the thin walls, drawing out his name like a neat might. 'Ryan.'

He covered his head with his pillow, despite how his ear burned.

'Ryan, I'm sorry.'

She had taken his blanket with her.

1 : 7

There was a knock at the door. He rubbed the gritty sleep from his eyes and shivered. He stamped his feet on the way to the door, trying to get some warmth back into them, to hell with the noise. The sunlight coming through the windows looked less than dawn-fresh. He'd slept late – she'd just slept.

He opened the door to see Bryn standing on the porch.

'Morning,' Bryn said.

'Is it? Well, that's something.'

'You look tired.'

'I feel tired,' Ryan said.

'Growing, most likely. I brought you this.' Bryn thrust a bag at him: bright-coloured things of all kinds of shapes. 'Fruit. It's for both of you.'

Ryan picked out a ball that sat in his hand and was the colour of the sun.

'You have to peel it.'

'Peel?'

Bryn took the fruit and dug his nail into the top, then wrenched off the outer layer piece by piece.

'It's like a lady's skirts,' Bryn said, laughing. Ryan didn't laugh. 'I'm— I didn't— I shouldn't have said that.'

Ryan held out his hand. The fruit was softer without its skin, just like a chook. He bit into it and juices sprayed all over his face. It was sweet, and made him wince. 'I don't know if she likes fruit,' he said.

'Can I see her?'

Ryan glanced at the bedroom door. 'She's not ready for guests yet.'

'We should finish the field today.'

'That's good.' Ryan could feel the sticky fruit on his hands and cheek.

The officer waited for a moment. 'Well, best get to it,' Bryn said.

Getting to it meant leaning on the fence and watching other men labouring. Those doing the hard work apparently didn't see that as a problem, though there was only one officer and a lot more of them. Didn't sit right with Ryan, but then, he wasn't in the army.

He tended to the chooks. The boys in the field started their calling and hawing, and somehow the house remained still and silent with not even a speck stirring in the morning heat. He scattered the chook feed on the ground but there was no frenzy of feathers and claws and beaks: they stepped around their pen as if worried to muddy their special gowns. He opened the egg hatch and took away their hard work. The biggest chook eyed him with some kind of fury. He was their officer.

His sole chore of the day done, he sat in the shade behind the house and watched the men clearing the field. They had a third of the field to go and were making short work of it. Their jackets were already on the fence and their backs were wet. Even from a distance they looked substantial: big knots of muscle straining and stretching with each swing of the sickle. Ryan pinched at the skin of his arms, still crisscrossed with welts and scratches from carrying the logs. He was plenty strong for their farm – now there were no neats to herd and no woollies to sheer. He'd wrung his share of chooks necks, though if he did that now there would be nothing to eat after a day, maybe two if he boiled the bones. He wrinkled his nose. There was nothing worse than boiled chook bones: the smell stayed in your clothes and coated the floorboards like a varnish.

He should collect more wood from McGraw's pile – collect anything useful the man – the *Walkin'* – had left behind. But there were men on their farm and it wouldn't be good to test the officer's word. If those boys with their broad backs and their sharpened sickles wanted to work at something different he doubted Bryn could stop them, even though he was their officer. He doubted he could either, but at least with Bryn there the soldiers might think twice about his young eyes seeing such a thing. Shame had a powerful sway on some men. He had to hope McGraw hadn't told the whole county he was leaving behind a bounty.

'Bryn?' Ryan called, moving the straw he'd been chewing to one side of his mouth. 'What do you know of Walkin'?'

The officer took his time turning round. At last he said, 'More than I should. Why?'

'Do they often up and leave their homes?'

'They call it the Walk for a good many reasons. I once knew a man who turned and the first thing he did was to wander. And then I knew others who barely budged an inch.' Bryn fanned himself with his hat. 'You thinking about taking off?'

'I won't become a bag o' bones,' Ryan said. 'Not me. I know someone who has, that's all.'

'Who do you know?'

'Just someone. What happens to their homes?'

'Goes to family, I suppose,' Bryn said.

'And if they have none?'

'Then whoever buys it from whoever is selling it. Can't say I've thought on it before.' Bryn squinted into the shade. 'You expanding?'

Ryan snorted. 'We don't need more bare ground.'

'Looting?'

'Would that be so bad?'

'You tell me,' Bryn said.

A shout went up from the field. It sounded like a curse word, but not one his mother used.

Bryn jumped over the fence. 'Fetch clean water,' he said, before racing towards the soldiers.

Ryan ran up to the well and worked the winch as quick as he dared. The bucket started full, but he lost some water getting over the fence and some more on the uneven ground of the field. When he reached the little group of men he hoped he had enough.

A deep voice moaned in pain and there were more curse words, some he knew.

The men parted before him. He could smell their morning's work – a clean kind of sweat from good honest toil, not the stale sweat of a bedroom. Their faces were grim.

Bryn was kneeling beside one of the younger soldiers. The boy's hand was covered in blood. His eyes were as big as two black saucepans with barely a sliver of white to them. Ryan put the bucket down and Bryn wet a scrap of clean cloth.

'Paul. Look at me, Paul,' Bryn said. The soldier boy was shaking but he met Bryn's eye. 'This is going to hurt.'

Paul was cradling his hand. The sharp whiteness of bone was clear through the blood and ragged skin. He had cut down the side of his forefinger and thumb. Somewhere in the field was a stained clump of corn, likely still stuck together where Paul had gripped it. His whole frame was wobbling with his big, quick breaths.

Bryn put the cloth over the wound. The other soldiers looked away. Paul didn't scream.

'Hot out today,' Bryn said, fixing Paul's eyes with his.

'Sure.'

'Hotter than yesterday, you reckon?' Bryn wrapped the cloth around his hand.

'Pissing nails, I don't know—'

'I'd say so. Though not as hot as last week. What were you working last week?'

Paul gnashed his teeth as the cloth went over his thumb again. 'Pots,' he gasped. 'Washing pots.'

'Ah, now that *is* hot work. Never liked kitchens – air's too close.'

Paul closed his eyes. He tried to wipe away the tears running silently down his cheeks.

'More water there, Ryan.'

Ryan moved the bucket closer. Bryn cupped a handful onto the bandage, which dripped pink.

'When he's good and ready, you'll take Paul over to the shade,' Bryn said.

'I'm no nursemaid.'

'I can see that. But you'll do this.' There was no bend in the man's tone and Ryan mumbled acceptance. Paul didn't look best pleased with the arrangement either.

'Just keep him talking,' Bryn said quietly as he passed the bucket back. 'About anything.'

Paul was in no hurry to stand. He didn't have much colour to his face. Ryan hunkered down beside him, but the other soldiers were all ignoring Paul, and making an obvious show of it too.

'This field isn't going to harvest itself,' Bryn said for all of them to hear.

The soldiers shook their heads. 'Where I'm from, nobody works after someone takes a licking,' one of them said and the others agreed.

'And do they leave crops to rot where you're from?' Bryn asked.

'Tomorrow—'

'We won't be back tomorrow. Or have you forgotten it's re-posting?'

The soldier spat from the side of his mouth. 'It's asking for trouble.'

'I'm sure Pastor Adams would be interested in all these superstitions,' Bryn said.

The soldiers grumbled at that idea. The one who'd voiced their objections was the last to take up the work.

Ryan helped Paul stand, feeling how uneasy he was on his feet. The soldier used his good hand to lean on Ryan's shoulder.

'Best pick that up,' Bryn said, gesturing to the sickle lying on the ground.

'Am I not carrying enough?' Ryan said.

'I don't touch that tool.'

'Why not?'

'Not for a long time.'

Ryan laughed, but Bryn just shook his head, his mouth set in a thin line. He had that faraway look Ma had sometimes, at quiet times, when she was remembering.

Making sure the soldier wasn't going to fall over, Ryan picked up the sickle. It was still slick with blood, though it was drying fast. He dropped it into the bucket and walked the injured soldier back to the house. The shade was welcome. They both sank down and leaned against the cool walls. Paul took some more water. He swallowed and closed his eyes. Keep him talking, the officer said.

'How old are you?' Ryan asked.

'Nineteen.' Paul didn't open his eyes. His bandaged hand was in his lap.

'You look older.'

'I left my farm when I was about your age.'

'Why did you join the army?' Ryan said.

'I just told you.'

Ryan took in the wonky fence, the empty corral and the flaking paint on the chook house. There were strangers cutting their crops. He stole wood to keep them warm and cook stale bread. 'They feed you good in the army?'

'Three times a day,' Paul said.

'*Three?* But none of you have gone to fat?'

'They keep us busy – all kinds of wasting time. Like harvesting this turning corn. Or worse: move that there, then move it back again. They come up with all kinds of ways of making us work.'

The crop wasn't turning. It wasn't so fresh, but it wasn't on the turn.

'Don't you ever get to fighting?' Ryan said.

'Maybe once a year. More if you got no luck.'

'You killed anyone?'

'My share.'

The soldier was falling asleep. Ryan shook his arm and he stirred and mumbled something. Ryan shook him again. This time he woke and snarled at the pain of his hand.

'The officer said to keep you talking.'

'He can go to hell,' Paul said.

'We all can – nothing difficult about it.'

'What would you know? You're just a kid.'

'So are you,' Bryn said, joining them against the house. 'Go on in now, Ryan. Your mother will be up and looking for you.'

Ryan doubted it. They'd have heard if that was the case. No such thing as a quiet storm. But he left the army men to their talking.

Inside the house the air was close and still. A lone speck drifted in with Ryan and buzzed once around the room before making for the door. It seemed to struggle; the air was heavier inside than normal and he nearly followed it out. But his stomach cramped at the sight of the empty saucepan. If he was hungry she'd be starving. She was sleeping late – or the soldiers in the field were keeping her quiet.

He started cooking some eggs; she'd hear the pan crackling or smell the mix of woken ashes and dry-frying eggs. He had a vague memory of Ma cooking with butter – that was a smell worth getting out of bed for. It had a thickness to it that was special. When the eggs were done he put them onto plates and put the plates on the table, making plenty of noise, but still she didn't come out.

For the second time in as many days he held the handle to her room. It was just as heavy as before. He steadied himself for thrown words or bottles before he inched the door open. The sheets on the bed were red – they only had white sheets, stained in places and washed to dullness, but white sheets. Not red.

She was sitting up in bed, gashes across each wrist.

1 : 8

The smell of blood was already familiar to the day. It was strong in the bedroom, and there was nothing else, nothing underneath it. He took two steps and fell onto the bed. He lifted his hands, expecting them to be covered, but they came away dry: it was all dry – she'd been there for some time. The last thing she'd said was sorry. She had said it over and over again. And Ryan had tried to ignore her, his pillow over his head, his ear ringing. But she wasn't sorry for hitting him.

He was crying without meaning to. He didn't want the soldiers to hear. He wanted them gone.

He took her hand in his. Where she'd cut was a mess: she'd dug deep, slashing many times. She must have wanted to be sure. There were frown lines on her face. She hadn't found calm, not even then. She wasn't wearing anything special, just her nightdress. He shifted closer and something sharp poked his thigh and, now he looked, he saw the bed was covered in shards of glass that caught the light; he'd thought that was the blood. A broken bottle: made a kind of sense.

A large shard was near her other hand, a curved bit where the body of the bottle tapered up to the neck, like a stubby sickle, and the same type of sharp. The green piece was elegantly lined in red. The neck was the right size for a small grip, though it was lighter than he'd expected. He stared at his own wrist. He wouldn't have to clean out the chook house or haul wood from McGraw's or sweep the ancient floorboards or winch buckets of water. He looked at her. Her eyes were quiet. There were things she didn't have to do any more.

He put the glass down and got up, wiped his eyes and closed the door behind him. Three eggs and two plates were waiting at the table. He ate them all.

Ryan was still at the table when Bryn appeared in the doorway. The officer took off his hat, but he stayed outside.

'Can I see her?'

Ryan shook his head. He'd been drawing a circle on the tabletop with his knife, over and over, until it was scratched into the surface.

'Is she awake?'

'No.'

'She won't eat?' Bryn said.

Ryan didn't look up. 'No.'

'She has to eat.'

'Not right now.'

Bryn fanned himself with his hat, though it wasn't so hot. 'We're done in the field. If she won't see me now I'll be back tomorrow to pay up.'

'What about your re-posting?' Ryan said.

'That's a keen memory you have there. Don't worry, I don't leave behind debts.'

'Tomorrow, then.'

'Tomorrow.' Bryn left the porch.

Ryan kept drawing his circle. The blunt knife barely made a noise as it wore away at the wood. As hours passed the light in the room changed, the shadows stretching and yawning across the floor. Ryan's back ached, but he sat there until his hand seized up and he couldn't hold the knife. The pain of cramp brought tears and he sobbed loudly; there was no one to hear him now – no one to be angry at his noise. He cried for longer than he thought a person could; any longer and he'd be as dried-up and used as McGraw . . . McGraw with his one hand and empty farm. It was the same empty as theirs now. His cheeks itched with old tears, but he let them be.

The sun started to set. He wanted to see the field.

It was colder outside than the heat of the day suggested. One of the soldiers had returned the bucket to the well. Ryan climbed the fence. All that remained of the corn were the stubs, left in rough bunches, each no higher than his boots. It looked like the view from the walls of Fort Davis, the rows of chimneys evenly spaced out and sprouting towards the sky. The half of the field they'd worked the day previous was just a field of low crop. It had recovered quickly. Ryan walked among the short chimneys, wondering if he might see where Paul had cut himself, and though he went from one end to the other he couldn't find it. The soldiers had done the job properly, not slacking at the edges. The land sloped away on all sides of the field to worthless scrub and rock. Their field was in the wrong place. It wasn't supposed to be there.

Nothing in the house looked different. Silence filled it. They didn't need more wood but he set off for McGraw's anyway.

'McGraw?' Ryan called. The cabin was dark, but the man, alive and Walkin' alike, had sat in the dark. He kept to the trees as he circled the building. The door was open and from this far away he could make out the chair, but not the Walkin'.

He was being a fool. The Walkin' would be long gone – he'd said as much himself – and the rufts too. He would look over the cabin to see if there was anything worth carrying home, then take as many logs as he could. They'd have a proper store then. He didn't rush up to the door. There was still the same tightness in his legs and chest as when there had been two vicious animals and one grumpy man inside. Some feelings stayed in a place, no matter what changed.

The porch steps were loud under his boots. McGraw's chair gaped at him like the mouth of a cave. It was a fancy chair for a farmer, with a big high back made of material. It was rubbed bald where McGraw's head had rested for years, but it held itself well. It was too big for him to carry on his own; he would ask Bryn to help – he'd say it was a gift from old one-hand McGraw. He wouldn't be lying.

The leather bag was gone, as was the rifle. He stretched to check the two shelves as best he could in the bad light. His fingers came away dusty as he picked things up. He didn't know what most of it was but it looked useless. He sneezed and shook his head. McGraw should've had a son. The stove was smaller than the one at home and he couldn't imagine how McGraw had ever kept warm. But beside it was the real prize: the axe. It was heavy, though he could lift it with one hand. The blade was polished and wicked in the moonlight. He tried to swing it and needed both hands for that; he raised it above his head and slammed it into the floor.

There was a yelp.

He looked down at the axe, checking either side, but it didn't look like he'd hit anything or anyone; for a start there wasn't any blood. From the far end of the room came a mewling sound, one he recognised, and he wrenched at the axe. Eventually it came free. Holding it in both hands, he crept forward, and the further he went, the more total was the darkness. It didn't matter how dark it got; he'd be able to see those eyes anywhere. The ruft was under a table, just the one, staring up at him. He checked each way and then behind, but he couldn't see the other. This mewling ruft was the one he'd caught with a log, the one that had given him a scar. And here it was, alone.

It got up – a landslide of sleek muscles. Ryan made ready

with the axe – he'd not used the rifle when McGraw said but he'd swing now if he had to. The ruft padded towards him like it was taking some effort. It sniffed at his boots and raised its huge head waist high and panted softly. Ryan lowered the axe and held out his hand. The ruft's nose was wet on his palm. He made to scratch behind the ruft's head but the animal reared up and bit the air. He kept his hands where it could see it, and apparently happy with how he smelled, the ruft slumped to the floor.

Ryan checked over the rest of the cabin but there was little else. McGraw's clothes were no better than his own, and worse-fitting. If there had been any food the rufts had found it. McGraw had little more to his name than Ryan did.

Outside, he was struck dumb by his own stupidity. McGraw had called himself a farmer, and not just a farmer of trees. Ryan hefted the axe and ran towards McGraw's fields. The ruft joined him, sounding more like a courser and almost big enough to ride. There might be neats or woollies or hogs in the fields: big animals, like the one next to him, all lined up ready to be eaten. He smacked his lips at the idea and ran faster.

At the fields he cursed himself for a fool again. The gates were wide open and the ground had been churned by hooves. The ruft sniffed all along the fence and Ryan had a pretty good idea what had happened to the animals, and the other ruft: Simmons, if he had to guess. He might even have paid for them.

Ryan wandered back through the trees, the ruft trailing

behind. He had an axe now, though he still took as many logs as he could carry.

He stood on the porch, just where Bryn had been earlier that day, and he hesitated for the same reasons, though he knew more than the officer had. She changed the way everyone behaved – it was something she did, but he didn't understand how. Was it the reward for cruelty, or just part of being vicious?

The ruft started to growl. Every muscle in its dense body was taut; even its stumpy tail was rigid. The growling rumbled through the whole animal.

Ryan looked over the room again, and it was still empty. He stepped inside and the ruft's growls got louder.

'Stupid. There's no one here, just me,' he said. He tried to pull the ruft in, but he might as well have been trying to move the house.

'Ry . . . an.'

He turned towards the bedroom.

1 : 9

The ruft started barking. Ryan still had the axe in his hand and he slowly crossed to the bedroom door. Any noise he made was too loud. He had an urge to bury the axe in the door, to swing at it and swing again until the whole thing fell apart. He wanted it gone for ever. But the axe was too heavy; it was a man's axe.

She was sitting on the edge of the bed with a gun in her lap: a small pistol. She looked as worn as he'd ever seen her.

'There you are,' she said. Her smile took some effort.

'You were—'

'And now I'm not.'

The sheets were still red. He hadn't dreamed it. He hadn't wished it to happen so hard that he'd fooled himself. Her wrists were still in tatters.

'Why did you do it?' he said. His throat burned and he was gripping the axe so tight his shoulder hurt.

'It's not done, not yet.'

'Was it me?'

She started to laugh, loud and hard, and her whole body

shook. He closed the door on her, but he could still hear her, even over the ruft growling. He could hear her on the porch. He got to the middle of the field before he found quiet. The ruft followed him, snapping at the air as they ran. He tripped on the stumps of the cut crop and lay there, curled up as small as he could. The ruft licked his arm and then lay beside him, panting, though it kept glancing back to the house. It could still hear her.

He was shivering. The sky was clear and full of stars; the moon was a thin sliver of itself. He watched his breath cloud. He rubbed his arms, which didn't help. As he headed back to the house, the silence was a relief. The ruft wouldn't go inside, though it didn't growl. It lay on the porch, its giant head resting on its paws. He sat on the pallet wishing he had his blanket, but at least it was warmer in the house.

'I knew you'd come back,' she said.

He lay down and hugged the pillow to him.

'You have to help me.' Her voice was muffled, but loud enough. It had always been loud enough. The pillow just made him feel better. Eventually he'd fall asleep.

The door handle moved – only a little, one way and then the other. After a time it turned and the door drifted open. She was there, her arms thrust out and crossed in front of her. They were thin arms – frail as a stalk of corn. Her bones were like mountain peaks, sharp beneath her nightdress. She'd put her rouge on and her lips were painted red.

'You have to help me,' she said. She sat back on the bed.

'Why should I?'

'Because you'll want to.' She awkwardly scooped up the pistol and it hung from her finger, swaying back and forth. 'I can't do it myself. I shouldn't have to; where I grew up they would have burned my body before ... this. Didn't happen all the time, but it was supposed to. My pa and the soldiers like him came back. Even the Gravekeeper's wife, pissin' hypocrites. I met her once, Lydia, on a God-forsaken mountain somewhere. She stared at me like she would cry if she could.

'You have to help me, Ryan.'

He got up and slammed the door. 'No!'

'Ryan. Help me.'

'No.' He rested his head against the wood.

'Ryan.'

'You did it once. Do it again.'

'I can't,' she said. 'My hands don't work.'

'Whose fault is that?'

'Ryan.'

He hit the door. 'I'm not doing it!'

'Help me, Ryan.'

He slumped back down on the pallet and stuffed his head under the pillow.

A thumping noise started up, regular and constant. Her bed used to make that kind of noise, but not for this long. It was her feet, marching on the spot, the floorboards bouncing along with her, the dust shaking loose, then settling, then clouding again.

'Ryan, *please*.'

He closed his eyes and tried to sleep, but his eyes itched and he was too tired. She was going at the same beat as his heart.

'Ry ... an.' She dragged his name out. 'You're good for nothing, you know that? Your pa was good for nothing, too.

'If he could see you now, he'd be ashamed, just as I am ...

'He'd think you some kind of little *girl*. Where's your braids, eh? Where's your dresses and your dollies?

'You and your pa: both *cowards*. He ran out on me as soon as it wasn't so easy, soon as you started making too much noise. Said he didn't want to be a father, like he had a choice. Well, you going to run out on me too, Ryan? Run off and play outlaw instead of being a man?

'Ryan. Come in here ... He told me that night how he took away my own pa, said he'd finished what the army started and burned him. I threw the heavy pan, caught his head enough to make it bleed ... and then I realised he was trying to get me angry.

'He was just making it easier for himself: so I wouldn't want him to stay.

'*Ryan*. Come and help your mother – I brought you into this world, don't forget; the struggle and the pain I went through for you. I was never the same after that, never. I was just a girl, you little shit, and you tore me up, coming out kicking and screaming like you did. And you've been hurting me ever since. It hurts to look at you, even ...

'My life before you. You stole that, Ryan: you and your pa stole it. Give it back to me. Ryan, *please*. Please help me.

'If I could do it myself you know I would – you said it right: I already done it once . . .

'You weak streak of piss! You could've stopped them, you know? Every night, *you* could've stopped them. So what if they were bigger than you? I was your mother! And you just let them come on in.'

All night she spoke through the door, sometimes shouting, sometimes whispering, and all night long she kept up her pounding march. The ruft couldn't take it for long. It left the porch; it might have even left the farm. Ryan's eyes itched, and no amount of scratching helped. His legs and arms burned; he was wound up tight.

'You're selfish, just like your pa was. He ran out on me, left me to bring you up all on my own. I did what I had to do. I didn't like it – none of it. What could I do? What *could* I do?'

She was repeating herself; there were only so many ways to say the same thing.

The sun started to rise.

'And if you weren't so weak, such a little girl . . . if you could do the right thing.'

He got up quickly.

'Ryan?'

He opened the door and grabbed the gun from her.

'"You know how to shoot?"' he said, in the voice of old McGraw. He cocked the little hammer.

'Higher, Ryan. The head, it has to—'

1 : 10

So I stood beside him and killed him, because I knew that after he had fallen he could not survive. And I took the crown that was on his head and the band on his arm and have brought them here to my lord.

2 Samuel

BOOK TWO

2 : 1

Ryan looked up from his pallet to see the officer at the door.

'I've got the coin for the harvest,' Bryn said. 'I know she doesn't want to see me, but I'd feel better giving it to your ma. No offence.'

Ryan pointed to the bedroom door that was still open.

Bryn stood there for some time. He was big in the doorway. His hat was in his hands. 'Who did this, Ryan?'

'The first one was her.'

'And the second?'

'She wouldn't stop,' he said. 'All night.'

'Stop what?'

'Begging.'

The officer closed the door and sat beside Ryan. 'She was a troubled woman,' Bryn said.

'What would you know?'

'More than I need to, but maybe not enough.'

Ryan sniffed.

'I see you have one of McGraw's old rufts.'

'He didn't want them on the Walk,' Ryan said.

'What will you do now?'

'What do you mean?'

'It's not my place, but I'd say you're a bit young to be on your own,' Bryn said.

'I'll manage.'

'Your pa will find out.'

'Why? Why would he?' Ryan said.

'Word travels. He'll come for you.'

'No, he won't. He doesn't care about me.'

'He will, because he's your pa.'

'That's made no difference since I was born,' Ryan said.

'You could come with me.'

'Join the army?'

Bryn laughed. 'You're too young for a rifle. I'm being assigned to the Gregory River crossing. I'll be in charge – a ferryman. I could use the help.'

'I don't know a thing about being a ferryman,' Ryan said.

'Can't be too complicated. But it's your choice. I'll wait where the track to Fort Davis meets the river. I'll be there until sunset.' Bryn put a stack of coins on the pallet which fell over when he stood. He put on his hat. 'Sunset,' he said, and then left.

2 : 2

Ryan slept the rest of the morning and when he woke the coins were scattered about him and the ruft was sleeping on his feet. He had to work to get free; the ruft was a dead weight. It rolled over and started wagging its tail against the floor, a steady thump. Ryan leaned over and stopped it. He rubbed the ruft's belly, which made the tail even harder to keep quiet.

'See this, this here?' Ryan said, pointing to the scar on his leg. 'That was you.'

And the ruft knew it. It looked from Ryan to the door and back again. It made a noise in its throat, half bark, half whine.

'Let's hope you know how to bite other people.'

He was hungry. The officer's bag of fruit was nearly empty. At the bottom something had turned bad. There was a patch of wet and something wrinkled. He took out an apple and looked it over. It was firm enough, so he ate it on the way to the chook house.

He lifted the hatch to find no eggs. 'Well, aren't we all out of luck.'

He stared down at the chooks, which were clawing at the ground, making the motion of pecking for food that wasn't there. No eggs and no food.

'Be a ferryman,' he said. 'Help the army.' And what would he do if his pa *did* come back? Didn't sound like Pa was a farmer. People said he stole things, but there was no one to steal from around here.

Ryan couldn't leave the chooks to starve. He opened up the fence and stepped in with them. They didn't like that. They made all kinds of noise, fluffing up their feathers. The ruft ran the length of the fence back and forth. When it barked the chooks warbled and Ryan jumped. He tried to shoo it away, but it was far too excited. Moving slowly he managed to pick up a chook the right way: claws down and out, wings clamped to its side. It wriggled and tried to flap and Ryan was ready for it. He had to clamber over the fence as he couldn't get it open without letting go of the chook. He made sure the claws were a good arm's-length away – it was awkward, but he did it.

He went behind the house, out of respect, and wrung its neck. He did it quick and hoped it was painless. The first few times he'd done it were different: they'd suffered and that had left a sour taste. He slung the chook on the low-hanging roof, out of the way of the ruft, and went back for the next one.

The chooks were nobody's fool. They'd seen Ryan go away with a chook and not come back with a chook and now they were trying to tear their way out. The ruft was just as frantic, barking at the bursts of feathers. He could get the pistol and try his luck – or the axe – but that wouldn't be right. As soon as he was inside the fence the chooks ran from him. Going slow was no good; he had to chase one down. He caught hold, but not properly, and when he tried to bundle the chook over the fence it clawed at his arm.

He cried out and dropped the evil creature, then clamped his hand over the blood as he cursed and kicked at the fence.

The chook was off, making a dash for freedom.

The ruft was sitting looking at him, tail wagging. It inched closer. He realised it was waiting for him. Ryan nodded and it tore after the chook. The crunching sound suggested it was quick – painful but quick. And there was one less chook to take with him.

But the ruft didn't eat it: it carried the chook back in its mouth, almost carefully.

'McGraw use you for more than biting me, eh?' He patted the ruft's head. This way he didn't have to chase the chook around and risk his veins.

He opened the fence. The last chook wasn't so bright and he had to herd it out of the enclosure. He waited a while longer this time, though he wasn't done nodding before the ruft was off: solid muscle moving at a terrible speed; beauty, of a kind. Once again it returned with the dead chook.

'You'll get a cut,' Ryan said.

He shook out Bryn's fruit bag and the few bits of rotten fruit slapped the dry ground which was covered in specks within moments. They liked the sickly-sweet – he didn't like the way it felt on his fingertips. He rinsed the bag. It was a thin kind of canvas and the fruit juices came free with a bit of scrubbing. The ruft lapped at the bucket when he was done; it was not a quiet drinker. He stuffed the dead chooks inside the bag and left it in the shade, figuring he didn't have to worry about the ruft.

He didn't take much from the house: his flint box and the smaller pan – in case Bryn forgot he was cooking for two. The axe. His hat; it would get cold by a river. He didn't have a jacket, or a second of anything. His pa's old boots would have to do for walking. The pistol was on his pallet. He opened the cylinder. Four rounds. He glanced at the closed bedroom door. He'd had no idea she had a pistol. Where she'd hid it – and any spare rounds – was anyone's guess. He wasn't going to start looking now.

He carried the axe and pan, one in each hand, with the bag slung over his shoulder. His flint and the pistol nestled against the heads of dead chooks. He didn't need to call the ruft; it padded after him, like it had at McGraw's. It must have been used to leaving empty farms.

The track wound out beyond McGraw's trees and onto scrubland. Ryan didn't like to look at the size of it – he couldn't see an end, just blue sky and yellow earth. There shouldn't be a river in such a place, but there was – showed how much he knew of the world. The ruft was happy enough snuffling through the low bushes; it didn't appear to notice the thorns and whatnot. When it felt it had tarried too long by a real interesting bush it barked and chased after Ryan, though the noise was lost in all the open air. He could fire the pistol and barely hear it. The farm and the house, the walls and fences, they made things loud. The ruft nipped at his boots and then raced on ahead.

They reached the river well before sunset. Bryn was already there.

'Earlier than I expected,' Bryn said. He held out his hand for the ruft to smell. His reward was wet fingers.

'Wasn't much to finish up.'

'You said your goodbyes?'

'In my way,' Ryan said.

Bryn had an old-looking courser and a shaggie that wasn't faring well in the early evening heat. It wasn't the courser he normally rode.

'I can't ride,' Ryan said.

'Just as well; the shaggie is just carrying and this old boy wouldn't take you.'

'I brought chooks.'

'That's good,' Bryn said. 'You can hitch your bag to the saddle.'

The ruft was sniffing around the shaggie until a swish of its furry tail sent the ruft scampering back. It barked, but the shaggie was none too impressed.

'Does she have a name?'

'Who?' Ryan said.

'The ruft?'

'Why would it have a name?'

'People give animals names.'

Ryan poked the chooks in the bag. 'Not much point in that.'

'Michael and String here disagree.'

'Do they now?' Ryan said. 'You named your courser Michael. And your shaggie String?'

'The shaggie was named before she was mine.'

'And that's important?'

'I'd say so. String, come.'

The shaggie took two slow steps towards the officer. It didn't drag its feet – that was the speed it moved.

Ryan looked at the ruft. 'Chunk, come.'

The ruft didn't move.

'Chunk, come. Come here.'

'Chunk?' Bryn said.

'That's what it took from my leg. Guess McGraw called it something different.'

'Well, she'll get used to it.' Bryn checked over all the straps and bags on String. He also checked the saddle on Michael.

A person's name for an animal. Ryan shook his head. 'Is it far?' he said.

'We'll be there before dawn. It's cooler to travel at night. But before we go, we pray.'

'What?'

Bryn held out a book. The edges were all battered and there wasn't much left of the cover. He put his hand on top of the book and waited for Ryan to do the same.

'You'd better get used to this,' Bryn said.

'But what's it for?'

'Asking the Good Lord to grant us safe passage tonight.'

'We passing through his lands then?' Ryan said.

'Always.'

Ryan shrugged and put his hand on the book.

The officer closed his eyes. 'Good Lord, see us safely to our new home. Watch over us as we start our new lives, ever in your service and understanding. Amen.' He looked down at Ryan. 'You have to say "Amen" too.'

'Why?'

'Didn't your ma tell you anything?'

'She did plenty of telling,' Ryan said.

'You say it to show the Good Lord that you agree.'

'And he can hear us?' Ryan looked round at the bushes.

'All the time.'

Ryan snorted. 'That don't sound likely.'

'Do you want to come with me or not?'

'Amen.'

'No, you have to ... Never mind.'

They walked for hours alongside the Gregory River as it twisted and turned. In places it was so narrow Ryan could throw a stone from one bank to the other, but in those places the sides were cliffs and the river angry enough to look broken, the surface like smashed glass. Where it was wide and fat a man might swim across, and he might even persuade a courser to do so, not a wagon though. And there were those who had a desire to cross a river and keep dry. He'd be helping those kinds of people.

'How will we eat,' Ryan said, 'if we're not going to be farmers?'

'Only thinking about that now?'

Ryan patted the shaggie's big belly. He'd hate to have to eat it. 'If I could, I'd have brought the chooks alive.'

'There's my officer's salary, and people pay to cross the river. We'll buy food.'

People pay to cross the river? Ryan scratched the back of his head, just under where his hat sat. Now there was a thing.

'They pay a lot?'

'We won't be making our fortune, no,' Bryn said. He smiled down at Ryan. 'But you'll have plenty of time to read.' He had that book wedged between him and the saddle.

'I can't.'

'Then you'll have plenty of time to learn.'

Ryan kicked a stone and it made the river with a hollow *clop*. 'What if I don't want to?'

Bryn pulled the courser up and the shaggie stopped too. He shifted in the saddle to get a better look at Ryan. 'There'll be things I make you do that you won't want to: chores and such. People cross rivers all times of day; doesn't matter whether we're sleeping, eating or whatever, we've got to help them. When I pray I'll expect quiet. But a man has the right to decide his own betterment.' He was staring at Ryan, his brow set serious.

Ryan shrugged away from how intent the officer was and started off again. The dull hooves on packed dirt sounded their march. Chunk had clearly decided bushes weren't as exciting as she initially thought. She – Bryn had said he was sure Chunk was a she – was happy lumbering alongside

Ryan. She wasn't panting so much now it was night. The moon didn't give them much light but the sky was full of stars. Clouds felt like someone else's memory.

When they stopped to drink from the river Bryn pulled him upstream from the animals. The water was cold enough to make his mouth ache but it tasted better than the well water at the farm.

'What's been done to this?' Ryan said.

'Nothing – well, not until Fort Davis, but that's a few miles in the other direction.'

'Why's it taste so clear?'

'Did you ever leave that farm of yours?' Bryn said.

'Sometimes.'

'The Gregory starts somewhere high in mountains that are a long way off and it's always running, that's why it's so clean.'

Ryan looked up the river. He couldn't see mountains but Bryn sounded sure of his words. Maybe rivers did start in mountains. He'd like to see that one day: see where a river started.

2 : 3

They came to the crossing. Bryn got down from the courser and they stepped onto the boards of the jetty. Bryn tutted: the wood was old and there were holes. Ryan ran his hand along the rope, which was rough and grainy and tied to a solid-looking post – no, not just tied: the rope went through it. He traced the many knots with his finger. The rope spanned the river. The dock on the other side was faint, just a dark smudge on the bank.

There was a small drop to the ferry, which wasn't so different from the jetty – a bunch of wooden boards bound together. It had just as many holes.

'We'll wait until tomorrow before we try crossing,' Bryn said as Ryan helped him back up. 'The man here before us was idle, that much is clear. Bone-idle.' The officer tutted again.

A track led from the crossing to the cabin and beyond. It was well worn, with obvious dents of wagon wheels.

The cabin was a sorry sight: sorry because he already knew such a place. There would be two rooms – one smaller and more private – and a pallet for him, a table and a cooking stove, chairs with broken legs.

'I didn't know it was . . . It's going to be better,' Bryn said.

The front door was off its hinges and propped against the outside wall, but they didn't make it inside. Ryan raised a hand to his nose as the officer snorted and tried to waft the air with his hat, though it did no good.

'What *is* that?' Ryan said, gagging.

'You want to find out?'

'After you.'

Chunk agreed; she put some distance between herself and the cabin. Grim-faced, the officer entered the cabin. Ryan peered after him and saw the air was dusty with specks. They didn't like being disturbed and Bryn had a job keeping them from his face. By the stove were baskets of rotted food, more than he had to eat in a season, but so far gone Ryan couldn't tell what it had been.

The officer brought the baskets out, followed by a cloud of specks. 'What soldier could live like this?' he said.

The door to the other room was also off its hinges and whatever Bryn saw made him pause.

'Is he dead?' Ryan said.

'It's not him.'

Bryn went into the room and came out slowly. He was holding a bedpan. It was brimming with all the kinds of offering a man could make. The officer had gone pale. His lips twitched.

Ryan took a few steps back.

Bryn walked a long way with the bedpan. He could have taken it all the way to Fort Davis and it would have been too close.

Ryan swallowed back bile. 'What kind of man?' he said.

They slept under the stars that night.

The shaggie was hitched to a post of the corral because the fence was broken in more than one place.

'She'd make a run for it if she could,' Bryn said. He offered the shaggie his hand, which was full of feed. 'She's a bit of a free spirit.'

He took off the saddlebags, dropped them at his feet, and opened up Ryan's.

'Hey, wait!'

Bryn looked at him. 'What's this?'

'Private is what.'

'I think I'll be looking after this.' He pulled out the pistol.

'But it's mine,' Ryan said.

'You can have it back when you're ready.'

Bryn moved to the old courser, which was happy to stand by dropped reins, though it did paw the ground a lot – Ryan had heard it in the night. Now he could see what the courser was up to. Two lines inscribed in the dirt: one through the other. The same thing was on the front of the book that Bryn carried.

'When you named this courser did you take it from that book?' Ryan said.

'Sure did. And it's called the Good Book.'

'What's so good about it?'

'Whatever you make it,' Bryn said. He scratched behind the shaggie's ear, though it didn't appear to like that much.

They took care of the animals before they took care of themselves. Chunk was given a fat, dried-out bone – neat or woollie, Ryan wasn't sure. The ruft wagged its tail and barked until the bone was thrown its way, and between the flat sound of her chewing, Chunk let out contented sighs.

Bryn gave him a bowl of watered oats and a bent spoon. A neat bone looked good in comparison. 'It's what we give to all our soldiers,' he said.

'No wonder you aren't winning.'

Bryn laughed as he spooned his own breakfast into his mouth. His scar was more noticeable when he smiled, like a big crease in a bedsheet.

'Was this posting a punishment?' Ryan asked.

'Why do you say that?'

'You were in charge of men back at Fort Davis.'

'I was,' Bryn said.

'And now you're out here alone.'

'Being in charge of men isn't always easy. And I have you now, don't I?'

'Was it because Paul hurt his hand?' Ryan said.

'No, though that was a bad business.'

'Then why be a ferryman and not a real Lieutenant?'

'I wanted to stay near enough to you and your ma and this was the only posting left in the county.'

Ryan concentrated on his oats, putting as much as he could onto each spoonful. He chewed little and swallowed quick. It might be slimy and tasteless but he wasn't going hungry.

'It wasn't like that,' Bryn said eventually. 'You must know that: you'd have seen me in the house a lot, otherwise.'

'I didn't see them all come and go. And if you weren't one of them, why stay close?'

'I cared for her in a different way. We had seen some of the same troubles and I wanted to help.'

'She didn't care for you,' Ryan said.

'No, she didn't.'

'That was her, though.'

When they were finished it was Ryan's job to wash out the bowls. He took them to the river. The bank was easy by the landing and he took his time swilling the brown water around the tin. The river was calm here, more like a field full of corn brushed by the breeze. It was cool too; he might walk right into it until it covered his whole body and then not feel the heat of the morning.

He put the clean bowls next to Bryn's saddlebags. 'Can you teach me to swim?' Ryan said.

The officer looked up from the supplies he was sorting. 'Which first, riding or swimming?'

'Swimming in the day and riding in the evening.'

'And when will the work get done?'

'Between,' Ryan said.

'Right.' Bryn held out his hand. 'You shake on that kind of deal. Like this.'

Ryan copied the officer. Bryn's grip was dry, even in the heat.

They spent the morning clearing out the main room of the cabin, which was piled with crates, mostly, and big jars, some open, some sealed – not that it made a difference. There was no point risking the kinds of things inside: bulbous-looking vegetables sloshing around in some kind of juices; something that had the appearance of a child's hand, and one jar that was worms – just worms, tightly wound together like a mess of string the man was keeping in case it was useful someday. The soldier before them had been a real hoarder: the jars were stacked two- or three-deep against every wall.

They threw the whole lot out onto the prairie, Bryn shaking his head with each new revelation, though he'd given up passing comment.

It was curious, no denying it. One large crate was empty except for three gloves: heavy gloves of thick hide. But when Ryan suggested the crate was fine for keeping, Bryn refused; nothing of the previous resident was to be left.

He'd asked it once: what kind of man was this? Old – that much was obvious: a young man didn't keep worms in jars. A young man didn't save an extra glove after he'd lost its partner. There was a loneliness about the situation, an old man trying to put what was around him into a proper place, to have it ordered like he wanted. He could do that, out here on his own, with no one in the other room to stop him, but somehow it had become twisted, a bad thing. Bryn's offer made a little more sense now: Ryan was here to stop that loneliness taking hold – in either of them.

When most of the crates had been cleared the room felt much bigger. There were still too many specks, but the smell was approaching bearable once they'd scrubbed the floorboards. Rather than a constant it spiked, bringing one or both of them up short at unexpected moments, then it rattled around the nose like a lost worker determined to find a hive up there.

Ryan picked up one end of the table to drag it out.

'I think we'll keep that,' Bryn said.

It was in worse shape than some of the things they'd tossed, with one corner burned black and something carved into the top surface, making it rough and uneven. Bryn claimed they were words.

'What's it say?'

'We'll wait until you can read them yourself,' Bryn said.

Ryan frowned down at the shapes. There were plenty of them.

The chairs were kept too, and the stove. The pokers and the ash shovel were so clean the light bounced off them, and when he ran a finger along the inside of the stove he came away with nothing.

'How'd he cook his food? Or keep warm?' Ryan said, thinking on the lonely, cold man, filling his jars and helping wagons over the river.

They ate Bryn's dried meat out on the porch. The wind was up, whipping across the front of the cabin, swirling the prairie around them. The dirt was loose despite the bone-grass. It was hard to imagine anyone ever coming over the rise and demanding a crossing – where would they be going to? Where'd they come from? Fort Davis was the biggest town in the county, far as he knew, and that had its own bridge.

The bedroom had two small beds, against opposite walls. The window was covered by a threadbare piece of cloth. On the floor there was a mark where the bedpan had been. Ryan scrubbed at it again. Bent over like that, he had a good view of under the beds, but there was nothing there; no jars, no crates, no hidden trinkets. He did the best he could with the stain.

Ryan threw the bucket of water out onto grateful ground.

'Your grandpa was a Southerner, did you know that?' Bryn said.

'No he wasn't.'

'He was. I met him – he still had his red coat.'

'Ma never said.'

'No, I guess not,' Bryn said.

'I never met them – my grandparents.'

'They were good people; lived through tough times and it left its mark. There was a hardness to them but they treated me fairly, that I can say.'

'Ma didn't have much of a good word for either of them.'

'Family is a complicated thing.'

'Is yours?' Ryan said.

'That's a story for another time. We'll start you riding, now you're done with your chores.'

The courser and shaggie were motionless in their broken corral. Bryn headed over, picked up Michael's reins and led the courser back to the house.

'Shouldn't I start on the slower one?' Ryan said.

'String don't like saddles much. She'd throw you before the first step. Michael here, he just wants to be sure of you first.'

'And how's that going to happen?' Ryan said.

'With this.' Bryn passed him the Good Book. 'Hold it and make the sign of the cross, right where he can see.'

'The courser wants to see me make them lines too?'

'He's a creature of faith, is Michael – we came to the Good Book about the same time. Both seen some things, haven't we, boy?'

The courser pawed at the ground, making the first of its lines.

Ryan knelt down and dug out the cross.

'Next time in the air would do, like this.' Bryn drew pretend lines across his body and Michael nodded his long head, sharing the joke.

'Well, why didn't you say?' Ryan's cheeks were hot. Who'd ever heard of an animal of faith?

Bryn smiled his scarred smile.

'We'll get you up using the porch. First thing: always mount from the left side of the courser. He won't like it the other way – he's not used to it. You know which is left?'

'I'm not simple,' Ryan said.

'This here is a stirrup. Put your foot in, facing Michael's

tail. Then push up from the other leg.' Bryn got on the courser to show him. It looked easy enough.

Ryan wedged his boot in the stirrup. He glanced at Michael, who was as still as the house; he could've been made of the same wood. Ryan counted to three, then launched himself up.

The saddle was smooth. He'd pushed too hard and went sliding across. His foot came free of his pa's boots and he was falling.

He hit the ground hard on his shoulder, and Bryn was there, helping him up. The pain was all across his back.

'Is there bone? Is it white, like Paul's?' he said through the tears.

'Who's Paul?'

'The soldier who cut his hand.'

'Nothing's coming through your shirt.'

Ryan took the shirt off slowly, wincing all the while.

'It's already bruising,' Bryn said.

'Would we know ourselves without them?'

'What?'

'Nothing,' Ryan said. He left the shirt on the porch and yanked his boot from the stirrup.

'Maybe we leave it for today?'

'No, I'm fine.'

'Let me look at those laces.'

'What are laces?' Ryan said.

Bryn looked down at Ryan's boots and sighed. 'They tie up your boots – see mine? There were some in one of the crates this morning.'

'Look like worms.'

'They're not worms. Wait here.' Bryn went over to where they'd dumped the previous ferryman's rubbish. Crates were tossed around, and so were words that barely carried on the wind, though they had the shape of curse words.

Michael didn't approve.

Bryn returned with long grey things hanging from his hand.

'They're not worms, are they?' Ryan said.

'They're not worms.'

He tried hard not to fidget as the officer knelt at his feet. The top of Bryn's head was red and dry-looking and his hair was thin there. He threaded the laces through holes that Ryan had always figured weren't supposed to be there, like the scuffs on the toes or the holes in the bottoms. Now he examined them, they were as regular as Chunk's teeth. She'd been watching them the whole morning but she was busy: there was a bone to see to. When all the holes were used up Bryn did something that made the laces look funny.

'What's that?' Ryan said.

'It's a knot.'

'No it's not – I've made my share of knots and they don't look droopy like that.'

'There's different kinds,' Bryn said, starting on the other boot.

'Why would I need different kinds of knots? What's the point in those extra loops? Just tie a proper knot and cut off the rest.'

'This makes it easier to untie them and then tie them again.'

'Why would I want to untie them then?' Ryan said.

'You ask a lot of questions.'

'Only when you don't make a heap of sense.'

Bryn looked up and Ryan tried to step away but the officer still had his foot. Bryn didn't look angry; he was grinning, in a 'finding something amusing' sort of way, not a 'Chunk taking to your leg' sort of way.

'Don't tell me you sleep in your boots?' Bryn said, laughing at his own joke.

'No one likes cold feet.'

'I'll show you how to make the loops.'

'Fine,' Ryan said, crossing his arms.

'This time, don't try and jump over a mountain.' All the same, Bryn stood on the other side of Michael, ready to stop another fall.

Ryan rubbed his shoulder as the courser nodded again, a kind of encouragement. He tested the boots and they felt as fixed to his feet as a tree was to the ground. There was still no leather to meet the end of his toes, but now he wasn't dancing on his own with every step. He put his foot into the stirrup and flung himself up, and there was the slide-and-pull once more, but this time his foot stayed in his boot. As Bryn hurried to right him Michael stayed dead still.

It took some scrambling, but he was on.

'Both feet in. Good, sit straight now,' Bryn said. 'You're leaning back too much.'

Ryan leaned forward a little. The courser's neck was strange from where he was sitting; it looked shorter, and the mane was thin, like the top of Bryn's head. Two old men together.

'Sit forward.'

'I am sitting forward!'

'More. And put your heels down,' Bryn said. He grabbed Ryan's leg and pulled it down. 'Good. Now I'll walk Michael a bit, get you used to moving.'

'I think this is just fine.'

'Don't worry.'

'Bryn, what are you doing?' Ryan said. His shoulder hurt – it hurt a lot now, and he didn't want to see white bone.

'Don't worry.' Bryn took the reins and they started forward.

The courser felt impossibly heavy underneath him. How did it move? It carried him with less effort than a man carried a tune. They rounded the corral a few times, Bryn giving orders like he remembered he was in the army: Heels down! Sit straight! Stop squeezing your thighs.

Ryan was tired when Bryn helped him down from the courser.

Michael made his lines in the dirt. Another one off safely.

'Amen,' Ryan said.

2 : 4

Bryn lit three candles that night – they were big, sitting in fat jars – and he was quick to say he'd brought them from Fort Davis. He put two of them on the table and the other in the bedroom. Ryan liked the smell of melting wax. He sat at the table, resting his head on his arm, watching the flames. The lips of the jars shattered the light, and if he squinted, it looked like dawn.

The Good Book was also on the table. It cast a long shadow.

Bryn took the other chair and picked the book up. 'Have you decided?' he said.

Ryan traced the words that were carved into the table. 'Will it be hard?'

'At first.'

'And there's more to read than just your holy book?'

'A lot more.'

'Can my pa read?'

'I'd think so. Your ma said he was the son of a preacher, although she said it like it was a bad thing. He probably learned with the Good Book too.'

'Can't hurt more than falling off a saddle, can it?'

Bryn opened the book and put it on the table where they could both see. 'There's pages missing, but that's a different story. See here? This big letter is where you start. It's an "N". The next letters are "o" and "w". Which means the first word is "Now".'

'Now? As in, right now?'

'Right.'

Ryan stared at the small black lines. They didn't sit still in the candlelight. The big 'N' wasn't so hard to spot. All the letters should have been that big – but then there wouldn't be much room for so many letters. 'Wait right there. You say that word is "names" and it starts with a "n", but it looks different,' Ryan said.

'That's because some letters change when they're at the start of a word.'

'Don't make much sense.'

'You'll get used to it,' Bryn said. He read each word slowly, explaining the letters and drawing their shapes with his finger in the air. He made Ryan do it too. It took a long time, and Ryan's head throbbed like each letter was being pushed in through his eyes and ears and there was only so much room. There were some words he didn't understand. Bryn said they were places. They were gone now.

Bryn closed the book.

Ryan rubbed at his eyes. They'd barely made it down the page.

'That's a good start.'

'It's harder than riding,' Ryan said.

'They both open up the world.'

There was a shout from outside: a man's voice calling in the night.

Ryan blew at the candle. It was foolish to have light so late.

'What are you doing?' Bryn said, moving to the door. 'We're here to work the ferry, remember?'

'Then why take your rifle?'

'I'll need your help, but stay here first.'

From the porch Bryn called out. A lone rider was making his way down the track at some pace. Ryan peeked out from the doorway. The rider was darker than the darkness. Bryn went to meet him.

'Messenger!' the rider yelled. He held something up.

'Ride on, we'll meet you at the ferry,' Bryn said. He turned to the house. 'Quick now, boy.'

They both ran after the rider. Ryan had never seen a courser move so fast. Could Michael do that? He didn't want to find out; he'd stick to his reading. Bryn was breathing hard when they got to the landing. The rider had already taken his courser on board and hitched it to the lone railing. The courser didn't look happy. It was stamping its front hooves, and not for any kind of faith.

Bryn took up the winch and the ferry started off from the landing with the three of them and the courser. Ryan tried not to look at the holes in the boards, though he couldn't help see the constant movement of the river – see it and feel it. The Gregory might look calm from the bank, but it was ferocious here.

'Who's it for?' he said.

'Ryan!'

The messenger ignored him. He was definitely a soldier; his uniform was heavier than Bryn's, with a coat for keeping out the rain. It made the man a funny shape, like a pine cone. The winch squealed. It was the sound all winches made – none of them were happy to work – and Bryn was hard at it. The fold of his scar was a dark line on his face and he was grinning that other kind of grin now.

The ferry bucked against the current and the courser tried to turn around – as if that would help. Ryan backed away, his hand still on the rail, then something snagged at the ferry and it twisted against the rope and shook Ryan loose.

Then he was falling.

He hit the water and the cold pressed the breath from him. It was an all-over cold, like he'd never felt. He opened his eyes but there was nothing to see. He flailed his arms and kicked his legs, and it was like fighting air.

Something caught hold of him, and even before he could imagine the monsters that might live in such a place, he was hauled out and dumped onto the boards of the ferry. He coughed up great buckets of water, along with what felt like his insides.

The messenger patted him on the shoulder. 'Any longer, and they'd have found you in Fort Davis.'

Ryan could only nod in thanks. He stayed very still and close to the boards for the rest of the crossing.

Bryn was sweating. He changed arms often and the last part was slow. It didn't help that the courser kept moving.

Even before they made the landing proper the messenger had loosed the courser's reins and was mounting. He urged the animal on and when they made the track he dropped some coins to the ground.

Bryn helped Ryan up. They stood on the landing and watched the messenger go.

Ryan shivered, his clothes clinging to his skin.

'How was your first swim?'

2 : 5

'Let me go,' Ryan said.

Bryn was already on the porch with the empty saddlebags over his shoulder.

'It's no place for youngsters. And I'll be busy, picking up orders and such.'

'I know Fort Davis! I'd have Michael – I could get away from trouble.'

'Some trouble is faster than that,' Bryn said.

'You know I can ride; you said so yourself.'

'I need you here, in case someone wants to cross.'

'That's a pissing lie!'

'Don't you curse at me,' Bryn said, his voice low. He headed out to Michael and checked his straps twice. Hand on the Good Book, the man and the courser said their prayers.

If there was so much trouble in Fort Davis, then why did he leave the rifle? Ryan kicked at the dirt. The best stones were by the river.

String whined as Bryn rode off. She didn't like being left behind either. At least he wasn't tied to a post.

'Don't forget the meat,' Ryan shouted after them, but if Bryn heard, he showed no sign. There were lots of reasons he was going, and going now. Ryan had seen it before – men all had the same face when they came to the farm to be with Ma. They were *eager*.

He'd better not forget the meat.

Bryn had left halfway through a hand of cards and they were still spread over the table. Ryan picked up the pack and flicked through. The game would've been won in a few turns. He took a couple of the cards and swapped them: give the old man something to think on. The carved words poked out from underneath the stacks of cards and he said each letter out loud, on their own, and then the whole thing: 'Never, the sea.' When he'd first read them it had felt good to finally read those scratchy lines, and Bryn had smiled. But the smile had faded when Ryan asked what it meant and they'd argued.

'You know what Israel is,' Ryan said. 'You know who Joseph was. All those complicated things in that book. Why don't you know what *this* means?'

'It's not that simple.'

'Why not?'

'The words could mean a lot of things,' Bryn said. 'Maybe the person who carved them hadn't seen the sea before.'

'"Maybe"?'

'I can't say for sure.'

'Then what good is reading if you can't be sure?' Ryan said. Bryn shook his head.

Chunk padded into the room and lay down with a lot

of huffing and puffing. The heat made her lazy, unless she was in the river.

He went to lie down himself. The bedroom was cooler – partly being distant from the stove and partly because of where the sun hit the cabin. Chunk found the energy to follow him and he scratched behind her ear until she started wagging her tail against the floor.

Bryn would be in a bed no better than his. And he wouldn't be alone either.

'Hello?'

Chunk was out on the porch and barking before Ryan could stand.

'Chunk, back!'

Outside, two riders waited on coursers that made Michael look young; they were breathing badly and foaming spit on their muzzles. And they weren't happy about Chunk.

Ryan pushed in front of the ruft. 'Afternoon,' he said.

'Where's the ferryman?' one rider said. They were of the same age, dressed different but close enough. Four pistols between them.

'Sleeping it off.'

They laughed. They were familiar with that notion.

'We need to be crossing.'

'Four for the both of you,' Ryan said.

They looked at each other. 'I think two would be enough.'

'Three, and that's offered 'cause I'm slower than him. When he's able.'

'Three it is.'

The coursers took some persuading – they had enjoyed being still – then the men made for the ferry.

Chunk was growling.

'Chunk, stay!'

The ruft looked at him.

'You can't be on the ferry with those coursers. Look, I'm taking this.' He showed Chunk the rifle and she shied away. She knew what kind of noise it made.

He followed the men at his own pace. He wasn't going to hurry for three coins. Hardly worth the effort. Wagons: that was what people paid proper money for, but they were rare. Bryn said it was the war; that no one wanted to move their lives with all that going on. Lucky if they had the choice.

'You need to hitch them coursers to the rail, not too close to the winch,' Ryan said as he approached the men, who were standing idle.

'Aye aye, captain,' said one as the other eyed the rifle.

The animals loaded on, Ryan took up his position. There was a courser between him and the men. He watched them as he turned the winch and they watched him back. The rifle was at his feet.

'This isn't so bad. Maybe I should have been a sailor?' the man said. His friend seemed to be a mute, or deaf, or both.

'It gets rougher than this,' Ryan said.

'I'm sure it does.'

He had to switch arms, but he didn't turn his back on them.

'That looks simple enough to me,' the man said. 'Don't really need ferrymen.'

'Times when the river is no good for crossing – can be dangerous. Some would load it full of coursers and shaggies and whatnot and then be surprised when they had to swim.'

'World is full of fools, and we're paying for them.'

Ryan agreed. The man kept quiet for the rest of the crossing.

When they bumped to a landing the men led the coursers off. The animals were shaky on the boards, their thin legs wobbling until they were on proper ground. The men mounted up.

'Three coins,' Ryan said, holding the rifle.

'I thought about that and decided against it.'

Ryan raised the stock to his shoulder and took aim. 'Three coins.'

'You're not going to shoot me over three coins.' The man grinned and turned his courser. They rode away at their own pace.

Ryan was shaking. He hadn't had his finger over the trigger. He gripped the rifle. *Useless.* She had been right to call him that. He was just a child – a helpless child. They hadn't even drawn their pistols.

Ryan waited on the porch. The sun was taking its time setting. It turned the sky a deep orange that had more colour to it than the land below. The rifle was on one side of him, Chunk the other, though much good either of them were.

A rider came into view. Ryan was fairly certain it was Bryn. He wasn't in a hurry, picking his way down the track, or more likely, letting Michael decide. The saddle-bags were full, which changed the shape of the rider, even at a distance. The breeze was soft and it played with the loose hair that was almost down to Ryan's eyes. Bryn was weaving through the uneven ground, and there was a beauty about it: the calm man and the gentle footfalls of a steady courser. Bryn held the reins to one side. It made him look delicate.

He hitched the courser and carried over the bags.

'You're back early,' Ryan said.

'Am I?'

'New orders?'

'Nothing new, no,' Bryn said.

'Then I hope it was worth it.'

Bryn put the bags down. 'What's the rifle doing out?'

'Two riders came. They crossed, but they wouldn't pay,' Ryan said.

'And you took the rifle?'

'They had pistols. Not that they needed them.'

Bryn stepped towards him and Ryan flinched and raised his arm. 'What are you—? I'm not going to hit you.' He sat down on the porch. 'One crossing isn't worth shooting a man over. I would have done the same.'

'Then what's the point?'

'Because some people understand that a service should be paid,' Bryn said. 'You do chores, help with the crossings, look after the animals. I give you a roof, food, and teach you what I can.'

'And if I had pistols I could just take it all,' Ryan said.

'Not all of it: I couldn't teach you to ride if I was dead. I could lie and tell you the wrong letters on each page. Not everything can be taken.'

'Did you visit a woman in Fort Davis?'

'Would you be angry if I did?'

Ryan looked out at the prairie. The sun was nearly gone. 'Not really.'

'I don't pay her, if that's what you want to know.'

'Is she married?'

'No.'

'Have you ever hit her?'

'What? No!' Bryn said. 'Why would you say that?'

Ryan shrugged. 'Men hit Ma.'

'Her name is Norma. She's a little older than I am. Her husband died a soldier before they had children. We take walks and talk and sometimes we share a bed. All right?'

'Fine.'

'We need to get you reading more of the Good Book.' Bryn stood with some effort and took the bags inside. Chunk followed him, tail wagging. She must have smelled something. There were noises of things being put on shelves and Chunk's claws on the boards. The next thing, Chunk came screaming out of the door and Ryan leaned aside just in time. A bone was flying through the air, more ponderous than any hood or even chook, and Chunk wasn't taking her eye from it. Too big to catch, she pounced when it hit the ground. Bryn was spoiling her.

Ryan picked up the rifle and headed in. He put it in the corner and tried to forget it.

'Hope you didn't give that ruft all the meat.'

Bryn pointed to the pan where two thin cuts of neat were starting to hiss and spit. Ryan sniffed hard at the thick smell and moved the cuts in the pan. Blood and water bubbled at the edge. 'Barely any fat on this,' he said.

'Norma says a growing boy needs good meat.'

'She knows about me?'

'I told you, we talk,' Bryn said.

Ryan flipped the cuts. They were browning, though the stove was a little too hot.

'Will she come to live with us?'

'Would that be a problem?' Bryn said.

'I asked first.'

'No, she won't. She has a nice house. And I don't think she wants another soldier for a husband.'

'So there's no problem then.'

They ate at the table, careful not to disturb Bryn's hand of cards. His losing hand.

2 : 6

Ryan opened his eyes a crack, trying to see the room without moving his head. Bryn's bed was empty and the muffled sound of voices came through the cabin walls. Bryn and Ryan were the only way across the river for some miles and that should've made them important men, but it didn't. Every prick with a pistol and a courser thought it was his given right to cross. They had no mind for how wide it was, how deep, or how strong, and no mind for how late at night it was. 'People are ignorant,' Ma had liked to say. She included herself and Ryan in that statement of fact.

He pushed down the sheet and scratched his thigh. Dots crisscrossed his skin like lines on a map: whatever was feeding on him was having a feast. The skin was turning pink.

Something started buzzing in the cabin, closer, cussing harder than the scrapers outside.

He wrestled his legs out of bed and felt the cold wood floor under his feet.

Michael was whinnying – Ryan thought he could tell the courser and String apart – and there was a thumping sound:

Michael was going at the ground as if a storm was coming. The shutters were open, though there was no breeze.

Through the window the sky was an ugly red and the clouds boiled and bubbled. It was a peculiar sunrise. The bushes and weeds were inky black scratches on the ground, like the Good Book's letters.

The buzzing kept on and he looked to the ceiling for a dead-lie or a worker; something with wings and a temper, but it was too dark to see in the corners, where such things preferred. He went through to the main room, scratching his head where some other beast had been eating at him. A smart number of them relied on him for food. When he used to go hungry, he hoped they had gone hungry too.

There was a wagon outside: a big one, too, with canvas stretched over the top. It had seen a brush of paint recently, but the wood was still crooked in places. No wonder Bryn was keen to get it crossed, though he should have woken Ryan.

He didn't envy the shaggies pulling – it looked like a whole house was in the wagon. Three men sat up on the driver's seat and there was another man talking with Bryn, a few hundred paces from the cabin. His courser snuffled the dirt.

'Won't find nothing there,' Ryan muttered.

The stranger waved at the wagon. Ryan couldn't see much of the man; he was a silhouette against the red sky, wearing a long coat and a wide hat. With a yell and a flick of the reins, the wagon rolled off towards the river. The stranger and Bryn watched it go for a while.

The buzzing broke the quiet. It was close now and Ryan

glanced down at the table. Bryn had finished his hand of cards. There was a candle next to the deck. Another buzz and he found the loud-mouth. He should have guessed from the desperate sound that it came from the candle. The wax was a murky yellow and dead specks floated in it like raisins in a fruitcake: not just on the surface, but all the way down. The latest was still jigging about on the top, wings or legs stuck.

The wagon was down at the ferry now, waiting. There would be coins handed over, and then Bryn would be back, grabbing the rifle and his coat. A heavy wagon, men moving the sum of their possessions; the charge would be twelve at least. That discussion was what was taking so long, Ryan figured.

Ryan pressed the speck further into the wax. Mercy. The Good Lord had it right: it was a mighty fine thing to do. He blew on his finger until the wax cooled and then peeled it off.

Outside, voices were raised. That happened when haggling and he didn't like it. The sky was heavy with something wicked. He glanced over at the rifle, still in the corner where he had left it.

Bryn spat, his head whipping to the side. If he was making a deal, he'd missed his hand by some way.

The spit hit the ground like a roll of thunder: a streak of red as dark as the sky.

Bryn doubled over. The stranger's elbow came down and cracked his head.

Ryan tried to yell, but he couldn't. Instead, he grabbed

the rifle. It was heavy, like the weight of years. His fingers were numb.

Something dark moved quickly. It was out of the cabin and on top of the stranger before Ryan had a chance.

'Chunk, no!'

The man grunted as he wrestled with the ruft and Chunk growled back. Ryan knew what those teeth were busy doing.

There was a gunshot. It rang across the hills like it was far away, and right up close in Ryan's ear, and Chunk was yelping, her leg not right as she limped away from the stranger. She was soon lost in the bone-grass.

Raising the rifle Ryan tried to take aim, but he couldn't keep it still.

Bryn was on the ground. That wasn't the end of it: the stranger was laying it on heavy, with fists and feet. A gurgling, choking sound came from Bryn. It ended with a splutter, and still the stranger kept stamping and kicking.

Ryan sighted the silhouette as best he could and closed his eyes. He had to kill a man. His arms were shaking with the weight. He pulled the trigger.

Nothing happened. The rifle wasn't loaded. But the sound of the hammer was as loud as gunshot. It was hard to tell if the stranger was facing him, or if he had tried to shoot a man in the back.

His legs locked like two fenceposts. He couldn't look away, and he couldn't say nothing either. His thigh felt warm and he knew he'd pissed himself.

It felt like days before the stranger gave up. He clearly hadn't seen Ryan, or heard him. The man got on the courser – the damn animal hadn't budged an inch the whole time – and rode down to the river.

Ryan finally breathed out, but stayed stock-still. He had seen men fighting before, been wailed on by his ma enough to know a beating, but this was something different. This was something a man didn't walk away from. He hugged the useless rifle.

The lump that was Bryn didn't move.

The yellow stain of his piss started at his thigh and kept going.

Useless.

He threw up on the table: stringy mucus and things he hadn't eaten. It covered the deck of cards. He kept spitting, trying to get rid of the taste, and remembered the arc of Bryn's blood.

2 : 7

Ryan wasn't sure how long he stood gripping the table edge. The sky hadn't changed, nor the stretching waves of bone-grass. He took the empty rifle with him out onto the porch and looked to the river, but the wagon and the stranger were gone. The ground between him and Bryn stretched on for days.

He took three steps on the cold, rough earth and wished he'd thought of boots. Taking them off at night: that was Bryn's idea. He was close enough to smell the blood, rich, like greased metal. His stomach lurched again.

Bryn was a gap in the bone-grass. He'd curled himself up best he could, but his head wasn't right: it was looking the wrong way, like he was being chased by something. All around his head was a bloody halo of spiky lines. There was an awful lot of it, painting the grass in sweeping, messy strokes. His hat was a few feet away and his hair was wet. His nose had more bends than the river. His cheek had split and teeth snarled through.

Ryan swallowed – he didn't have anything left to bring

up. Bryn wasn't breathing, but he was looking right at him.

He crossed himself. "'And Joseph died, and all his brethren, and all that gen-er-ation.'"

He was answered by a whining sound, off in the bone-grass. 'Chunk?'

The whines got louder and higher in pitch. She was lying in a similar way to Bryn, the grass around her pressed down and stained with blood. She didn't raise her head as he came close but followed him with her eye. She was panting hard. *Hurts*, her whine said. *It hurts.*

The blood was coming from one of her back legs, which was raw, slashed open by the bullet. He looked away, remembering a different wound, then took off his shirt and tried to rip off a sleeve, but the stitches held strong. Kneeling down, he wrapped the whole shirt around Chunk's leg. It turned red.

Chunk raised her head and barked with difficulty.

'Sssshhh, now, girl.' He pressed down on the shirt, ignoring the blood staining his fingers. For a long time he watched the steady rise and fall of her chest until the blood started to dry. It changed colour, growing darker as the sky became lighter, and at last she fell asleep, despite her pain. He couldn't carry her, even if she let him. He made sure the shirt was tight and went back to the cabin.

The nearest Law-Man was a long way off. So was the nearest soldier, two days there and back – and that's if they even cared about an old officer. That's if they believed

Ryan. Candle in hand, he went to see Bryn again, keeping his distance this time. The blood was still obvious, though Bryn looked more at peace than he had close up. He might come back, like she had; he might ask for the same help – but there was nothing wrong with Bryn's hands.

And if he didn't come back, then he should be buried. There was a shovel – Ryan couldn't remember if it belonged to Bryn or the man before them. He'd wait till morning proper, then he'd know what to do.

In the bedroom he took off his wet trousers. He could live with the smell; it hadn't left the room from before, not entirely. It was worse when the sun came through the window and heated the middle of the floor. He only had one pair of trousers so he'd have to wash them, or use a pair of Bryn's – if that didn't feel strange. He was used to wearing another man's trousers; did it make much of a difference if the man was dead instead of a long way off?

His body buzzed like a speck, his muscles feeling angry, vibrating. He was too awake to get into bed. He gathered what he had, which would barely fill a saddlebag. He wanted to be ready to leave, when it was right. He searched the cabin for his pistol, dragging a chair over to the shelves and looking in every pot and jar. He checked under the stove and even tried the floorboards, in case one was loose. He found it in the bedroom under Bryn's pillow. Reaching for the Good Book he knocked a candle off the bed – he had a vision of the room in flames but by some miracle the jar didn't smash.

*

He slept later than he had meant to. The bed bothered his bare skin – sleeping naked was a bad idea – and the bites that covered him didn't help either. He scratched, and that only made it worse. He pulled on a pair of Bryn's trousers and cast around for his shirt – but it was Chunk's shirt now. He took one of Bryn's. It was huge. He tucked it in, but he could still grab two handfuls of its width on either side of his belly. He rolled up the trouser legs so many times he lost count, until they were finally at his ankles. If he had time he'd stitch them. His things were piled on Bryn's bed, ready to be packed.

Moving to the main room he noticed something outside. Some*one*. The door was wide open. They noticed him too. Bryn was back.

'Hello.' It wasn't Bryn. It was a big man. 'You Ryan?' he called.

Ryan glanced at the rifle in the corner. The empty rifle.

'On your own now, then?'

He ran back into the bedroom and got his pistol. He had four rounds; that had to be enough. He went outside, keeping the gun levelled in front of him.

'Hey! Easy now.' The man raised his hands. 'I'm not here for trouble.'

'Trouble is all there is.'

'I can see. That your ruft over there?'

'So what if it is?' Ryan said. His thumb was on the hammer.

'Needs water or it'll die.' The man's concern sounded genuine. He was old for someone so big. He had an orderly white beard that covered the bottom of his face.

'What you want?' Ryan spluttered.

'Right now I want to save your ruft. 'Cause I can't save this man.'

'Stay there. Right there.' Ryan backed into the cabin and picked up the bucket of water. It was a day old at least but Chunk would drink anything at the best of times. He carried it in one hand and the pistol in the other. The man had lowered his hands, but Ryan made sure the gun was always on him. Water spilled from the bucket onto thirsty ground.

When he got to Chunk she was still panting and her eye was half-closed. It was hard to see a patch of white on the shirt at all. She made no sign that she knew he was there. He crouched down and tilted the bucket until the water was right on the edge and she lapped at it, slow at first, as if getting the taste, and then urgent.

'She's lost some amount of blood,' the man said. He was close.

Ryan turned, pistol ready, and the man put his hands up again.

'Were you just going to let her die?'

'I didn't know what to do,' Ryan said.

'I'll bring her in; she needs to be out of the sun. And there's a storm coming.'

Ryan followed the man's gaze. There were clouds in the distance.

'You're not coming in.'

'If I wanted to hurt you, you think I'd be helping? Even with that pistol of yours?' the man said.

'I know how to use it!'

'I'm sure you do. Let me carry her inside.'

Chunk was still drinking, but she did look dried out. She had less shine to her than the man.

'You be careful with her,' Ryan said.

The man picked Chunk up as if she weighed no more than a crate half-full of worms and laces and all. Her eyes were fully open now and she tried to snap at him, but she didn't have the strength. He held her firm but not tight and started towards the cabin, Ryan walking behind.

There was a huge black courser by the broken fence looking right at them. It didn't have a saddle or any bags, and no reins either ... no reins, and it wasn't tied to a post. It had thick bundles of muscle, like Chunk, just ten times the size. There was something monstrous in the way it stood so still, so big. Michael was at the other end of the corral, his rump pressing hard on the fence that was still there. He was going at the ground like he was trying to dig his way out. String was pulling at her tether; she had the post half out of the ground. Neither animal made a sound beyond Michael's digging.

'Is that your courser?' Ryan said.

'In a manner of speaking.'

'But it's got no saddle.'

'Don't need one,' the man said.

That wasn't right – how could a man stay on a courser without stirrups? Or tell it where to go without reins? He hadn't been riding long but they were clear necessities.

'Stop!'

The man did so without turning. His back blocked out most of the cabin. All Ryan could see of Chunk was the tips of her feet.

'How did you know my name?' Ryan said.

'Let me get—'

'How did you know?'

'Your pa told me.'

2 : 8

'My pa? How do you know my pa?'

'You could say I work for him,' the man said. 'This ruft ain't getting no lighter.' He started for the cabin again.

Work for his pa . . . only one type of man would do work for his pa. Ryan had to hustle to keep up with him.

'If you work for Pa, what are you doing here?'

The man was careful on the porch steps. He had to angle himself to get through the door, and even then it was a close fit. He sniffed when he got inside. The table still bore the marks of Ryan's weakness and so did the trousers piled in the bedroom. The man laid Chunk down on Ryan's bed and rested a hand on her chest.

'She'll be all right, won't you, girl?' the man said. Chunk's ears were flat against her head. She wriggled at his touch.

'I asked you a question,' Ryan said.

'Tenacious. Just like your pa.'

'I'm nothing like him.'

'And how would you know?' the man said.

'Why are you here?'

'To come and get you, of course.' He took off his hat. It was expensive, with silver circles on the band – nine that Ryan could count. 'Name is Knox. Now we're introduced, I'd be a happier soul if you lowered the gun.'

Ryan put the gun in his pocket but kept his hand on it.

'That soldier – he looking after you?'

'He's dead.' It was a simple thing to say. The truth was simple, sometimes.

'So I saw.'

'I'm waiting until he comes back,' Ryan said.

Knox brushed past him. 'Come.'

They stood by Bryn's twisted body. The blood had dried to a muddy colour – a more natural fit for the bone-grass.

'Makes you wonder what He's got planned for *you*, seeing something like this,' Knox said. They both stared at the body for a while. Knox appeared deep in thought. Not a thing stirred.

'I didn't know him long,' Ryan said, 'but he never raised a hand to me.'

Knox cleared his throat. 'You see it happen?'

'No,' Ryan said. Seeing it meant he should've taken measures to stop it. Seeing meant admitting he'd been afraid.

'They take anything?'

'There's nothing worth stealing here.'

'Not to most folk, no,' Knox said. 'They didn't take your animals neither.'

'No.' Michael and String were still trying to put distance

between themselves and Knox's courser. The fencepost was almost out.

'This one's not comin' back, Ryan.'

'How do you know?'

Knox pointed to the darkening sky. 'They wouldn't be interested otherwise.'

There was a group of blightbirds circling, shadows against the clouds. They were getting lower all the time.

'You're scared,' Knox said.

'I'm fine.'

Knox took a step towards him.

'I'm here to help you.' Another step closer. He was talking soft and slow. His big black eyes were deeper than the river. It was hard to look anywhere but those eyes.

Knox put his hand on Ryan's shoulder. The red sky behind the man seethed and broiled like a knot of hushts. 'I'm taking you to your pa,' he said.

'Pa? He never wanted me.'

'He does now.'

'Why?' Ryan said.

'Because he's all you've got.'

Knox dragged Bryn's body to the side of the cabin. 'Needs to be done before the storm,' he said. He took off his jacket – he wore black braces instead of a belt – and set to with the shovel. The dry, packed dirt wasn't easy to move and he was soon sweating.

After the ground was broken Ryan offered to help.

'You'll only slow me down.'

'I want to bury him,' Ryan said. 'I should be part of it.'

Knox handed him the shovel.

Ryan tossed out each load of earth as he'd seen Knox do. When his shoulder started to ache he ignored it. Then his arms started to feel loose and lifting the shovel tested them; each action took longer and moved less earth. Knox let him decide when he'd had enough, so he worked more than he should. He had to leave the shovel in the hole, doubting he could hand it over. Knox finished the grave. It was anything but deep.

Ryan recovered enough to help lay the body down. He took hold of Bryn's feet and they piled the dirt on top.

'Want to say anything?' Knox said.

Ryan knelt so he could touch the turned soil. 'I'm sorry I didn't shoot. I'm sorry.' He crossed himself. 'Amen.'

'That's a habit you might think on losing. Your pa doesn't go much on faith.'

They passed the storm on the porch watching the rain. The sky grumbled and there were far-away flashes. Chunk made noises when the sky did and the coursers wouldn't stand still. Knox fell asleep first. Ryan slept in Bryn's bed. The pillow smelled of the man. He had kindness where she had cruelty and they both ended the same way. He got up and closed the bedroom door.

Ryan was hungry. He had spent days hungry before; feeling his belly fold in on itself until a single egg would fill him up. This was different: there was an emptiness to it. He groaned.

Somebody was making a racket with the pots and pans. He had the brief hope he had dreamed the whole thing; slept so long that his stomach and Bryn were now cursing him.

'I know you're awake.'

That wasn't Bryn. Bryn was dead and buried. The voice was thick and rich. It belonged to a bigger man. Ryan got up. He had slept in his clothes. His foot snagged on a trouser leg that had rolled loose. He caught himself on the wall before he fell.

'You're hungry. Meat won't be long now.' Knox was tending the stove. The yellow light cast strange shadows on his bearded face. It was all together wrong for Knox to be there; he didn't look comfortable, and neither did the cabin. The man was too big for the single room, and the walls shuddered whenever he went near.

'There's a difference about you,' Ryan said.

'That right?' Knox didn't look up from the stove.

'Strangers don't help people.'

'No, they don't.' He dropped bits of meat into a pot. 'But I'm no stranger, remember?'

'A stranger killed him.' The smell of the meat cooking made him wince.

'Takes a savage man to do that. One day it'll catch up to him,' Knox said. He stirred the pot.

'But I should have stopped it.'

'You would have, if you could. That's not the same as doing the deed.'

The man led him over to the table. It was clean – Bryn's cards and other belongings were neatly piled in one corner.

'Good to you, was he, that soldier?'

'He was.'

Knox sat down on a chair. It creaked and strained as if a neat had jumped on. He stared at his hands. 'I know you saw him get beat. There's no shame in it.'

Ryan's stomach pinched at him.

'Things happen to the best o' people.' Knox went to the pot, poured water in and then chopped vegetables over it. There were splashes when bigger pieces fell.

The smell pinched Ryan's stomach again and he couldn't stop himself moaning.

When it was done and Knox brought over a portion of the stew, Ryan spooned it down even before the man had turned away. He ignored the stinging in his mouth and held out the bowl for more. The meat was tender and the vegetables were fresh, best he could tell, though he had little experience of the growing and eating of vegetables. They had needed more than the farm could give.

'Growing boys need plenty of feeding. This might be your best chance for a while.'

'Why?' Ryan said.

'Taking you to your pa will be rough going.'

'What if I don't want to go?'

'You'd rather stay here? Alone?' Knox said.

'No. Not alone.'

His stomach felt a little better – a different kind of tightness, a better kind.

'Your shaggie is long gone,' Knox said from the porch. 'My fault, I s'pose.' He lit a pipe. The smoke was a mix of burnt dust and damp wood. He'd loosened his neck-tie and his braces, but he still didn't look right there; the porch was about to buckle. Men made an impression on a place, some more than others.

'You smoke?'

'Never have.'

'A fine habit. Wish I'd thought it up myself. Still, can't be in every business,' Knox said, sighing out grey wisps.

'You're in the thieving business instead?'

'I'm a man who likes to keep it interesting. I've known your pa for a good long time; long before you were born. Anyways,' Knox said, tapping out his pipe, 'you need rest before we start out.'

Ryan stared out at the black courser, a silhouette against the grey sky. It hadn't moved an inch. Michael was still stuck between trying to get as far away as possible and not turning his back.

'I can ride just fine,' he said.

'There's no rush.'

'I'm already packed.'

2 : 9

Ryan made sure the saddle straps were firmly in place, though he wasn't certain how tight they should really be. They weren't troubling Michael, but Knox's black courser still held his attention. Ryan's saddlebags were heavier than he'd expected. The Good Book was weighty, and so was the pistol. He led Michael out of the corral. There were marks on his rump from backing against the fence. Any longer and there would have been sores, or worse.

'Didn't like your chances with String?' Ryan said. He held out a handful of feed. The courser's lips were dry and hairy. He put a bucket down and Michael drank, though he still had one eye on Knox's animal. They both did.

Knox was sitting on the edge of the bed stroking Chunk. The ruft's ears were still flat against her head. She was as still as Ryan had ever seen her.

'Is she okay?' Ryan said.

'Fine.' The bed groaned as he stood.

When he left the room Chunk's tail started wagging and Ryan stroked her. She lifted her head to see him better. 'You did your best,' he said. 'Better than me.'

He peeled away the layers of his shirt, which was all stuck together by dried blood. There was an odd satisfaction to pulling the cloth apart, the give and pull of the material. Chunk's leg was already scarring. It looked fairly clean.

'Saved these for her,' Knox said, bringing some fatty pieces of meat over.

Chunk laid her head back on the bed and sighed.

'Put them on the floor,' Ryan said.

'I'll see to my courser.'

Suddenly Chunk got real interested in the meat. She leapt off the bed, but fell in a scrambling of claws, her body making a heavy thump on the floor. Her back leg wasn't moving right. She stood without putting weight on it, leaving it hanging there, useless. She ate like it was her last meal. She kept checking on him, as if she knew what he was thinking over. He let her finish in peace.

Knox was ready to ride. His black jacket was buttoned halfway and he wore his hat against a sun that wasn't there. With no reins to hold he rested his hands on his thighs. Another kind of man might have laid them on pistols at his waist, but he didn't need them, not for show.

Michael had put some distance between him and Knox, though he was too well trained to make his escape. Ryan took the courser back to the porch so he could mount up. He rubbed his shoulder to remind himself this was a courser and not a mountain. His mounting was not a thing of grace, like a hood taking flight, more like the wobbling blightbirds, but the result would do. Michael drew his lines and Ryan prayed alone.

They started towards the ferry and Chunk came running as best she could. She barked. Neither of the coursers were bothered by her noise.

'I gave her the choice. She doesn't want to stay,' Ryan said. 'Would you?'

He looked at the cabin. He was getting used to leaving.

'If she can't keep up, there's greater mercies,' Knox said.

'I'm tired of mercy.'

Despite hobbling, keeping up wasn't Chunk's problem; she was too excited to be outside and moving again. She went fifty or so paces ahead of them before realising, then dashed back, all the while barking as if they might have missed her. Then she did it again. They weren't going fast enough for her.

Knox guided his courser onto the ferry first, then lumbered off the beast and left it at the very end. The ferry lurched under his weight. Ryan hitched Michael at the opposite end. Coursers and ferries were trouble at the best of times. Chunk lay near Michael, licking her wounded leg.

'I'll winch,' Knox said.

'No argument here.'

It was no surprise the ferry moved at some speed with Knox doing the work. He had to crouch low, like a giant hiding something small and precious.

'I'd have made quite the ferryman,' Knox said.

'River is calm today.'

Knox was breathing heavily when the ferry bumped into the landing. 'I know what you're thinking. Quick, eh?'

Ryan pointed back over to the cabin. 'There's rarely a queue.'

Knox walked off the ferry and his courser followed: no reins, no command, it just knew. Michael wouldn't move until they were well distant. Chunk wasn't too keen either.

'What's got you so sour?' Knox said.

Ryan stopped at the landing. 'It's different getting off knowing you're not getting back on.'

'Be grateful to leave things behind.'

The track wound up the rise. The ground was rockier on this side of the bank, no sea of bone-grass. *Never, the sea.* He didn't look back at the cabin.

Not once.

2 : 10

Get up, go away!
  For this is not your resting place,
because it is defiled,
  it is ruined, beyond all remedy.
                    Micah

BOOK THREE

BOOK THREE

3 : 1

Ryan shifted in the saddle. His bones were grinding against the polished leather and his thighs burned. He'd never been in the saddle so long and it was barely midday. Michael wasn't suffering, clearly used to heavier loads. He picked his way along the rough track with thoughtless skill, like a farm-hand at harvest time. But farm-hands can be cut. Ryan patted the courser's neck, making sure he was awake.

The empty land dipped and rose and stretched out in front of him. If anything grew, it was as dusty and dry as the ground around it, and no use to any man. The only sound they didn't make themselves was the rocks shifting. They rode through canyons and stones skipped down the cliffs as if the great earth shivered in the heat. Birds followed them soundlessly above.

'They're patient, have to give them that,' Knox said, looking up.

'Where are you taking me?'

Knox turned in his saddle. '"Taking you"? Is that how you see it?'

'I didn't have much of a choice.'

'Well, here you are then.' Knox spread his hands to the horizon. 'I ain't stopping you.'

There was nothing out there and nowhere to go that Ryan knew. The only directions were back – where only bodies waited for him – or forward, to his pa. The rest was as blank and unknown as the scrubland.

'We all have choices,' Knox said. 'This here's the best one for you, and you know it.'

'Where are you taking me?' Ryan said.

'To your pa.'

'But *where*?'

'What's it matter?' Knox said. 'If I tell you a town or a county, will you know it?'

Ryan shook his head.

'Then you'll just have to trust me.'

'Can we rest yet?'

'Not until we're on open ground,' Knox said.

Ryan glanced up at the cliff walls. He couldn't imagine another man in such a place. It wasn't for men.

He pulled his hat back down to shade his eyes. It was Bryn's hat. Knox had considered Ryan's old one, with its dead-lie holes and ragged edges, and tossed it into the stove. It didn't burn, it shrivelled and blackened. Going without a hat wasn't an option. Bryn's was too big but Ryan's sweat was keeping it in place.

The land tapered back down to level. They were out amongst the blank hills again.

'Long time ago this here was a river.' Knox motioned back along the canyon. 'Not a big one – not like the Gregory.'

Ryan's mouth watered. He uncapped his water-skin and took a slug. He was careful not to spill a drop.

'You drink too much,' Knox said.

'Runs in my family.'

'Gimme that water-skin.'

'And what happens if you decide to leave me here?' Ryan said.

Knox rode on a little before getting off his courser. He used the beast for shade – it was barely big enough – and fanned himself with his hat. Ryan got out of the saddle, but when his feet touched the ground his legs crumpled. He fell on his bruised shoulder and cried out at the pain.

Knox didn't move but a stubby black muzzle nudged Ryan's forehead. Chunk licked him, her tongue feeling like old leather. He sat up and stroked her, remembering how she didn't like to be scratched behind her ear.

'Done well to keep up, that girl,' Knox said.

At the sound of his voice, Chunk dropped low and started to growl. Her whole chest shook.

'She doesn't like you,' Ryan said.

'Not many do, not at first. Except these. They're real regular and happy to see me.' Knox put his hand on the ground. A hairy huntsman ambled over his fingers until it covered the whole of his hand. He lifted it up, looking at it face-to-face.

'They grow big out here,' Ryan said. He'd caught huntsmen

in the house and taken them outside before she could kill them.

'Isn't he something? But he's looking for someone more special than me. And she'll be even bigger.' He put the huntsman down. He had to encourage it off his hand. More were making their way towards him. Ryan counted five. The black courser didn't move, but Michael was getting skittish.

'Why do they come to you?' Ryan said.

'Don't know – have since I was your age. You're not scared.'

'They're just huntsmen.'

'Folk come up with all kinds of stories about them to justify their own fear,' Knox said.

Chunk sniffed at a huntsman that came close to her and it reared up and waved its legs. Chunk gave a snort and let it be. Ryan poured a little water into his palm and let her lap it up. They ate dried meat and got back on the coursers. After two paces the huntsmen were gone, hidden by the rocky ground.

'If he finds her, she'll eat him, right after,' Knox said.

They passed the rest of the day riding. The occasional cloud brought a reprieve from the sun and Ryan began to appreciate the canyons and curse the open trail. But when bluffs rose on either side of them Knox started getting restless. He kept checking both sides the whole time and let his courser do the walking.

Ryan could smell himself: a bitter tang. His shirt clung to his back. Where his trousers met the saddle they were a different shade of blue.

When the sun started to set Knox led them off the trail, heading uphill. Michael slowed a little over the rough ground but didn't complain.

'Where are we going?'

'Shelter for the night,' Knox said.

Ryan looked ahead to where the hill rose up to a cliff-face.

'Where? Up there?'

'Don't that book of yours talk about patience?'

'Might do. Haven't got very far,' Ryan said.

There was a track up the cliff that was wide enough for a single rider. It wound round and up until they couldn't see the original trail. The hills were turning a pale blue and the evening chill made Ryan rub his arms. His sweat was cooling all over and Bryn's hat started to slip from his head, but he caught it.

Knox turned his courser into a large cave and was quickly swallowed by the darkness. Ryan pulled Michael up short – the courser wasn't too keen on following either. A spark came from inside and grew into a torch as Knox came to the mouth of the cave.

'Where did you get that?' Ryan said.

'Are all boys your age so full of questions?'

'I don't know many boys.'

'We use this cave here, sometimes. Can be a useful spot,' Knox said. He took Michael's bridle and walked the courser inside. Michael was no happier; no doubt the animal wished he was back at the cabin where a walk to Fort Davis was his biggest worry.

The black courser was standing beside one wall. Knox led them to the other. Along it were crates and barrels. They looked old in the torchlight, the wood like dusty, brittle stone. One crate they passed caught the light and Ryan jerked away and started to slip off the saddle until Knox steadied him. The crate was full of knives. There was a barrel that bristled with rifles – the kind soldiers used.

'You leave all this here?' Ryan said.

'Times it's useful, times it rots.'

Ryan dismounted carefully, hanging on to the saddle until his legs were steady. At the back of the cave were some logs, neatly stacked, and a pile of kindling ready chopped. Black marks on the stone showed them where to set the fire and Knox took to the task with some enthusiasm while Ryan tended to Michael, like Bryn had shown him. He fed his courser, then took the oats over to Knox's beast.

'How did something get so big on oats?' he said.

Knox used the torch to light the fire and, when it caught, a warmth rolled out that made the cave feel smaller. It was full of shadows that didn't sit still. The smell of dried wood burning was strong, but there wasn't much smoke. He found a pan, added beans from a sack, filled it with water and set it to cook.

Ryan settled by the fire with Chunk resting her head on his leg. Knox lit his pipe and sat smoking as they both watched the flames.

'Lose yourself in it, couldn't you?' Knox said.

'I made a fire every day and I don't understand it.'

'Not many do – well, not more than an understanding not to put your hand in it.'

'But how does it work?' Ryan said.

'Were men who knew, once. Little good it did them.'

'Where are they now?'

'Dead. All dead. Happens to everyone, understanding or no,' Knox said. He stirred the beans.

'Not everyone.'

'No, I s'pose not. Haven't decided whether those are the lucky ones or not.' The man scratched at his cheek.

'Nothing lucky about it. Nothing good about it,' Ryan said.

'Your soldier friend didn't come back. But your mother did, didn't she?'

'Don't talk about her!' Ryan snapped.

Knox held up his hands.

The beans were salty and hard. Ryan said so, but Knox kept on chewing – and they took some chewing.

When they'd eaten their fill and given the rest to Chunk, Knox leaned against the cave wall and lit his pipe again. 'Why don't you tell me a story? I like stories,' he said.

'I don't know any.'

'Then read that book to me.'

'I don't read so well,' Ryan said.

'Then you need the practise.'

Ryan stood slowly. His legs ached. His back ached. Even his fingers ached – and the book felt heavier than he remembered. He sat and angled the book into the firelight.

'You're missing a bit,' Knox pointed out. 'Hope that's not important.'

Ryan cleared his throat. '"And the King of Egypt sp— sp—"'

'I like stories 'bout kings.'

'"—spake to the He-brew midwives, of which the name of the one was Ship-rah, and the name of the other Pew-are."'

'Never met a Ship-rah before,' Knox said. He blew his smoke into a ring.

'"And he said, When ye do the office of a midwife to the He-brew women, and see them upon the stools; if it be a son, then ye shall kill him: but if it be a daughter, then she shall live."'

'Isn't that rich? You'd have been for the chop.'

'So would you,' Ryan said. '"But the midwives feared God, and did not do as the King of Egypt commanded them, but saved the men children alive."'

'This Egypt – where's that, then?'

'Do boys your age always ask so many questions?' Ryan said.

'Just trying to understand the story.'

'It's an old country, leastways, that's what I was told.'

'Know a lot about this stuff, do you?' Knox said.

'Only what I was told.'

'I imagine that's the way of it.'

'"And the King of Egypt called for the midwives, and said unto them, Why have ye done this thing, and have saved the men children alive?

'"And the midwives said unto Pharaoh—'

'Who? Who's this faery-oh?' Knox said.

'That's the king's name.'

'Oh.'

'Should I carry on?' Ryan said.

'Please do.'

'"Because the He-brew women are not as the Egyptian women; for they are lively, and are delivered ere the mid-wives come in unto them. Therefore God dealt well with the midwives: and the people multiplied, and waxed very mighty."' Ryan closed the Good Book.

'Well, that's a story we can all appreciate. Lively women. Very sensible.'

Michael scratched out his Amen on the cave floor.

'There must be a lot of stories in that book,' Knox said.

'There's a lot of names – and a lot of stories too, I think.'

'Just started, eh?'

'Just started.'

There were blankets in one of the top crates, smelling like dried mud. As Ryan shook out the dust at the cave-mouth he saw there were many stars in the sky, many more than people below them.

He fell asleep to the sounds of crackling wood and huntsmen tickling the stone.

Breakfast was a thick porridge – there were plenty of oats, but little water to spare – and they ate it at the entrance to the cave. The air inside was heavy with the smell of coursers and woodsmoke. Afterwards, Knox handed Ryan a shovel;

it took them two trips to clear the coursers' leavings from the cave.

As they packed fresh supplies into their bags Ryan asked, 'Shouldn't we leave something? In trade?'

'You ain't got a thing that's not already here.'

They picked their way down the bluff, Chunk running ahead in her difficult gait. She disappeared into the bushes and when they passed her a few minutes later, she was going about her business. She looked away.

'Bryn said it was better to travel by night – not so hot.'

'I doubt Bryn was ever a wanted man, then. Can't see what's coming at night,' Knox said.

Ryan looked around. 'There's no one out here.'

'I doubt that too.'

The early morning sun was at their backs when they reached the trail. Ryan pushed the front of his hat up to shade his neck; he could still feel the heat on his shoulders and he was already sweating. The ground ahead was hazy.

'Why does that happen?' he asked.

'It's the heat: like frying meat – the ground is cooking.'

Ryan looked down at Michael's hooves to see if the courser was stepping lightly or any different, but it was the same easy plodding. He didn't like the idea of walking barefoot on cooking ground. 'Good boy,' he said, and patted Michael's neck.

They didn't stop at midday; it was too hot and there wasn't any shade. Ryan tried to sink into his hat but the sun was relentless. He drank little – he knew he had to save the water, but the urge to drink it all, or to splash it over his face, was strong. Every time he uncorked his water-skin Knox turned round and watched, so he made a show of only sipping.

'You don't feel hot?' he said.

'This ain't real heat.'

Knox was made of stone – that was the only explanation. He was living rock on top of a stone courser. Or there was something more obvious.

'You're a Walkin',' Ryan said.

Knox was suddenly covered in shadow: they were entering a canyon. 'Do I look dead to you?'

'A Walkin' wouldn't feel the sun – they don't feel anything.'

'They don't eat, neither, and you've seen me do that.' Knox got off his courser and Ryan followed suit, glad to be out of the saddle. 'Here, I'll prove to you I'm no Walkin'.'

Ryan sat down and took a gulp of water while Knox was rummaging in his bags until he found what he was looking for: a knife, so clean it was almost see-through, like rain. The edge was wicked, though, that much was obvious.

Knox raised it to his neck and Ryan said quickly, 'What are you doing? Don't – you don't need to—'

Knox flicked the knife.

Ryan was ready to catch the man's body, but instead, white hairs drifted between his fingers. Knox cut again, and as more of his beard fell to the floor Ryan saw it was not all white; there were black and brown hairs too. He took his time, checking his work in the reflection of the knife and evening up the other side for every cut he made on this one.

'You've done that before,' Ryan said at last.

'Many times. Won't be long till you have to.'

Ryan rubbed his own smooth, hairless chin. There was no way he'd be growing a beard. Beards were for old men.

Knox worked until there was just enough hair left to frost his cheeks and chin.

'I don't understand,' Ryan said.

'Walkin' don't grow hair – no matter how long they make a nuisance of themselves. When my beard grows back you'll know I'm no Walkin'.' He put the knife away.

'And what about until then?'

'You'll have to take my word on it.' Knox scanned along the top of the bluffs. 'We need to keep moving.'

'We only just stopped.'

Knox mounted up. 'Have to keep moving.'

'Are you scared or something?' Ryan asked, although it was hard to picture a man so big being afraid of anything. But he sure was doing a lot of looking around.

'I don't like waiting for trouble.' He moved off down the canyon.

Ryan glanced back along the track and saw a stone skipping down the bluff. Another followed, and he tracked where it came from up to the top of the canyon wall. There was a face: a woman, looking down at him.

3 : 2

She stared at Ryan: dark eyes, like peering down a well –
a touch of blue to them, but otherwise black. Her cheeks
were swollen and saggy. Her lips looked ready to burst, they
were so big. She was old and she was fat and she was out
here, which was nowhere. Chunk was growling, her tail
low between her legs. She took a very slow step forward.

Knox was still ambling down the canyon.

'Knox,' Ryan hissed. He checked back: the woman was
still there. She shook her head and he ignored her. 'Knox!'
he shouted.

'What?' Knox started riding back, but when Ryan looked
again she was gone.

It was more than just that she'd ducked behind the cliff-
edge. Ryan was pretty sure that if he rode as hard as he could
back out of the canyon and up to the top she wouldn't be
there; they could search for miles around and not find her.
She was gone as if she'd never been there at all.

Chunk was sniffing the air, as confused as he was.

'She's gone,' he said to the ruft, 'but she *was* there.'

Chunk barked.

He told Knox what he'd seen.

'You sure? Swollen cheeks?'

'Sure. Wouldn't want to be carrying fat around in this heat,' Ryan added.

'That ain't fat, boy.' Knox kicked his courser into a trot. 'Quick now,' he called back.

Michael was only too happy to move. He didn't like the closeness of the canyons.

Ryan tried to keep an eye on their tops, but it was difficult. And he couldn't shout above the noise the coursers made – what did Knox mean, it wasn't fat? That's what she looked like. Ma had said there were men and women in Fort Davis who had the money to grow to all kinds of sizes. If you could eat enough to get fat, Ryan reckoned, you'd be pretty happy.

They cleared the canyon with Michael working hard to keep up, but Chunk was falling behind. She wouldn't be able to manage any distance, but he wasn't going to leave her behind. He pulled on the reins and slowed Michael to a walk. Looking back he saw Chunk still struggling along the track, with no sign of a woman of any shape.

Knox had also stopped. When they caught up to him, he lifted his hat to fan himself. 'Now, tell me again what you saw,' he said.

'A woman. She had dark eyes and wobbly cheeks.'

'She say anything?'

'No.'

'You see a rifle? Or a pistol? Or two pistols?'

'No. She just shook her head.'

'Jus' shook her head.'

'Like this.' Ryan shook his head.

'With wobbly cheeks?'

Ryan puffed out his cheeks.

'This ain't a time for fooling about,' Knox said.

'I wasn't fooling,' he said. 'That's what she looked like. What's the problem? Why are you scared of a fat woman?'

'Never you mind.' Knox put his hat back on.

'Is she following us?' Ryan said.

'Always. Ride on a little and I'll catch up.'

Ryan checked he still had his water-skin and his pistol. He didn't move too quickly, for Chunk's sake – that, and his back ached. The land ahead was mostly flat – a speck would have trouble sneaking up on them – but Ryan kept his pistol in his hand. He understood this wasn't a time for fooling about. *Pistols* weren't for fooling about.

He watched the ground cooking around him. Bushes blurred out of the distance, slowly taking shape, and there was the occasional tree, stripped bare and bent, like living was hard work – well, it sure was. His back would end up the same, there was no doubt in his mind. He was out here riding across a place he didn't know, on his own, in a way – if this was better than the farm it wasn't by much. And it wasn't better than working the ferry, so he'd taken a step back. Finding his pa would be another – or two, or a hundred, and each step would be accompanied by the bite of old leather.

'Did you need that?' Knox asked, pointing at the pistol, 'or you just like the way it feels?' When Ryan put it in his pocket he added, 'We'll have to find you a holster, too.'

'I don't want one,' Ryan said.

'You can't keep it there. You'll shoot your own foot.'

'Did you see her?'

'I wouldn't be here if I did,' Knox said.

They rode through that day, slept, and rode through another. Ryan didn't see the woman again – didn't see anyone or anything except rocks and dust and sky. Knox kept them on the track as it rolled along hillsides, between walls of burnt earth and across plateaus. When they were up high there was wind, strong enough to cut through Ryan's loose shirt and trousers: not winter-cold, but a shock nonetheless. Chunk snapped at it – she must have forgotten how it felt too. Ryan was keen to forget it all over again. When the path started to slope downwards they found a valley covered in short trees, their green so bright he thought he was dreaming.

Knox brought them to a stop. 'You hear that?' he said.

All Ryan could hear was the dry wheeze of the coursers, it being louder than his own. 'Hear what?'

Knox clipped the back of his head. 'Open those ears of yours! It's water, for pity's sake.'

He led them down to the wash. It couldn't have been more than a few inches deep but it was a good ten or fifteen paces wide. Like the colour of the trees, the grey of the water didn't seem real – too thick, too flat, even. It put him in mind of paint rather than water; the kind Farmer Simmons used on his barn. Chunk lapped it up without asking permission and her muzzle came away stained by silt.

'Drink it like that if you feel the need,' Knox said. 'Though you'll bring it back up most likely.' He bent to fill up his water-skin. 'We'll cook it later.'

Being so close to water, feeling it in the air and trees around him, gave him a strong thirst. When Knox wasn't looking, he sneaked a handful from the wash, figuring he could handle the consequences. It was like licking the earth and little bits of grit stuck in his teeth. He came away with muddy knees, a full water-skin and the same kind of thirst he'd started with.

He'd have liked to stay by the wash but Knox insisted they press on. Leaving the valley behind, the closeness of the dry ground with its shimmering heat made Ryan's eyes heavy and loosened his grip on the reins. More than once he caught himself just in time to stop slipping from the saddle.

That night they cooked the water, then the food, but Knox preferred to let the fire die. He grumbled something about being watched and Ryan didn't press him on it. Chunk insisted on lying beside Ryan; he was glad of the warmth, but the ruft's breath was enough to make him roll over and clutch his nose. He spotted Knox, standing by the coursers, his hands resting on his pistols.

When Ryan woke with the sun drying his lips, Knox was

still there. He patted Chunk's ribs, reassured by how solid the ruft was, and Chunk licked his chin. Her tongue was worn as a week-old cob of corn. Shaking life into his feet Ryan fetched his water-skin and before the cork was even free the ruft was at his side, her tail sweeping up a dust-storm. He took a swig and then cupped his hand for Chunk to drink from.

'Did you sleep?' Ryan said.

'As long as I needed,' Knox said.

Ryan gave Chunk another handful and then stroked the ruft's big head. He wouldn't sleep longer than necessary either, not if huntsmen were his only company.

'You were watching for that woman?' he said.

'Amongst other things.'

'She didn't look so dangerous.'

'Looks got nothing to do with it,' Knox said.

'You should tell me why she's following us.'

Knox pinched his nose and then snorted hard, like he was trying to dislodge something. 'She don't like your pa.'

'Why not?'

'I don't stick around long enough to ask. And besides, she does more shooting than she does talking.'

'Are there a lot of people like that – people who don't like my pa?'

'Plenty, but she's different. She comes looking for him.'

'We eating in the saddle again?'

Knox pointed to the horizon. 'I thought we'd let this resolve itself first.'

There was a small muddy-coloured cloud approaching down the track. Knox was staring at it, making no move for the coursers.

'You don't think it's her?' Ryan said.

'Only one kind of person makes that kind of dust.'

'That's just one rider?'

'Going at a pace,' Knox said. 'That's a messenger, and I'll wager my hat and holster it's an army boy, too.'

'What are you going to do?'

'We're going to say hello.' Knox kept his gaze fixed on the track as the rider came closer with every beat of Ryan's heart; both were picking up pace together. Amongst the dust Ryan could see a movement of darker colour that grew into the shape of a courser. Knox eased himself to the edge of the track as the rider became a single blue grain in a whirling crop of beige and brown and orange. When Ryan could see him properly, face and all, Knox took off his hat and started waving it. The quick beat of the courser's hooves pulled Ryan's chest even tighter. The rider was also waving his hat, as if it were the right and natural thing to do, and Ryan joined them. He could see the rider's smile as the messenger closed the last thirty paces.

Knox pulled his pistol and fired. The noise of the shot was swallowed by the hoofbeats.

The rider fell, hit the ground limply and didn't move. His courser stopped a short way off and waited.

Knox put his hat back on and motioned for Ryan to follow.

'What did you do that for?'

'Come see,' Knox said without looking back.

The track felt uneven beneath Ryan's feet, as choppy as the Gregory River. He concentrated on walking those few steps. He left Chunk behind – she was growling at no one and as low to the ground as she could be – and tried to focus on the man lying in front of him. The outline of his blue uniform wouldn't stay still, maybe because the air was alive with the dust-storm the courser had brought.

He snorted to clear his nose, but that just made his eyes water.

The rider was lying face-down and making a bad kind of sound that Ryan recognised: the low moaning sound of something eating away at a person from the inside.

Knox knelt and took the rider's only pistol. He emptied the rider's pockets: a handkerchief, a small pouch of coins, a comb. He tossed them aside.

'Please ...' the rider said. His voice was wet, and stuck in his throat. 'I don't have—'

'Shhh.' Knox worked his way up the man's chest. 'Ah.' He turned to Ryan, something small and golden in his hand, like he'd found a piece of the sun in the rider's coat. 'This is why. This, and that courser over there.'

'Please ...'

'You have a watch, young Ryan?'

Ryan shook his head as the rider coughed, blood muffling the sound as it stained the dirt.

'Your ma must have shown you one?' Knox took a step forward.

Ryan shook his head.

'A good way to mark any man's day. We'll start marking yours right now.'

'I don't want it,' Ryan said softly.

'What's that?'

'I don't want it.'

'Nobody *wants* it, but everyone *needs* it.' Knox put the watch in Ryan's hand. It was as cold and solid as a stone from the bottom of the river, but it was so bright to look at . . . He closed Ryan's hand around the watch.

'Do you have a watch?' Ryan asked.

Knox reached into his coat pocket and pulled one out. 'Look the same, don't they? All messengers in the Northern Army carry them, and Southerners have them too, though they're different. You'll have your pick.'

'Please, please,' the rider whimpered. 'Listen, I . . .'

Ryan looked at the watch sitting heavily in his hand and opened the clasp at the side. Numbers, like those in the Good Book, were written on a pale circle. The sun was on the outside, the moon on the inside. It made the sound of a courser walking slowly. So this was how a man marked the days.

Knox turned the rider onto his back and found he was holding a small leather bag to his stomach. His fingers were lined red and so were his teeth. He eased the bag out of the rider's grip.

'No—'

'Shhh.' Knox pulled the strap over the man's head and

said to Ryan, 'He'll die, but it'll take time, and it'll be hard.'

'You shot him,' Ryan said. The rider was wearing a pair of black boots – they were marked by the dirt of the trail, but they were good boots, with laces.

'Did my best to make it clean. You still have that pistol?'

'You know I do.'

'It would be a mercy,' Knox said.

'I won't.' Ryan shook his head. He couldn't keep back the tears.

'He'll suffer.'

'You do it.'

'I can shoot a man – we both know that,' Knox said.

The rider coughed more blood and it dribbled out of his mouth, bubbling like a watery stew.

Knox rested a hand on Ryan's shoulder. 'You can make it quick. A mercy.'

'It's always a mercy, once the cruelty is done.'

'It's a cruel world.' Knox walked away.

Ryan had the rider's watch in one hand and his ma's pistol in the other. The rider's eyes were large and didn't stop moving. He opened and closed his mouth and no words came.

'I know how to shoot.' Ryan raised the pistol. '"Higher. It has to be the head."'

This time the shot cracked the earth. The coursers stamped at the unexpected sound, but Knox was there to calm all three of them.

Chunk came to Ryan's side and nuzzled his hand.

The rider had stopped moving. A black hole above his ear was bleeding thick and black.

A watch and a courser.

3 : 3

Ryan rode a good distance behind Knox, who was leading the messenger's courser. They were going slowly, on account of it having been pushed so hard. The day was shaping up to be a punishing kind of hot. There was no air to speak of; when Ryan took his hat off to try and create a stir there was nothing except more heat and he soon regretted letting the sun reach his face. Chunk padded alongside and kept to the courser's shadow when she could. Her panting was the loudest noise. Knox stopped with some regularity to water the mounts. Ryan wondered how often that might be, but he didn't take out the watch to look; it stayed heavy in his pocket. Chunk lapped what Ryan spared her from the water-skin, which was getting light. He took sips himself, and left his neck and face parched.

The bluffs were bigger now, and there were more canyons, their shade gratefully received. The horizon was higher and somehow further away, but even as hills replaced the shimmering flatlands there was no end to the dryness. Ryan couldn't remember the taste of river air, or the smell of trees as they dropped their leaves.

They came out from a winding canyon, no different from any of the others they had plodded their way through, and without warning Knox left the track. They drifted for twenty or so paces, then he turned and headed towards what looked like nothing more than another set of bluffs. Chunk raced to the very spot Knox had veered away and started barking; she kept it up until Ryan reached the place, but he could see nothing special about it, so he just followed. Chunk didn't let up for a good while; neither Ryan or Knox looked back at her and at last she gave in and joined them.

The going was slow off the track. Ryan let the reins drop into his lap, trusting his courser would know the best way through the rocky outcrops and bowl-like gullies. There were no straight lines across this place unless you had wings. Knox and the other two coursers were close enough to talk to one moment, then out of calling distance the next.

It was well past midday when Knox finally stopped. The bluffs were still some way ahead, but now they loomed large over their heads, eating greedily at the sky with every pace. Knox handed out bread; it was hard and robbed Ryan's mouth of the little saliva it had, but it did stop the stomach cramps he'd grown used to.

'Another cave?' Ryan said.

'No. Viv is up there.'

'What's Viv?'

Knox sucked his cheek between mouthfuls. 'Not what, *who*. And don't expect no warm welcome from her.'

'Viv,' Ryan said, looking up at the bluffs. 'She lives way up there?'

'Up where she can't cause too much trouble.' Knox mounted again, and his black courser barely flinched.

Michael looked less pleased and started stamping the ground. Ryan patted his mane and whispered to him, 'Viv will have some hay. And water. Plenty of water.'

Knox turned in his saddle. 'Just don't mention her neck.'

'Her what?'

But Knox was already moving off. The messenger's courser stepped gingerly over the rough ground, keeping one eye on Knox's black beast and pulling its tether as tight as it could.

The trail up the bluff forced them into single file. Chunk was last in, but she didn't like it and kept trying to sneak between Michael and the edge. But the height of the fall was growing and she soon clearly thought better of it; the ruft wasn't a fool. The trail was steep in places as it wound its way higher and Ryan couldn't help clenching his thighs at each bend. Michael ignored him.

Knox whistled, sending the sharp sound rippling along the rock wall. He was pointing to the sky where a group of blightbirds were circling. They were getting lower as Ryan rode higher and he realised they were back along the track, where Knox had shot the messenger. Where they had both shot him.

At the next bend Knox pulled his courser to a stop. Ryan drew level and followed the man's gaze.

'Surprised it took them so long,' Knox said.

'They'll eat him.'

'Nothing goes to waste out here.'

'He did nothing to you,' Ryan said.

'You know by now how little that matters.' Knox spurred his courser on and by the time they reached the top the blightbirds were no longer circling in the sky.

Being so high up made Ryan feel small. He shrank down into the saddle. It was difficult to swallow as he looked from one edge of the world to the other, and at everything between. This was a scarred, bruised place – the same heat that was wearing away at him had made it that way. If he stayed long enough he'd have canyons running through him, patches of parched surface and random scrub.

'You can't knock the simplicity of it,' Knox said.

'There's nothing here.'

'Nothing and no one. Almost.'

Knox rode away from the cliff edge. They were on a large shelf easily bigger than the plateaus they had crossed days before. There was a copse – how many trees was difficult to say, but their washed-out green caused Ryan to rub his eyes. There wasn't a breeze, not even as high as they were. They were riding towards the splash of colour. A house came into view, two storeys tall, peeling away from the orange-brown of the bluffs to have its own lines and shape. The glint from windows was sporadic as gunfire. Viv's house.

Nobody came to greet them as Knox angled for the hitching posts. He tied his black to the post furthest from the house and they hitched Michael and the messenger's courser at the other end. Knox slung his saddlebags over his shoulder and headed for the house, Ryan unsteadily following on, his own saddlebags slapping against his knees as he walked. There was a sweet, sticky smell to the air that he couldn't place. He ran his hand through his hair, as much as it would allow. If Viv had a pair of scissors and a mirror maybe she'd let him do something about the bigger knots.

He was grateful the house wasn't far. It cast a huge shadow, even so close to noon, and looked sturdy: put together by someone who knew what they were doing. Fort Davis had big houses, though most weren't. Considering where this house was, that the only other option available to a traveller was a tent or a cave, it was like a fancy saloon.

Knox didn't wait on the porch; he didn't knock and present himself. The door was open and he strolled right in.

Ryan lingered near the door. The shade of the porch was welcome. His shirt stuck to him in more than one place. Chunk wouldn't put a paw on the first step, no matter how much he called her; the ruft paced back and forth, sniffing and huffing at something. A rumble of voices came from inside but when he peered in he couldn't make anything out: it was dark, and his eyes were still used to the brightness of bare rock.

She – *Viv* – came out. 'Is he coming in then?' she said. There was a grumble from inside. 'Don't tell me he has manners?'

'He's just confused. Or scared. Or both,' Knox shouted.

'Well, don't be both. One is enough.' The woman smiled, which made her look older, crinkling what had been a smooth face. 'Come on in. It's your house, one way or another.' She turned from the door. Her brown hair was pulled back into a long, thick ponytail which swayed a little as she walked. He focused on that instead of her red neck.

'Drop the bags and take yourself a seat,' she said, and he did as he was told. She handed him a battered cup and the smell of water was enough to stick his tongue to the roof of his mouth.

She refilled the cup from a bucket as Knox took off his boots with a sigh and wriggled his toes.

'So this is Callum's son?' she said.

'You can't call him prodigal, Viv.'

'Looks bright enough to me.'

'Exactly,' Knox said. They both laughed, but Ryan didn't understand so he took another gulp of water.

Viv sat in the chair opposite him. She reached out and took the cup, then held his hand, inspecting it. She ran a fingertip over his nails and he found himself wincing as she pressed calluses and the little blisters that came from holding reins.

'He's not lazy like his pa,' Viv said.

'Farm-boy, ain't he?'

'I see why you brought him to me.'

'That's not what I've done,' Knox said.

There was a quiet then. Viv took Ryan's other hand and looked them both over, palms and backs.

Knox slowly lifted his pistols from their holsters. They made a thud big enough to send up dust.

Viv put a plate of dried meat on the table. It was tough to chew and tasted more of salt than anything else. 'That's from our own hogs,' she said, arms crossed and waiting.

'It's good.' He was losing teeth, he was sure of it.

There was stew in the pot hanging over the fire, though he couldn't feel the fire's heat, which was something. Viv chopped herbs that filled the room with a healthy smell speaking of things that grew in soil rather than died in it. Ryan regretted the dried meat, touching his sore cheeks with a tentative finger. He should have waited for the stew. Knox was chomping away.

'Your ruft won't come in, not with me here,' Viv said. 'Here, take her this.' She held out a bowl of water.

Ryan couldn't help looking. Her neck was as uneven as the ground they'd crossed to get there. The red was bright where the skin peaked and faded to an angry purple in deeper parts. It was more than a bruise; it ran the whole way around. He waited to see her throat move as she breathed. She pushed the bowl at him.

'You're a—'

'That's right.' She turned to Knox. 'Don't miss a thing, does he?'

He took the bowl out to Chunk. The ruft barked when she saw him, and stayed low to the ground, snuffling. He stroked her as she lapped at the water. He held out a half-chewed piece of meat in his hand, but Chunk didn't appear to enjoy the challenge, which was unlike her. He tried to encourage her inside, but she wouldn't move.

He returned to the house and stood in the doorway. 'How did it happen?'

'What I tell you?' Knox burst from his chair, his hand going to his belt buckle, but she stopped him with a sharp word.

'It's all right. Nothing meant by it.' She mouthed 'later' to Ryan.

The stew was ready. They ate in silence.

Knox was the first up from the table after slurping the last bit, taking the bowl to his face, somehow without leaving a trace on his close-cropped beard. He left his boots, gathered up his saddlebags and headed up the stairs, his feet shaking the house. Viv looked to the ceiling and followed the footsteps until they stopped and there was a loud noise that could only have been Knox falling onto a bed.

'Help me wash out these dishes, then I'll show you to a bed,' she said. They used the same bucket they'd drunk from. The oily stew cast streaks through the water that caught the light and he tried to pick them up as if they were stray hairs, but they slipped between his fingers. As he scrubbed the bowls the days of riding shed from his skin and turned the water black. Viv took the bucket and tossed the water outside amongst the trees. He watched from the small window as the visible roots greedily drank the unexpected downpour. He heard the sound of smacking lips before realising it was him making the noise. Staring hard at the new leaves he wondered if they were growing right in front of him, or if they waited until night when nobody was awake to see.

Viv came back inside, followed by a series of barks.

'That's going to get old real soon,' she said.

'Chunk's first owner started the Walk,' Ryan explained. 'She didn't like it much.'

'What's to like?'

Ryan scratched behind his ear. He opened his mouth to speak, but closed it again.

She laughed. 'I wasn't expecting an answer.'

'Then why ask?'

She put the bucket back by the fire. 'I bet your ma had a belt ready more often than not,' she said. She picked up his bag and led him up the stairs. 'There's only the one proper bed and Knox isn't the kind to share.'

'Don't you have a bed?' he said.

'Don't need one.'

There was a short corridor with a number of doors. Ryan tested the floorboards with a foot: they were sturdy enough, and they'd taken Knox's weight with little more than a groan, but floorboards weren't to be trusted at the best of times and there was a way to fall in this house. Viv just smiled as he reassured himself of their integrity.

She opened the nearest door and ushered him in. 'The choice is yours,' she said.

There were pallets lined up against every wall – enough

for twenty men at least. Some of them had straw poking out from seams that had split. He pointed to the one closest to the door. He wanted to be able to turn his back on so many empty beds.

'This time of year you use the outhouse.' Viv covered the single window with a patch of ragged cloth, pinning it to the wall. It softened the sunlight, but the room was no darker.

He stood by the bed.

'Go on then,' she said. 'I've seen it all before.'

He looked at the bed and then back at her.

'Fine.' She turned around.

'How old are you?' he said as he took his shirt off. His own stink wafted into the air and he rubbed his nose to be rid of it.

'I was twenty-six, or thereabouts. That was some time ago.'

He paused at his trouser button. He pulled faces at her back, grotesquely pulling his nostrils up, sticking out his tongue, making slits out of his eyes, but she didn't move. Quickly he took off his trousers and jumped under the sheet. The creaking of wood made him wince and he waited for the floor to go from under him and to find himself dropped square on the table. Or the fire.

The straw was softer than what he'd grown used to the last few days. The sheet smelled mostly of soap, though there was something underneath – a musk that was older than him and maybe older than Viv, depending.

She sat on the bed. His back was to her and the rest of the room and he flinched at the coldness of her hand on his forehead. She whispered like he was a frightened courser as she ran her sweatless fingers through his hair. She was careful of the knots and as he sank further into the straw bed she began to hum a tune he didn't recognise.

3 : 4

There was a different kind of light flooding the room. The many beds were dark shapes lined in silver, looking like the coffins of rich folk, and he listened hard, wondering what might have woken him in the night. But he heard only his breathing and the shifting of straw beneath him. He rubbed the bites on his shins, wishing he'd slept in his trousers no matter how filthy they were.

As he was closing his eyes again he heard a door close, then footsteps. There was a good inch gap under the door and he saw the shadow of feet pause there for a moment, then move to the stairs. It wasn't Knox, judging by how the house didn't shake. He got out of bed.

In the dark his skin was as pale as Viv's, though prickly with the unexpected cold where hers had been smooth. He hurried to put his shirt and trousers on, muttering curses as he cast around for his boots. He was sure he'd left them at the end of the bed, as he did wherever he slept. He lifted the pallet, not really believing they might fit unnoticed there but because there was nowhere else to look. No point searching under the other pallets.

The door opened on quiet hinges. He did his best to tread lightly, but his heels felt leaden on the boards. A shuddering roar made him stop, one hand clenched around the banister. It rumbled out from the far room like ten ringed-neats were beyond the flimsy door and making good to charge, then it softened for enough heartbeats that Ryan turned back to the stairs. He made it down three steps and had to stop himself falling as the noise blasted out behind him; only his hand on the wooden rail kept him upright.

Before he reached the bottom he saw Viv, busy at the table, and shadows cast by the fire, the banister's thin lines dancing against the wall. He sat on the stairs, pulling his knees up under his chin and working his cold toes with his hands. She was rolling something into little bundles before tying them off with something, string, maybe. She was humming the same tune from that afternoon, but it was different with her hands so busy.

'You're no use to nobody sitting there,' she said, not looking up.

He stood and saw his shadow; its blurred edges made it look mean and he was glad to lose it as he made the kitchen proper. There was a door in the corner that he hadn't noticed before.

'Warm yourself by the fire and then you can come help me,' she said.

His toes uncurled like claws and he wiggled them clumsily.

He reached out his hands close enough to singe the colour-less hairs on his arms. 'Someone stole my boots,' he said.

'Only to walk to the porch and deliver them next to Knox's.'

'I prefer them at the end of my bed,' he said.

'Preferring has less to do with it than sweeping. Now, see here?' There was a basket on the floor next to her. It was a mess of browns and blacks.

'Is that all your hair?' he said.

'It's not hair at all. Feel for yourself.' She took out a handful.

He fingered it. 'Looks like you shredded some dead leaves.'

'That's right.'

'Why?'

'Not a smoker, then?' she said.

He shook his head.

'Well, don't start. It tastes horrible and makes you smell like only a man can smell.'

He stared down at the wasted leaves. 'Tastes? You don't eat them, do you?'

'Some do.'

'Eating dead leaves. I'd have to be real hungry,' he said.

She laughed and pulled out a chair for him. 'Here, take enough to fill your palm – for you, you'll want a little bit more, that's it – and then work it against the table like this.' She pressed down the leaves, pushing the edges in until she made straight lines, or straight enough. When she'd finished there was a little door made of leaf on the table.

She waited for him to do the same, though it wasn't easy to get the lines straight.

'It keeps sticking to me,' he said.

'You got too warm. Wipe your hands on the cloth there.'

That helped, and eventually he got his to look a little like hers.

'Now we roll it,' she said, and that was easier, though his wasn't nearly as tight. With one hand she took more of the leaves and rolled them into a thin line. 'Then we tie it off, like this.'

He watched closely, but she was too quick. He'd never thought of his fingers as fat before, and he struggled to tie the leaf fastening around his roll, which was growing looser with each attempt. He put his finished work next to hers.

'You'll get it,' she said, taking another handful. 'Or you'll fall asleep trying.'

The sound of a door opening woke him: he was back in the straw bed, although he couldn't remember getting there. He scratched the edges of his mouth, crusty with dried dribble, and white flakes rained on the sheet. He caught a bitter whiff of dead leaf on his fingers.

'We rise early here,' Viv said. 'No one likes a bath in the middle of the day.' She unpinned the cloth over the window. The sun wasn't up yet.

Ryan licked his lips to get rid of the taste of sleep, but his tongue was too dry – though it was still better than waking up with a desert's worth of dirt up his nostrils and in his ears. He pulled back the sheet to find he was still wearing his shirt and trousers. He got up and followed her downstairs. She paid no attention to the noise coming from the far room. He was still surprised just how loud a sleeping man could be.

'Go on in – it's almost done; just another bucket or two.' Viv motioned to the closed door.

Ryan stood in front of it: the door off the kitchen, his fists balled. He could feel his pistol heavy against his thigh.

'Go on,' she said. She was holding a bucket of hot water, the steam curling around her wrists and up her arms. He was back at Ma's door again, reaching for the handle. It was wet. He pulled his hand away and looked for the bright colour that would be on the bedsheets and dripping onto the floor, but his hand was empty.

'You want me to?'

'Yes.'

She held the bucket against her with one arm and opened the door with the other hand.

He stared at the empty floor and blank walls: there was nothing inside, except for a large metal trough and enough steam to make the air drip. The trough wasn't like the ones he'd seen on farms crowded with neats or woollies: one end was higher than the other.

'You'd better try it,' Viv said. She poured the bucket of water in, then stirred it with her hand. 'The heat doesn't bother me.'

He stepped slowly towards Viv. The heavy metallic smell

was impossible to ignore. As he got closer he saw Ma propped up against the back. He glanced at Viv, who was stirring the water between his ma's knees. Red water. Ma's face was slack, her eyes open but not looking at anything in particular. Her mouth fell open.

'It's just a bath,' Viv said. She pulled her hand out of the water and there wasn't a mark on it. His ma was gone.

He shivered as Viv helped him take off his shirt. 'Look at your arms: your hair's all standing.' She touched his shoulder, and he flinched away. 'Make sure the water isn't too hot. I'll face the wall, see?'

He squinted through the steam. The bath was empty, no one leaning against the high back; the water was clear, showing the metal through it. He touched the surface and the heat made him pull away. A fat drop ran down his middle finger, but it was just the colour of water. He sniffed and couldn't smell it. She wasn't there. It was a different room. He stirred the water and his hand came away pink, but it wasn't so hot it hurt.

He took off his trousers and carefully stepped into the bath. The bottom wasn't hot, not like a pan on heat was hot. The water came halfway up his shins. Viv turned around and he cupped his prick in his hands.

'You know how to wash yourself?' she said. 'There's soap on the stool.'

He'd missed the stool: it was next to the bath, in easy reach, and on it was a square of dirty cream with dark flakes and a cloth of the same colour, and a thick towel.

'I'll just be out here. Make sure to wash that tangle of yours,' Viv said, and left him standing in the bath.

The door was almost shut when he said, 'Could you leave it open?'

3 : 5

The water was starting to get cold. He was lying with his legs mostly out and the water-line above his top lip, imagining what it would be like to have a moustache. Days of grit and grime made patchy floating islands. When one came close he blew out through his nose and watched it sail on until it hit the side of the bath and was grounded for as long as he kept still.

Viv came in, holding a folded set of clothes. 'These will be too big for you, but it looks like you're used to rolling hems,' she said. She added the towel to the clothes and sat on the stool, placing the pile in her lap. He watched her, his face still half-submerged. 'Took six men to carry that bath up that trail. The wagon was too big, but your pa insisted.' She touched his hair, pulling strands loose, checking for knots. 'I doubt he ever thought you'd be in it.'

Ryan pushed himself up. 'Why am I here?'

'Knox didn't tell you?'

'Said he was taking me to my pa.'

'So he is. This is as good a place to wait for your pa as any.'

'He's coming *here*?'

'He will eventually.'

'You don't know when?'

'I'd be surprised if even your pa knew that,' she said, standing. 'Don't worry, there's plenty to be doing before he comes.' She left, keeping the door open.

He dried what he could while standing in the bath, but he still got the floor plenty wet. She was right, the shirt was too big, so he rolled the sleeves until there was a thick bundle of cloth resting on each wrist. The trousers were the same. When he was dressed – barefoot and wishing for his boots again – he edged out of the door.

Knox was sitting at the table. In front of him was the messenger's small brown bag. 'Breakfast before business,' he said.

There was a plate set on the opposite side of the table and Ryan sat, relieved to see a slice of bread and not dried meat – though there was something greasy spread across it that smelled similar, and tasted similar too, but it eased the passing of the bread from lip to stomach and didn't leave him gasping for water.

'Soon enough you'll have had so much hog you'll be rollin' in the muck with them,' Knox said.

'Be my guest.' Viv's voice carried from outside. Ryan glanced at the windows but couldn't see her. Chunk added her own opinion.

'Damn it, woman, come in if you're going to be listening.'

'Busy,' she called, and there was a series of rattles and bangs as demonstration.

Knox sighed. Good as his word, he waited until Ryan was finished with his food, staying quiet as the last mouthful was chewed and swallowed. Then he opened the bag. 'We split the spoils. You have the watch and I have the courser. And then there's these.' With a delicate touch he lifted out a folded piece of paper. Ryan could make out the whispers of writing inside. Knox placed the paper to one side and lifted out another; this letter was on paper too thick to see through, and it had been sealed with blue wax. Of the seven he ended up pulling from the bag, only two were sealed.

'These are mine,' Knox said. He gave the remaining five to Ryan. 'Burn them if you want, or practise your reading. They're worth more than that book of yours.'

Ryan followed Knox's example, handling the letters with a kind of reverence. 'Whose are they?'

'The names won't mean a thing,' Knox said. 'You can bet they're from soldiers to their sweethearts.'

'And those?'

'Won't be as exciting; they're from one soldier to another.' He returned the sealed letters to the bag.

Ryan pushed his chair back.

'Rinse that plate first,' Viv shouted, accompanied by more barking.

'Those two had better get used to each other or I'm going to shoot one of them,' Knox said.

Ryan managed to sneak upstairs without further orders. He chose a different pallet, this one bathed in sunlight from the uncovered window. Lying on his front, his bare toes enjoying the heat from the window, he unfolded the first letter. He only touched the edges, in case he might smudge the thin, tall words. They were as different from the writing in the Good Book as Chunk was to a courser, but like the Good Book, the letter started with numbers that he assumed placed it in some kind of order. He read it aloud taking each word slowly.

Dear Father,

This is my third at-tempt to write. We are stuck on the banks of a river. The specks carry something here; the men make a lot of noise before they go. We mark the graves. The locals seem un-interested. You wouldn't know the place, even if I could say its name. I under-stand you and the len-ders are eager for news but I cannot be spe— spe— sif—

'He can't be "specific". Means he can't say details.'

Ryan got up and went to the window. Viv was hanging clothes on a line that ran from the house to the hitching posts; his shirt and trousers were amongst them.

'This is private,' he shouted down to her.

'Don't go reading it aloud then.'

Chunk dashed out from the porch, sat so she could see them both and barked, happy enough.

'If you're going to listen, just tell me when I get it wrong.'

'I am,' she said.

but I cannot be spe-ci-fic. Just know there is no end. The
South-ern-ers are as stub-born as they are ig-nor-ant.
We are the van— van—

'Viv? I don't know this word.'

'What's after "van"?'

'It's a g, I think,' he called.

'And then?'

'There's a u.'

'Vangu? That's no word I know.'

'Blood and ashes,' Knox shouted. It sounded like he was still in the kitchen. '"Vanguard". Word is vanguard; fancy way of saying front of the army.'

'Then why didn't he say so?' Viv said.

'I didn't write the damn letter, did I?'

the van-guard for some great movement. The moun-
tains don't sleep — none of us do. I saw two men shoot
each other, right at the same time. I asked those near-by
what the quarrel was. They said there was none. I felt no
surprise — there is a heaviness here in everyone. Not least
Col-on-el Web-ster.

I met with the Col-on-el, as you asked. I realise you
were once friends. He is a troubled man, Father, prone to
silences. His hands shake when he pours — something he
does often. The Col-on-el is ada-man-t

'—means?' Ryan called.

There was silence from Viv.

'Really? Simple serving-girl. Means certain.' Knox was standing in the doorway.

ada-man-t he won't sell more than ten ac-res

'Acres,' Knox corrected.

acres. He says he has more than enough Walkin' to man-age the holdings. Though, later in the evening he described a bleak future in great detail. He can smell them burn-ing in his fields, so he told me. And yet he would not be moved.

I have failed to meet your cond-i-ti-on. Father, please, do not make Mad-e-line and Paul suffer for my shortcomings. Have mercy — they too are Baxters.

I will continue to write, hopeful for a reply.

Your faithful and loving son,

Captain Frederick Baxter

After a while Knox cleared his throat. 'Don't read another unless it starts "My dearest love".'

3 : 6

Ryan read the letters until the light started to fade. He didn't understand much of them, with names he took to be far-off places, not people, though it was difficult to tell at times, and numbers that must have meant something to the person writing and the person who should have been reading, although not to him. As the house creaked around him, Ryan glanced at the doorway, expecting to see a man in uniform: a soldier, rifle ready and itching to take back what was his – his sweetheart, his sickening little boy, his disappointed father. The blightbirds should be finished with the messenger by now ... didn't the army want its letters back? Wouldn't they be looking for them?

Ryan folded the letters one by one, lifted the pallet and put them under the corner, but they were too big: the pallet bulged, and bulges were no way to keep a secret. He put one letter under each of the other pallets that lined one wall: one soldier each.

Downstairs, he found the kitchen empty. The fire threw live shadows onto the pots hanging from the ceiling – the pots were all different sizes and shapes, far more than one house could need.

Knox was sitting out on the porch, slouched on a chair, with Chunk beside him. He scratched the ruft's head.

'I read all the letters,' Ryan said. 'On my own.'

'No more vanguards to be had?'

'Where's Viv?'

Knox waved towards the trees. 'Shouldn't be long now. He'll come late in the day, but before dark; and you'll see: he'll cut a fine figure against the sun.'

Ryan looked across the deep orange plateau and was calmed by the solid colour. He turned away before it could be broken by the silhouettes of men on coursers. 'You're hoping he comes soon?' he said.

'Ain't you?'

'I don't know.' He slipped his feet into his boots and sat down to tie the laces properly. His fingers weren't right for it somehow; he pictured them as bigger, older, a soldier's hand: fingers that'd held a rifle for days at a time, pulled the trigger, reloaded even; fingers that had written letters. He tied one loop too big and had to start over. The thump of Chunk's tail sent shivers through the porch boards. His fingers were slick now with a dampness that covered his palms. He checked the horizon. He would meet his father wearing his father's boots, with the addition of the laces, tied tight, steady as a man's footwear should be. And he would practise tying them quickly so he wouldn't be caught out. He pulled hard at loops of an acceptable size and stood up.

The plateau was as empty as the kitchen, the sun as tired as the embers. He would practise tying his laces.

A few paces from the porch he felt strangely alone, and then realised Chunk wasn't following him. He glanced back and the ruft was lying there alongside Knox, her big head resting on the boards.

'Come on, Chunk,' Ryan said, slapping his thigh. The ruft just closed her eyes.

'Looks like she's happy right here.' Knox scratched behind her ears and her tail started up again.

'Chunk!'

When the ruft didn't move, Ryan spat like he'd seen Knox do – like men did when they were trying to show they didn't care about nothing. He kicked every stone he could find on his way to the trees. It was cooler under the leaves, despite their closeness. He had to duck under the lower branches and was soon surrounded by leaves that curled like claws around their yellow fruit. He felt bold and touched one: it had the kind of soft, sleek feel of a well-fed courser. He ran a finger from top to bottom and it fell, knocking against branches until it hit the ground. He winced at the rattle, expecting a bang rather than the soft thud. He peered between the leaves as best he could, ready for the flash of Viv's white shirt, her scolding. He bent down to see better, to catch her legs quickly coming his way under the branches before she found him, but she wasn't there.

He snatched up the fruit and turned it over, prodding it where he figured it landed. Making a sound like that, it should have a bruise at the very least, but nothing was showing. The fruit was round, though not perfectly; one half was larger, and the bottom was red, like it had been dipped into a hot bath – red like Viv's neck. He raised the fruit to his mouth—

'I'd give that a week yet.'

Someone was standing between the trees; he could see patches of dark brown amongst the leaves. Ryan pushed his way through and came out onto what felt like a path between the trees.

'Hello, Ryan.'

The folds of her face settled down after his name. Her skin was so pale it made her black eyes shine. She held up her bloated hands unencumbered by pistols, though the same wasn't true of her hips.

'You know my name,' he said.

'And who we're both waiting for.'

'Knox is scared of you.'

'But you're not.' She smiled. It pulled her face and hid her lips and eyes.

'I don't know you.'

'Are you only scared of things you know?'

He rubbed his thumb along the fruit. How could you be afraid of something you didn't know?

'You look just like her when you're thinking,' she said, reaching down into her long coat.

Ryan readied to bolt – she might miss if he made it back between the trees quick enough.

'You like candied drops?' She ignored her holsters, instead filling her hand with what looked like coloured pebbles: reds and greens and blues, all brighter than a thing had a right to be. She held them out to him. 'Go on, take one. They're sweet on the tongue.'

'They're for *eating*?' He couldn't tell if she was making fun of him or wishing him to eat rocks for some other malicious intent.

'Didn't your ma ever give you candied drops?'

'She never gave me anything. She took things,' he said.

'All the more reason to have one now.' She stepped forward, hand reaching out.

He was leaning towards the colourful drops – and drops was the right word; they looked like late summer rain which was somehow bigger and fresher than the rest of the year's; it made dust spring up from the ground and knocked on the roof like it wanted to come in.

'I'll take one for Viv,' he said.

'No.' She closed her hand, but not all the way. She was bleeding a rainbow between her fingers. 'Candied drops are for young boys and girls.'

'She's not much older than me.'

'Why don't you take this nice red one? Red is my favourite flavour,' she said, opening her hand again.

He stared at the red drop against her pale skin, wrinkled as it was, like a bedsheet. 'Blue, please,' he said.

He tried hard not to touch her as he picked up the drop. He held it in his palm, like she had. It was a different kind of smooth to the fruit, which he'd left forgotten on the ground. 'For later,' he said.

Her face was pulling upwards, easing out some of the folds. It might have been surprise. 'You're a very good little boy. Your ma must be proud.'

'I don't think so.' He turned and walked towards the house. The going was easier with some space between the trees. They were in rows, he could tell that now, though some were growing bigger than the others. Near the end he glanced behind, but she was gone. He felt the candied drop in his pocket to make sure he hadn't imagined her: the woman who was waiting for his pa.

Knox and Chunk were still on the porch. There wasn't much light left in the day.

'What's Viv cooking for dinner?' Knox said.

'She didn't say.'

'I heard you talking.'

'She didn't say.' Ryan unlaced his boots. They were quicker to take off than put on. He hadn't noticed that with trousers or shirts – he would check that night.

'There are places in this world where a man can buy a slab of neat, big as a plate, butchered out back of the kitchen – you can see it done, if you're so inclined. They'll ask you how long you want it cooked.' Knox whistled. 'I'd take it raw if they'd let me. "Just show it to the pan," I say, so when you stick it with your knife it runs red. Mind, have to take your time with it, or your jaw suffers. Seen many youngsters ruin a meal that way.' He sighed. 'It occurs to me I don't spend enough time in those kind of places.'

Ryan waited, but that was all Knox had to say on the subject of neats and the eating of them. He examined Knox's face. 'Your beard has grown some since we've been here,' he said.

'So we can agree I'm no Walkin'?'

'No, not a Walkin'. But there's something else about you, Knox.'

'I should hope so.'

Ryan took a spot at the table. Every so often he touched the candied drop in his pocket. He might put it under a pallet, like his letters, but he didn't want to hide everything there. That was the cunning of nibblers: he'd watched them, even tried to follow them in McGraw's woods – it was easier there; no fruit trees, and not so many leaves. One nibbler had many places to hide his treasures – so many, it was a wonder they didn't stumble on each other's hoards. Or maybe they did – maybe they helped each other, with or without knowing it. Or more likely, they fought in the highest branches, where he couldn't see, and put their claws to good use. They had a funny way of eating when they got around to it, like they were talking into their little hands. He did the same, pretending he had a bigger treasure than the candied drop – big enough to fill his hands so he had to spin it over and over as they did.

'What are you doing?' Viv said. She was standing at the head of the table.

'Knox is hungry.'

'Is he?' Viv crossed to the fire and poked at it. She put a split log on top. 'Unless he wants hog muck in his food, he'll have to wait. Make sure this doesn't go out.' She left carrying empty buckets.

He tended the fire as he was asked, the quiet embers pulsing in time with his breath. They appeared to ignore the log, but that was only appearances; a blackness was creeping up the underside of the log. It came at a steady pace, no hurry about it, until suddenly the whole thing was covered – and then the flames came, small and bright.

Knox was rocking in his chair, just his square shoulder and arm visible through the doorway, Chunk and him like old companions now. McGraw had given the ruft to Ryan, but how much did that really mean? Knox was more like her old master and maybe she needed that.

When Viv returned she hung the buckets over the fire on a sturdy metal pole. The fire hissed as drops fell from the bottom rims. Some hit the blackened log, but that didn't halt the flames.

'Don't touch,' Viv said. 'The handles get hot.'

'But they don't burn you?'

'No,' she said, sitting by the fire.

'You don't feel it?'

'No.'

'Then why heat the water?' he said.

She rubbed at her neck, all along the red and raised parts that Ryan was trying so hard to ignore. He looked away as she said, 'I can still tell the difference. I know when the water is warm and when it's cold. It's not the same as feeling it, but still.'

After a while she carefully took each of the buckets and went into the next room. The hollow ring of the water hitting the tub was louder than he remembered any river. Then there was just a soft splashing. She had left the door open.

He stood square to it, intending to push it closed, but didn't. He listened hard for the noise of water on skin – a sound that meant she was still in there, still moving. The room off from the fire, off from the table, off from where he slept, that was *her* room, not his. The door should be closed – it was always closed, unless she made it not closed; there was no leaving it open. He couldn't touch the handle.

He edged closer. He could still picture her dresser, covered in trinkets that had no use or value. The rugs and covers that were softer than his bed. The heavy smell of incense that couldn't cover everything like she wanted. It was all there, and then it wasn't.

It was just Viv, naked, leaning over the tub.

Her ponytail was pulled loose, her hair wet and straight and covering most of her face. She ran her hands through it and her fingers snagged on knots. She didn't wince, just worked them free. Steam plumed from the bath but not enough to cloud the room. It was too big and too empty.

'No reason to be scared,' she said. She wrung out her hair and leaned back.

He blinked, suddenly aware how wide his eyes were.

'Didn't your ma tell you about girls?' she said.

He shook his head.

'Didn't she show you?'

'The door was always closed,' he said. He grunted, slow at first then quicker – he knew the noises a woman and a man made well enough.

'Come here.'

The floorboards were thunderous under his feet. He looked only at her face, not the red ring around her neck, or below. She shifted round to him and held out her hands. There was nothing to do other than take them. Her palms were damp, but she wasn't breathing so fast – she wasn't breathing at all.

He glanced at the tub. The water was only the colour of water, not blood.

She moved his hand until it touched cold, dry skin. 'Look,' she said.

His hand was on her chest and he flinched, trying to pull away, but she held him there. 'It's nothing special,' Viv said.

'You're wrong,' he said quietly.

'Just skin, flesh, and underneath all that, bone.'

It felt different. There was a roundness, a weight. He marvelled at it – knowing there was nothing on his body that felt the same.

'Nothing special,' she said.

Knox sat at the head of the table. It was big enough for eight, maybe ten people, and instead of sitting bunched at his end they spread out. The space made Ryan more conscious of his elbows, of his mug of water, and how he put down his fork between mouthfuls. The chewing of his food made enough noise to make him blush, even though it was outdone by Knox's wet smacking.

'Do you have to make that noise?' Viv said.

'What's that?' Knox said, his face half-buried in hog rib. Viv sighed.

'You don't like it? Then git. Not as if you're eating anyway.'

'I was brought up to know eating at the table was only polite – brought up with those kinds of manners.'

Knox sucked at the end of a rib and then used it to point right at her. 'That's just it: you aren't eating, are you?'

'Still,' she said.

'And don't go putting on airs, not for the boy's sake. He might be green, but he knows enough to know you ain't much of a lady.'

'And what's that mean?'

'Why don't you tell him?' Knox said. 'Tell him how a girl like you gets rope burns round her pretty neck.'

Viv stood so quick her chair fell over, though she left the room more deliberately.

Knox grinned over his ribs.

'You said I wasn't to mention it,' Ryan said.

'But you want to know.'

'I don't care.'

'I'd work on the lying before trying it again,' Knox said.

Ryan picked up his plate and took it to the porch. Exaggerated lip-smacking followed him. Chunk was resting in the shade of the side of the house, slumped against the wall, but she lifted her head when Ryan came close. Her nose twitched and she crawled forward a little, letting him rub her head, her eyes fixed on his plate. He couldn't see Viv, but that didn't mean she wasn't watching. She wouldn't like Chunk eating from a plate. He spilled the ribs onto the ground.

The ruft made less noise than Knox as she worked over a rib, one paw keeping it steady.

'You remember these meals,' he said, but Chunk only glanced up at him, flight in her eyes in case he had a change of heart and wanted his ribs back.

He left her to eat in peace and with the last of the light he read through his letters again. He had to sit on a different pallet this time, angling the pages to be able to make out the words. He read slowly, to make sure he got every one right, and to ignore the raised voices downstairs.

3 : 7

Something was jabbing his ribs and Ryan rolled over, hoping whatever it was would go away. The back of his head bloomed in pain and he sat bolt upright and rubbed it. 'What in—?' He looked round and found himself staring down the barrel of a rifle. There was a greyness to the mouth of it and he could see a little way in – enough to imagine a ball rolling down and out. It would be fast, but he saw it slowly.

Knox, a great mountain of proper black, stood behind the rifle. 'You know how to use one of these?' he said.

Ryan kept on rubbing the back of his head until his hand was all he could feel. 'When I'm older people will stop asking me that.'

'They'll stop asking and start shooting.'

'You've seen me do it,' Ryan said.

'From this close.' Knox rapped Ryan's forehead with the barrel and Ryan cursed and tried to snatch the rifle. 'Eat, then meet me out front.'

Ryan's eyes were streaming and the whole top of his head was throbbing. He checked his hand, expecting blood, but there was nothing. 'I don't like rifles,' Ryan shouted after him.

'Neither do I.'

Ryan thumped his bedding until his arms got tired, then he wiped his face; the tears had mixed with spittle – another thing that would change when he got older. His anger would be cold and dry, like Knox. He went to the window, not wanting to go down just yet and let Viv see. The distance was already shimmering; bushes were blurred and the hills weren't smooth lines but jagged, like the heat had torn their edges. He imagined what a lone rider might look like out on the trail: tall in the emptiness, but suffering under the sun just like the hills.

He rested his forehead on the glass and enjoyed the coolness of it. Closing his eyes, he could still see the rider – his father – coming closer, one tired courser step at a time. He tried to push the rider away, but the hooves were steady, their *clop-clop* as predictable as the blood beating in his ears.

A gunshot brought him to, and Chunk started barking. His breath had fogged the window a little, and there was nothing different out there: no riders yet. The sun had warmed the edges of his eyes until they almost stung from the dryness. If he touched them they'd only get worse, but it was hard not to and what would Viv care? She wasn't likely to bring up red skin.

She wasn't downstairs. There was a single plate, scraped clean, on the table. The fire was still burning with nothing hanging above. He warmed his hands, trying to ignore his head; it had now turned to a kind of prickling, a dropped-into-a-bush kind of feeling.

On the porch he laced up his boots. Chunk was still on guard, her legs stiff to shaking and tail rigid. She *humphed* at Ryan's patting. They were both looking out at the man with the rifle – the man they thought they knew well enough, who now had a rifle. Ryan glanced back inside at the long table, free from candles or playing cards, and at the door to the next room that was neither properly open nor closed. Chunk next to him, heavy and immediate. He stepped into the sunlight and pulled down his hat so he didn't have to squint. He was sweating some; if the hat wasn't sweat-logged already he reckoned he'd add a layer before midday.

Knox looked comfortable in his shirt and waistcoat – comfortable and dry. He held the rifle cocked in his arm and it appeared broken, as if the big man had missed his shot and snapped it like a twig. He was facing towards the cliff trail.

'That there's our target,' he said. Thirty or so paces away was a branch from one of the fruit trees, stuck into the ground. There were fruits bending the thinner branches and one broken sphere said Knox hadn't missed. Even from that far the smell of the juice was strong, but tinged by something like the fire.

'First it needs to be loaded.'

Ryan kicked at the dirt. 'No use otherwise.'

'With your pistol you have six shots. You can count that high, can't you?'

'I ain't simple.'

'It's harder than you'd think sometimes,' Knox said. 'But with a rifle you only have to count to one. With some of the boys we ride with, I consider that a significant advantage.'

Knox loaded the rifle, moving through the process slowly and twisting bits round for Ryan to see. Everything had its place, and it all fitted together snug. There was something to admire in that. He was leaning in close when it was snapped back together and he flinched.

'You try,' Knox said. He held out the rifle.

Ryan braced himself, remembering how heavy such a thing was, but his arms were shaking before he even had it in his hands. He handled it like he would a husht: at arm's length and with gritted teeth. He took his time, and Knox smiled at his being so deliberate.

'Now, lie down.'

'Lie down?'

'On the ground.'

He stared long enough to make sure Knox wasn't fooling with him, then, carefully holding the rifle in one hand, he got down on the ground. He was thinking it would be warm, but he was wrong. He lay down on his back, looking up at a towering Knox.

'How many fruits can you see like that?' Knox said.

Ryan craned his neck but could see only sky.

'Blood and bones, boy, roll over.' Knox hunkered down, grabbed Ryan's arms and put them into some kind of position, then he took the rifle and jammed it none-too-gently against Ryan's shoulder and into his hands. 'Look down the barrel and line it up with that tree branch there.'

'But who shoots from their bed like this?' Ryan said.

'Men who get to shoot until they die of old age. If that tree was shooting back, what good would it do you to be standing up big and tall? And besides, see how steady your arm is with the world beneath it?'

Knox took a few steps back and Ryan closed an eye and sighted down the long black of the barrel. It wasn't quite straight, and there were nicks and scratches the whole length. The fruits started small and got smaller the longer he looked, until they were just stars against the darkness of the gun's metal. He was back there, at the cabin, looking out into the night, the long grass stunned into a stillness, the moon unblinking and unable to look away, the river silent against the sound of bones breaking and blood hitting the ground.

He pulled the trigger: this time it was heavy, as if the rifle was making sure *he* was sure; that it meant something now – now, when he didn't need it to. He recognised the noise from before, even though it was different. It *lasted*. The rifle pushed against him; it was backing away, making itself scarce now the deed was done, and he'd have let it, too, except that his whole body was in the way.

'Were you aiming for a leaf?' Knox said.

'No.'

Chunk was barking from the safety of the porch, rushing from one end to the other in a strange kind of shuffle, never taking her eyes from Ryan and the rifle.

'Could've been worse. Reload and go again.'

'I can't,' Ryan said.

Knox sighed. 'I'll show you again.'

'It's not that. Say you won't laugh.'

'Laugh? Boy, nothing you could do would make me merry.'

Ryan eased the rifle down, though he could still feel it on his shoulder and on his fingers. He pushed himself up, revealing a damp patch where he'd been lying. Both of them stared at it, at the way it caught the sun in the middle and was already drying at the edges. He had a matching patch on his trousers, crossing both legs.

'You put a man down while he begged,' Knox said.

'I don't like rifles.'

Knox scratched his chin. 'I've seen plenty of things in my time. Nothing to be ashamed of.'

'I'm not ashamed.'

'This happen every time?'

'The two times I've tried,' Ryan said.

'Take them off,' Viv called, and the two of them turned to see her coming round the side of the house.

'He can't only shoot half-naked.' Knox glanced at him. 'Though it's one way to make a name.'

'You think he won't run out eventually?' Viv held out a hand expectantly.

Ryan started to untie his trousers. 'Nothing special,' he said.

Viv took them, wet as they were, without reaction. His thighs and prick started to chill despite the morning sun.

'Best stand up this time,' Knox said, taking a few extra steps back, and Viv also waited, likely to see if she was right. He reloaded the rifle. 'Just put it—'

But Ryan had already braced the gun against his shoulder, like before; it was a neat enough fit, like it was supposed to work that way – that not only the rifle but his shoulder was made with this in mind. Standing, the barrel wavered and he concentrated on keeping it still. He couldn't, though he could make it so the movement was small, less than the leaves were moving in the breeze. This time he did aim for a leaf, figuring that way he might hit the fruit. He pulled the trigger and pissed in a high arc.

There was less darkness around him and the sky beyond the branch stayed blue. The crunch of bone wasn't so loud, his shoulders eased a little against the weight of the remembered cabin and the smell of old candles tickled his nose only briefly. He'd knocked a smaller branch clean off.

He loaded and went again, and again, and each shot took a little more away from the target and brought a little less piss. There was a single orange globe and a handful of leaves left when he ran out.

'Twelve shots,' Knox said.

'It'll be fewer tomorrow,' Viv said. 'He's getting the hang of it. But start without the trousers.'

'He's got a good eye.'

'I don't like rifles,' Ryan said.

'One day you might,' Knox said.

*

He scrubbed his trousers in a bucket of cold water. It wasn't like cleaning off muck or dirt, the kind that lifted clear and either sank to the bottom of the bucket or lined the top. His trousers started the colour of wet and the water didn't change that. But he scrubbed nonetheless, and when his fingers wrinkled he judged he was done. He tossed the water out and hung the trousers on the porch. His own trousers were still wet too, so Viv found him another pair from upstairs. They were even bigger, in every way: he rolled up the legs until they bunched so big he could barely see his toes, and when he tied the cord around his waist there were clumps of itchy cloth every couple of inches. They felt altogether uncomfortable.

He helped Viv fetch more water from the spring, where there was a hand-pump of a kind he recognised; he remembered the need to dry-pump it a few times before even a dribble came out. Viv cleared out the metal trough underneath first, shifting a handful of old leaves and debris. Surrounded by yellowed rock, the water was twice as bright as any river he'd seen, and twice as cold on his face and neck.

Viv left him to it. Once he got a good flow going it wasn't hard work, but he had to wipe his brow enough to make him curse and wish he'd thought to bring his hat. Eventually he'd filled the bucket, despite drinking more than a whole herd of shaggies.

As he ambled back through the orchard, she appeared again.

'He's not here yet,' Ryan said.

She was leaning against one of the fruit trees, her hat casually low over her eyes as if she was trying to sleep standing up. 'You think I don't know that?' she said. Her face wobbled so much when she talked that he wanted to look at anything else, but couldn't. 'What happened to your trousers?'

'So maybe you don't know everything,' Ryan said, starting towards the house again.

In a few strides she was in front of him.

'Maybe I wanted to see if you'd tell me that you'd wet yourself at the sound of a rifle.'

'It's not the sound,' Ryan snapped.

She leaned forward so her face was level with his. 'Oh?' She smelled ... of *something*. He hadn't been expecting that – Viv didn't smell, not unless she'd been wrestling hogs. It was sour and sharp and made his eyes water a little. It wasn't her breath – she wasn't breathing – but it came from her mouth, mostly.

'You wouldn't understand,' he said.

'Would you tell me for another candied drop?'

He narrowed his eyes.

'A fair trade, surely?' she said.

'I still have the blue one.'

'If not the sound, maybe the kick made you?'

Ryan shook his head and brushed past her.

'He's not far away,' she said. 'You'll need more than a little rifle practice.'

'What will I need?'

213

But she was gone, the woman with folds in her face who smelled of bad milk, gone, along with her offer of candied drops.

Ryan gave a start as someone touched his shoulder. It was Viv, and he was on the porch. His trousers were almost dry and there was no trace of their dripping on the boards.

'You were somewhere else?' Viv said, sitting down.

'Not so far.'

'You've seen things, haven't you? Things that were hard to see.'

'That's all there is,' he said.

Viv turned his face to look right at her. 'Someone else would say you're too young to be talking like that,' she said.

They sat crosslegged on the porch for a time. The sun was high overhead and the shade was welcome. Chunk slumped her way from somewhere, but didn't come closer than she had to. She kept an eye on Viv, every so often growling to herself. Out in front of the house the broken and battered branch from the fruit tree stood guard, but it wasn't alone: ten feet or so away was another, smaller, bristling with leaves and fruit. If they were waiting for Pa long enough, they'd plant a whole new orchard blocking the way to the house.

But the wrinkled woman had said it wouldn't be long now, though she hadn't sounded eager when she said it, not like Knox.

'I was older than you when this happened,' Viv said, rubbing her neck. 'Of course, now I'm old enough to be your ma. I was strung up – you probably figured that much already. They chose a huge old tree with branches thicker than my waist, so no chance of them snapping before I did, so they thought. But I didn't snap.'

'Knox told me not to ask.'

'And you didn't. I worked in the big house – that's what it was called by anyone I had the chance to talk to. No doubt it had a better name, but that's what we all called it. He was kind to me – little things, like looking at me when I cleared his china cups and saucers. I didn't know any better then. His wife did. She accused me of stealing her silver.'

'Did you?' Ryan said.

'Not in the way she meant; I wasn't so stupid to take earrings and such. But the occasional spoon, or a butter knife – funny how you can forget about things like butter knives. That kind of silver bought me a new dress, or something sweet to eat in town.

'He didn't have the nerve to do it himself, she watched, though. Up I went, in total silence. I remember seeing hoods perched in the nearby trees, two of them, eyeing me. Two is supposed to be lucky. I would have laughed, if I could.

'When I came to, the hoods were still there but the people weren't. It was dark, and the sliver of moon gave an awful gleam to their feathers, to their eyes. They stayed there in the branches, even when your pa cut me down.'

'He must have seen your silver,' Ryan said.

Viv shook her head. 'He wasn't in charge back then. The man he rode under had seen the big house, but it was your

215

pa who cut me down and pulled me along by my arm, with thirty or so men behind us. They took what they could carry and burned the rest. They killed the men. The women – well, the wife couldn't keep her silence. Your pa made me watch. Everything.'

'You couldn't have stopped him?'

'I didn't want to. And now that colours me with shame.' She motioned to his trousers. 'You weren't scared of the rifle, were you?'

'No.'

'Was it something you saw or something you did?'

'It was something I didn't do,' Ryan said.

'Maybe you couldn't have stopped it.'

The sun was beginning to set when the first rider came out of the haze: a giant emerging against what Ryan had come to see as an empty view, totally out of place. There were more, and they blurred together so he couldn't count them.

Knox got up from his chair and Viv came to join them on the porch. She must have heard the soft rumble of hooves.

'They'll be hungry,' Knox said.

'So they'll eat.'

'He'll be wanting a bath.'

'There's water ready.' Viv shaded her eyes. 'So few.'

To Ryan it was an army that spread across the horizon, but when they reached the house the horizon wasn't so big: fourteen men; fourteen coursers. They were a sorry-looking bunch, their faces streaked with dirt, shoulders slumped.

Many had a vacant air to them, as if they weren't too sure what they were about or where they were.

Ryan turned to go back inside, but Knox caught him.

'Where you going?' Knox said.

'I don't want to.' Ryan glanced at the riders. 'He won't—'

'Won't what?'

'He won't want me.'

'You wouldn't be here if that were true,' Knox said, putting Ryan firmly in front of him.

One man dismounted and hung his hat on his saddle. His hair was a mess of curls, but cut close. He took a moment to steady himself and then took his time walking up to the porch. His shirt was loose, and Ryan caught a glimpse of something around his neck.

'Hello, son.'

3 : 8

Ryan stared at the face that was like his own. He understood the defined lines and rough skin, that these would come to him in time, and he understood where they came from: to hear a man's quick breaths become slow in the wake of the trigger; to see a purple bruise rise and then set on the horizon of a woman's back; to feel the heat of a house burning. When he looked at his father these were the things he saw. And from the softness of his pa's eyes, the resignation there, Ryan knew he saw the same would come to his boy.

'Pa.'

A small thing to say, but a big thing to admit. Here he was: not a giant, not a shadow. Not a masked bandit. He was all of these things, just not in the way Ryan had imagined.

Pa put a hand to the side of Ryan's head, tilting it to get a better look. He pursed his dry lips and nodded. Then he walked towards the house.

'See to the coursers,' Pa said, loud enough for his men to hear.

Ryan felt the remnant of heat from his father's hand. The thirteen remaining riders dismounted and led their coursers in a weary silence to the hitching posts. The length now made sense; even so, there was space for more animals. Michael wasn't crowded, though he was more obliging of the new arrivals than Knox's beast. Ryan watched as the men fed and watered the coursers before they thought of themselves – perhaps that was because of the order from his father, but they stroked necks and patted rumps in an unconscious way, and took off saddles with care.

He stood with Knox as the men filed past. After the first few it was a task to tell them apart. They were all of the same shape: a lean hardiness that produced clear cheekbones and large knuckles. This was more noticeable than small variations in height or the way they wore their hair or how clean-shaven they were. It was likely the work, but Pa appeared to attract a certain kind of man. And they were all men.

When he followed them inside, the room was covered in them: men sitting at the table, leaning against the wall, perched on the stairs. Those standing shifted every so often, testing legs that had been long in the saddle. Apart from the clearing of throats, they kept their silence as Viv busied herself between them. His father was sitting at the head of the table and looking right at Knox.

'You were right,' Pa said.

Knox shrugged. 'Could've been wrong.'

'The Northerners are pushing, quicker than I thought they would.'

Many of the men murmured at this – a soft kind of growl that sounded a lot like Chunk.

'We were lucky to avoid them at Hark Pass. In Lowerton they weren't looking for anything but food. If they'd caught us out on the open plains ...'

'It's not all bad,' Knox said.

'How's that?'

'Ryan brought down a messenger. Made for interesting reading.'

Everyone was looking at him, even Viv, and each face was blank, but the surprise was obvious. He wanted to back away, but Knox was behind him. He was caught between the man and his lie.

'He was alone,' Ryan said.

'Get some rest,' his father said to the men. 'Eat.'

Viv took Ryan by the arm and led him outside as chairs scraped the floor and men moved about heavily. What had felt like a house awkward in its size and too big for just the three of them now had the kinds of noises that seemed to suit.

He followed Viv through the orchard. She was in no rush. In her hand was a knife that caught the fading light from time to time. Chunk joined them from nowhere. Her tail was low between her legs and she kept looking back.

He rubbed between her ears. 'They won't take interest in you,' he said, but Chunk wasn't so sure and kept close.

It was quiet between the trees. He looked for the woman with the folded face, but she wasn't there. With his pa arrived, maybe she'd finished her waiting and moved on. She wouldn't give candied drops to the men; she'd said that. Viv cut between two trees and Ryan had to move quickly to keep up. She was taking a well-worn path – one he'd avoided until now. The hog pens were a good distance from the orchard and the house. Chunk found their scent and perked up a little; for him it had the opposite effect.

'What are we doing?' Ryan asked.

'Isn't that obvious?' Viv waved the knife.

'I don't like hogs.'

'Don't like hogs. Don't like rifles. What kind of a boy are you?' As she hustled him along the stench got stronger. It was a rough smell, abrasive, like chooks but not. It had the same texture just thicker, scratching the back of his nose and getting caught in his throat. He snorted to try and clear it, but that did no good.

The hogs were penned in by a waist-high fence. The posts were huge and squat and the boards looked to weigh more than any single man could carry. What kind of tree gave that kind of wood? Certainly not the spindly fruit trees or the tall, thin trees of McGraw's forest. Between each board there was only an inch or two of a gap, just enough to give a sense of movement to the hogs within – he caught the occasional flash of an eye or a snout, but mostly it was their dull pinkness that stood out against the faded wood. There was no telling where one started and another ended, so they appeared monstrously long. He judged the proportions of the fence entirely appropriate.

Ten paces from the fence he started to gag.

'My washing my hair doesn't look so strange now, does it?' she said.

He wiped spittle from his lips and was glad he hadn't brought up anything more.

She gave him the knife.

'Why me?' he said.

'I can't do it; it has to be someone else.'

'You're scared to?' Ryan said. He looked at the knife rather than at her.

She laughed. 'Not me. *Them*. The hogs run from me as quick as their stumps allow – and when they do, that's when they'll come to you.' She ran a finger across her throat, the gesture rightly red on her.

'I've broken chooks' necks before,' he said.

'There's not much difference, just more blood. You go in first.'

'How do I know which one?'

'Any you like, just not the big one. And take your time – better to do it right the once,' she said. She motioned him forward and he took a few unsteady steps, then glanced back at her. The knife felt too light in his hand for this kind of job, little more than a fruit peeler. He almost dropped it when the hogs started their racket: deep, rumbling honks that grew to a frenzy. These were as much hogs as Knox's beast was a courser. The fence started to shake and clouds of dust swirled in the air.

'They think you're going to feed them,' Viv shouted.

He wasn't carrying any food – unless he was the meal. He reached the fence. The hogs weren't so big – except for the big one, anyway; he was as round as he was tall and stood a good few inches above the rest. All eyes were on Ryan, and their snouts wiggled and twitched. There wasn't a gate – he'd have to climb over and hope they didn't try to bite his foot before he could defend himself.

They didn't give him much room. As soon as he had one leg over the fence he could feel their breath on his trousers. He wasn't sure why, but he decided it best to hide the knife as much as possible. Once he was in the hog pen maybe as many as ten fully grown hogs stared at him, kicking up dirt and honking to each other.

'What now?' he called.

'Get to the far side.'

That meant squeezing past the hogs: past their dusty bellies and their hairy ears. Some lost interest and went back to amusing themselves by rooting around in the dry dirt. Those closest followed him with their snouts, one going into his pocket before he could push it away. The big hog watched him. If he'd been a man, Ryan would have said he was squinting as old men do. The only part of him that was no bigger than the other hogs was the eyes – they'd be small for candied drops.

Ryan wedged himself in the far corner of the pen. Only one hog followed him so far; it was snuffling at his feet and flapping its head.

Then they all went very still as Viv appeared at the fence.

The hogs rushed towards him and the only sound was the *thud-thud-thud* of trotters on packed dirt. They didn't try to rush the fence; they just got as close as they could and then turned to face the Walkin'; it was a kind of courage. They bustled around him, and more than once he was forced to brace himself against the heavy wooden boards. The big one stood his ground in the middle of the pen. Viv was still on the other side of the fence.

'They don't like you,' Ryan said.

'One of them won't like you much, either.'

The smaller hogs were shivering and he put out a hand to one, half expecting the hog to squeal in fright, but it went right on with its shuddering. Its skin had the feel of bark more than anything.

'Best cut towards you – easier that way,' she said. The big one snorted his own response to that.

Ryan knelt down beside a good-sized hog. It wasn't so scared; it'd seen plenty of days in this pen, plenty of Viv bringing food, and plenty of things it didn't want to remember. Ryan plunged the knife in and pulled quickly back. The hog gave a wet cough, and then the blood came, drenching his hand and all the way up to his wrist. Blood on the wrist was a job half done. He stabbed the knife in again, this time higher, but it caught on bone and he had to wrench it clear. The hog had nowhere to fall; it slumped forward.

Then the others must have smelled the blood, which was all over his trousers and his shirt. They started shrieking, high-pitched yells, just about the most terrible sound he'd ever heard. He covered his ears, smearing hog blood across his face, not realising he still held the knife.

Viv was over the fence. The big one, clearly shaken by the noise, decided it was best to let her pass and the others scrambled in all directions, trying to get away from the smells of the dying and the already dead. Ryan greeted them like friends, people he'd grown up with, people who'd been away, but only for a few days.

He smiled up at Viv. 'Ma went like this, the first time,' he said. He showed her the knife and the warm blood between his fingers.

3 : 9

Viv lifted the dead hog over the fence. The heavy slap the body made when it hit the ground was utterly final. She followed. The hogs were still cowering on the opposite side of the pen, but at least they had stopped their noise. The blood was starting to dry on Ryan's hands, though he still left red prints on the fence.

'We'll get you cleaned up,' Viv said, carrying the hog in her arms. Ryan wasn't sure if she was talking to him or the hog, but he trailed after her. Sunlight played between the trees, the different-coloured patches dancing uncomfortably. He sneezed, then his nose started running and when he wiped it he couldn't tell the blood from the snot. His hand started to ache – he was still gripping the knife and he could feel the resistance of the hog's neck; the sensation ghosting its way along the underside of his arm all the way to his elbow. He scratched at it until there was only the burning left by his nails.

He focused on Viv's back and the sneezing stopped. The hog's bulbous head and its four short legs stuck out. It would have been funny to see if it weren't for the dead eye that was staring right at him. He didn't look away; this was something he had done.

Viv laid the hog down a few feet from the pump and started working the handle. The water was a shock, stinging his knuckles as it washed away the worst of the blood.

'You can put the knife down,' Viv said. Her face was calm. He dropped the knife into the trough. Flexing his hand under the water he saw there were bits that wouldn't come clean, between his fingers especially: no matter how hard he rubbed, his skin was stained.

'It will go with time. Always does,' she said.

'Not always.'

'You said, "The first time".'

'She came back. But she didn't want to,' he said, still rubbing at his hands.

'I doubt many want to.'

'But it was her fault,' he said, 'not like you.'

'Isn't always that simple.'

He glanced at the hog. 'So why does it happen?'

'You could waste a lot of time wondering "why". Why does the sun rise and set? Why does the wind blow?'

'Someone must know,' he said.

'It's a big world.' She stopped working the pump.

'Why don't you go find out?'

'Another "why". It's easy here, few surprises. Out there' – Viv motioned to the horizon – 'that's where it gets complicated. But you know that – it's *why* you're here too.'

'What do you mean?' Ryan said.

'As Knox tells it, no one made you come here, and no one is keeping you here.'

Ryan scuffed the dirt with his boot. 'I've nowhere else to go.'

'Me neither.'

'You're older. You can do what you want,' Ryan said.

'Is that what you think? You think it's that easy?'

'I just go where I'm told.'

'Be grateful someone cares enough to do the telling.' She stared at him for a moment and then sat on the edge of the trough and motioned for him to join her. 'When I was a girl, working at that house I told you about, I heard things, stories. I couldn't hear enough of 'em, but especially those about a place where Walkin' lived, and only Walkin'.'

'Like a town?'

'That's what the cooks said. The oldest one, she liked to tell stories – made her feel important, I guess,' Viv said.

'What kind of town is it? Like a fort?'

'Up in some mountains. She said that only Walkin' could find it and that normal folk had looked and found nothing.'

'Then how did the cook know?'

'Nothing gets past you, does it? I asked the same and the cook didn't like that. Said I was calling her a liar. She didn't tell me stories again.

'Still, we girls made up plenty of our own wondering what their town would be like. Mostly it was either witchcraft or fornication; that's how little we knew.'

'You could go there now you're a Walkin'.'

Viv stood and brushed off her trousers. 'What'd I just tell you? Out *there* is complicated. I wouldn't know how to live with one person like me, let alone a whole town.'

'What was it called?' Ryan asked.

'The town? Black Mountain, so the cook said.'

'I've never seen a black mountain before.'

'Me neither. That's what I'm saying: you can waste your hours thinking of where you *might* be, or you can get on making the best of where you *are*.'

'But I—' From the corner of his eye he saw Chunk creeping towards the hog, and Viv saw it too. She ran a few paces towards Chunk and the ruft stopped, caught between hunger and fear.

'Don't push it. You'll get some,' Viv said. 'I'll roast you up a couple of ears.' She went closer, which sent the ruft running into the trees. 'You don't want to be here when I cut it up. Just watch it while I get my things.'

He shifted to face the hog and stared hard at its chest; he was almost sure he could see it moving. Little bubbles of blood still escaped from the gash he'd made. He wished he could have made it cleaner, made it so there wasn't any pain. He lifted one of its legs. He hadn't really looked at the feet before – they were a strange mix of hard and soft. He fought the urge to prod and poke bits of the dead animal; instead, he patted its flank like he would a courser. Chunk watched it all from the shade of the trees. He could hear her panting; she sounded more hungry than usual. If

Chunk had a mind to have the hog, he wouldn't be able to stop her. He scratched his shin, remembering where she had bitten him.

The knives Viv was carrying caught the sun so that he had to shield his eyes. The edges were a different kind of bright, as if sharp enough to cut through the light. She also had a stub-nosed saw, two-toned: its teeth were white-gold like the knives but the top half was a flaked brown. No point sharpening that part. Each fleck might serve for a previous hog, sawn like lumber and chopped up into usable bits. At least there was something to mark their passing, instead of just the forgetful bellies of men.

'Go on now,' she said as she set down her tools. Draped over her shoulder were bloodied rags which she damped in a bucket. There were other empty buckets too, which she kept nearby. How many would a hog's insides fill? There was little to be gained in finding out, though Chunk had decided otherwise; she was edging closer in that odd awkward shuffle of hers. She must have thought the shadow of the trees to be an effective cloak, and he dissuaded her of that idea on his way past. She grumbled at his unwanted stroke. Behind him the crack of bones rang hollow around the trees, cut off by the more persistent sound of the saw.

He wasn't alone in the orchard; some of Pa's men were taking their ease. He passed one asleep under a tree, his hat covering his face. As Ryan approached he wondered if it was the wrinkled woman, but the figure's shape was all wrong and there was only a single pistol at his hips. Another of the men was examining the fruit. He offered one to Ryan.

'I've been told to wait a week or two,' Ryan said.

The man shrugged. 'They're not at their best, but better than hungry.'

'There's hog coming.'

'The first few days here and the fruit is everything you prayed for out on the trail. After that it sours and you get the squits.' The man frowned at the fruit in his hand, then he took a large bite out of it.

'I killed the hog myself,' Ryan said.

The man offered the fruit again, but Ryan left him to it. Other men were wandering between the branches, drawn there by the fruit or the shade or the fresh air. Those who wandered together appeared respectful of the place, whispering in hushed tones, and only then when necessary. It was hard to think of them as bandits – as thugs, ruffians, outlaws; the men from Viv's story.

When he got to the house the main room was empty except for Pa and Knox, who sat close together at the table, speaking softly. They stopped when they noticed him, watching him with blank faces as he went upstairs. He waited, silent, at the top until he heard their voices again. If he could have made out the words he might have stayed to listen.

In the bedroom most of the men were lying on the pallets, many quietly snoring. Just looking at the room made Ryan yawn. One man was standing at the window; he turned, and in his hand was a letter. Other men were reading too, propped up on elbows or resting against the walls.

'What are you doing?' Ryan said.

'Sshhh.'

'Those are mine!'

'Oh, I'm sorry' – the man at the window stared at the letter – '*Margery.*'

Those awake chuckled and Ryan flexed his hand, feeling for the knife that wasn't there. He looked at his own pallet. His belongings were piled neatly in the middle – all there, but none untouched.

The man in the window came over. 'You didn't hide these very well, Ryan.' He was smiling, though he still looked tired. His dark hair hung loosely to his jawline in strands. It put a lot of his face in the shade.

'You know my name.'

'Your pa talks about you often enough. I'm Lee.' He put out his hand.

Ryan hesitated.

'Don't worry, I've shaken my fair share of bloodied hands,' Lee said. He sat down and motioned for Ryan to do the same. Behind him two men exchanged letters. Someone – awake or asleep – let out a sigh.

'They're not for entertainment,' Ryan said.

'No.'

'Then why are you reading them?'

Lee scratched his face. 'To see how other people live.'

One man tutted loudly and threw down the letter he'd been perusing.

'And you?' Lee said.

'For practice.'

'That explains this.' Lee picked up the Good Book. 'Though how it came to you must be an interesting story.'

'I haven't got very far,' Ryan said.

'I'd stick to the letters.'

'Sometimes they're harder, written by hand and all.'

Lee put the book back next to Ryan's pistol and the candied drop. His hand dwarfed both. With the sombre men there it felt like a ridiculous collection – a child's toys. But the men weren't laughing. Lee wasn't even smiling any more. He was staring down at the pistol.

'You've used this.'

It didn't sound like a question, but he answered anyway. 'I've had to.'

'I suppose there is no such thing as too young. Can you read without saying the words aloud?'

'Sure.'

'Then join us.' He passed Ryan a letter. 'We all need the practise.'

Lee was shaking his shoulder. Around him, men were stretching and yawning as the light through the window painted their faces a dark orange, like fruit long fallen from the tree.

'Time to make good on all your efforts,' Lee said, pointing to Ryan's red hands.

The smell of roasting meat was fat in the air, overpowering the stink of dried sweat and unwashed clothes, and his mouth watered despite his cracked lips. He tried to rub the sleep from his eyes but his head felt woollen and his neck ached. He was slow getting up; the last few men were already making their way downstairs. The blankets showed the shapes of men in their wrinkles. The white shapes of carefully folded letters were at the end of pallets, on pillows, on the windowsill. Captain Baxter's was among them somewhere. Ryan wanted it back, perhaps to keep in his pocket, but he was hungry. He would find it later, when all the men were sleeping.

The hum of conversation almost covered the sound of men gnawing on bones and open-mouthed chewing. Ribs were wielded to emphasise a point, sleeves used to wipe away grease. Ryan squeezed by the table on his way to the fire. He stepped on someone's boot and apologised, but they were too engrossed in their meal to notice. His pa and Knox were still at the end of the table, though talking openly now. Pa had an easy smile as he cut his meat into sensible pieces; his beard was unmarked where others' glistened.

Viv, presiding over the spit, armed with two large knives, waved him forward. The fire hissed and crackled under the hog – if it was still right to call it that. What hung on the spit was headless and striped, the colours ranging from black to brown to almost yellow: lines of dawn, played out across its back.

'Something, isn't she?' Viv said.

The trotters were bound and stretched forward and back. It had the impression of mid-leap, with a grace that was far from the hog pen. Viv handed him a plate with a crack branching through it. She cut thick slices from the hog's hind. It was more than he could eat. He felt like he should thank the animal but didn't know how. He raised his plate in a kind of salute and Viv nodded as if that was the right thing to do. He turned to find somewhere to sit when he noticed a bucket by her feet. The hog's head was inside; its snout poking up like it could smell itself cooking. Ryan looked away, not quickly enough to stop bile rising in his throat. He swallowed hard and pushed his way out to the porch.

The air was clearer outside, even with the smell of sizzling fat following him. It was on his scalp, underneath his nails, between the fine hairs on his arms. His skin crawled with it and he couldn't stop his nose, like the snout, searching for the scent. He wasn't lying when he'd spoken of wringing chooks' necks and plucking their scrawny limbs – but a hog was so much bigger.

He stared at the slices on his plate. He could toss them out onto the ground, but what good would that do? It wouldn't help the hog none. Better to give the meat to the gaunt, hungry figures around him, those who might not have eaten for days.

'Funny what can get to us, what can make us stop,' Lee said. He was leaning over the railing, watching the slow sunset. He scratched at his beard.

'What do you mean?' Ryan said.

'We rode through a town, I forget the name, and I saw this shaggie that was missing a leg – not the whole thing, just about below the knee, if they have knees. It was still pulling a cart, still working. Someone had strapped a metal pole to the leg, but it didn't move right.' He spat and then worked something out from between his teeth. 'I left the town with my eyes streaming. With all I've seen and done . . .'

'Do you want this?' he said, offering Lee his plate.

'You eat it. You'll get over whatever spooked you, but don't forget it. It's important.'

He picked up a piece of meat. It felt rubbery. The stain of the hog's blood was still marking his fingers. The back of his throat stung from the bile he'd swallowed back. And despite it all, the meat was tender and the taste made him groan without meaning to.

'That feeling, that's important too,' Lee said.

'The killing was easier than the eating.'

Lee shrugged. 'Funny what gets to you.'

As Ryan finished his food more men came out onto the porch. Each of them sat down and started doing something with their hands. Ryan peered over the shoulder of the nearest one. He had a wad of smoke – the kind that Ryan had helped make. He was pulling bits off and putting it into a small piece of paper. A candle was passed around and then Ryan couldn't smell the meat any more; instead, the air turned grey, his eyes started to sting and he began to cough. It burned to breathe, and strangely, everyone felt far away, except for their faces, which were leering at him, close enough he could make out the veins in the whites of their eyes. He swiped at them, but his hand met nothing.

He stumbled away from the porch, shaking his head to clear it.

He wasn't the only one out there. A few paces from the house he felt something move quickly by his leg. It went by so fast he almost lost his balance: Chunk was tearing across the ground like a rifle round, dust shooting up in her wake. But she wasn't quick enough to catch the short branch that bounced ahead of her once, twice, and then stopped. She exploded onto it, her head shaking viciously. Not so long ago that was his leg. She trotted back, wagging her tail, to drop the stick at the feet of a man, who sighed and said firmly, 'No more.'

Chunk growled. She barked and pawed at the stick.

'What are you doing?' Ryan said.

The man picked up the stick and threw it.

'It was the only way to distract her from the hog.'

Ryan shielded his eyes as he watched Chunk chase after the stick. It wouldn't last long at this rate.

'You take over,' the man said. He had patches under his arms.

Chunk dropped the stick at Ryan's feet, tail still wagging. He took the least-chewed end, leaned back and threw. It didn't go nearly as far and Chunk managed to catch it before it hit the ground. She brought it back and he did it a few more times. Then his arm started to get tired, and Chunk met this stoically, as if she'd expected as much – that he was a poor substitute to start with. He rubbed behind her ears and she was content enough to occupy herself stripping the stick's remaining bark.

Ryan slept poorly that night. The room was stuffy with so many bodies making so much hot air – and not all from their mouths. What had been the soft purrs of dozing mousers that afternoon were transformed by night into great shuddering roars. He kept waking in a panic, half-dreaming of landslides. Sweat made the sheets stick to his arms and his pillow was damp no matter how regularly he turned it over.

When dawn finally came he could take no more. He got up, and wasn't too quiet about it, either.

He found Pa downstairs. He was rolling a loose bundle of smoke unevenly along the tabletop. What was left of the hog was at the other end, finally free of the spit. He sat beside his father.

'Up early,' Pa said.

'And you.'

'I don't sleep.'

'Viv doesn't sleep,' Ryan said carefully.

Pa laughed. 'Not like that. You'd think I'm too old for nightmares.'

'I don't have bad dreams,' Ryan lied.

'They'll come.' The certainty in his pa's voice made Ryan fidget. He glanced at the hog remains. He could imagine that as a nightmare: the head sniffing so hard the bucket tumbled and somehow moved across the floor leaving a trail of blood, coming straight towards him.

'Tell me what happened with your ma.'

'She didn't want to keep going.'

'She did it herself?' Pa said.

Ryan picked at a thumbnail, taking off enough so it was no longer red. 'The first time.'

Pa pulled him into a hug. His shirt was worn smooth and felt cool against Ryan's cheek. He could hear his pa's heart beating.

'I'm sorry it had to be you,' Pa said.

His top few shirt buttons were undone. Again there were flashes of something around Pa's neck, something on a leather cord. When the cloth bagged it was easy to miss, but now there was a definite lump – like a locket, or maybe a big ring.

'Did she speak of me at all?'

'Yes.'

'I didn't make it easy for her, and she had her troubles.'

'And you have nightmares,' Ryan said.

'That's different.' Pa looked him in the eye. 'Or maybe it isn't. But you're here with me now, and that's all right.'

'I didn't want to come, not at first.'

'I understand.'

'I have my own courser,' Ryan said.

'You'll need it.' Pa stood and stretched. His elbows made clicking noises above his head. 'Knox said you were practising with the rifle.'

'I don't like rifles.'

'He said that too.'

'Did he tell you why?' Ryan said, looking out the door, but he couldn't see the targets.

'He did. That's the kind of thing a man has to overcome, not run from.'

'Did you have those kind of problems?' Ryan said.

'I grew up very different to you.'

'Did your pa help you?'

'He didn't help me with anything,' Pa said.

'You said it was different.'

There was a moment of silence. Ryan waited for the sound of a belt unbuckling, the herald of a whipping from his pa, the kind of whipping Ma could only manage on her better days. But she moved quick when her leg allowed, or she waited for him behind corners. Beads of sweat ran down his ribs, cool despite how hot he felt, and his hands started to tremble as Pa moved round the table.

'Wait here.' Pa went upstairs. Perhaps he had a special belt for beatings? Perhaps it would be wider to make a bigger mark, and with jagged edges. Was Pa's tread heavier on the stairs, weighted down so by the belt?

His pa wasn't carrying a belt; he held a rifle and a large pouch of rounds.

'I'm the better shot anyway,' Pa said. 'Had you shooting fruit, didn't he?'

'Branches stuck into the ground.'

Pa put down the rifle and motioned Ryan over to one of Viv's buckets. It had all the innards of the hog.

'You told her to keep that?' Ryan said.

'Just bring the bucket.'

'You want the head over there?'

'No.' Pa took them a good way from the house, past the shaggies and along the ridge, whistling the whole way. Ryan didn't recognise the tune – not that he knew many. He wet his lips and tried himself, but got nothing except short of breath. Pa didn't notice his efforts.

'Okay, this'll be far enough,' Pa said. 'Empty the bucket out.' Then he led them thirty or forty paces back towards the house.

'I won't be able to hit the hog's mess. I can barely see it,' Ryan said.

'You won't be aiming at the hog.' Pa looked up into the sky. 'Best take them trousers off.'

Without his pa watching he loosened the ties and wriggled out of his trousers. The dirt was cold on his toes so he put his boots back on, though they looked huge against his pale shins. The dawn air made the hairs on his legs stand up. His prick was going in the opposite direction.

'Is it loaded?' Pa said. Ryan checked the rifle and said it was. 'Good, here they come.'

Ryan strained to see what his pa was talking about. He was glad not to be looking directly towards the sun, which was behind them, but all he saw was the pale blue of a clear sky. He tried not to blink in case he missed whatever was coming. Then there were dots in the sky: a loose circle of marks that were getting closer. He struggled to count them as they danced into one another.

'Take your first shot before they land,' Pa said. 'If you miss, you might get a second.'

'You want me to shoot a blightbird?'

'Men don't stand still like a tree branch.' He put his arms out and stood rigid to demonstrate.

'Where should I hit it?' Ryan said.

'Anywhere you can.'

The birds had changed from dots to lines and were growing. He hefted the rifle against his shoulder, feeling the true weight of it. It didn't matter what he'd seen or what he'd done, it was a man's weapon – too big for a boy. His arms were short, his thin finger small and light on the heavy trigger.

The blightbirds were above the hog's mess now, and big enough for him to make out their beaks and claws. They didn't flap their wings, just tilted one way or the other and gradually they came lower. It wasn't any easier to count them but he reckoned there were at least six separate birds. There was a smoothness to their descent: not a single bird wobbled or strayed from their perfect lines. No other animal moved in such a way – not a courser, not Chunk, and definitely not a man – though it didn't last. Close to the ground they started beating their wings and faltered. It was a strangely wooden sound, their wings punching up dust.

'Now,' Pa said, and Ryan sighted along the rifle, trying to

keep the bold outline of the blightbird solidly in place. He pulled the trigger. The sound of the shot was lost amongst the beating of wings and the brief, shearing squawks. A few heads turned in his direction. But the only real evidence of his firing was the line of damp ground that started near his boots and was almost as long as he was tall.

The noise brought men out onto the porch. They leaned on the fence or sat against the wall. Some smoked, and all were silent as they watched without comment. He didn't doubt they could see his bare legs.

He reloaded the rifle as the blightbirds shuffled amongst themselves, each trying to find the best spot from which to tear at the innards. Their legs were covered in ruffled feathers that gave the impression of baggy trousers, which made him laugh.

'You think missing is funny?' Pa said. He still didn't look round at Ryan.

'No.'

'You wait until one skips off or goes to fly away. Anyone can hit a heap that big.'

Ryan raised the rifle, took a step back and stared once more along the barrel. Pa was right, it wouldn't be difficult to aim at the tumble of wings and without much choice, kill a blightbird. It would be no harder than plunging the knife into the distracted hog – and less blood on his hands.

There was a scuffle as a blightbird hopped right in the middle of the mess. The others didn't take to that and it was chased off. It turned towards Ryan as if accepting what

244

was to come, that it'd made its choice and was now dealing with the consequences.

'Well?' Pa said, his voice sounding distant.

Ryan shot the blightbird, hitting it square in the chest, and this time the sound was the only noise in the silence, and all the bigger for it. The other blightbirds scattered, running awkwardly as they flapped their long wings, but he didn't have time to load and shoot again.

His pa was looking at him.

'No piss,' Pa said.

There was only a single line in the soil.

'It usually takes me a lot longer to run out,' Ryan said.

'This was different.'

Ryan stared at the dry earth. The blightbird had known, somehow: it had faced him. That *was* different. In the darkness at the ferry there was nothing like that. He was as good as hidden in the cabin and Bryn and the man had been hard to separate. They had both ignored him and his useless rifle.

'Put your trousers back on.' Pa started towards the blight-bird.

When Ryan joined him the bird was dead.

'Did you—?'

'Did I what?' Pa said.

'Did you finish it?'

'No. You got it good.'

That didn't make sense, not with how the bird looked. The only sign was a small redness to its chest. But staring long enough made it clear the thing was dead, though its eyes were open. Pa got a hold of its claws and hauled it up. The wings, each easily as long as Ryan's legs, opened and closed as Pa walked: one final flight. They weren't the solid black he'd been expecting from how they appeared in the air. Streaks of yellow and white ran along the feathers. He hadn't figured blightbirds would be pretty.

The men on the porch kept their silence, no cheers or slaps on the back. They blew their smoke and looked more at the blightbird than Ryan. These were strange men – he was starting to understand that.

Pa lifted the blightbird onto the table.

'Viv!' He cast around for the woman. There was movement upstairs. 'Viv, get down here.'

She appeared, unflustered by Pa's racket, with a bundle of sheets in her arms.

'This bird needs gutting and plucking,' Pa said.

Viv wrinkled her nose at the tangle of feathers taking up most of the table. 'Hardly worth it: not much meat on a blightbird.'

'That's not the point. Dry it if you have to.'

'But there really isn't—'

Pa picked up a large cleaver and slammed it into the table and she nodded and went to get the bird.

'Wait,' Pa said. He'd cut off more than Viv's protests. He held up one of the blightbird's claws. 'Now take it.'

Viv wrestled the bird out of the door, though she wasn't too careful about it, judging from the complaints coming from the porch.

'You should keep this,' Pa said, offering the claw to Ryan. It was almost as big as his hand and the skin was like an old man's, loose-looking and wrinkled. But it was actually firm, and dry to the touch. The claws themselves were wickedly smooth, with tips that weren't knife-sharp but sharp enough.

'It died so you could grow: that's worth your respect.'

'Is that why you keep something around your neck?' Ryan asked.

'You noticed that?'

'Sometimes it makes a bump in your shirt.'

'That talon would make a bigger bump. We should cut it down,' Pa said.

He pulled the leather cord over the top of his curly hair and put it on the table with some care. It made a soft thud, like a knuckle tapping the top. It was an eye, perfectly round. The cord ran right through the middle of it. The bottom edge was blackened, but otherwise it was the complicated white of a chook's egg.

'Is it real?' Ryan said.

'You think it's painted wood?'

'It looks like wood – dry in that way.'

'Pick it up,' Pa said.

Ryan hesitated. 'Is it a person's eye?'

'It was.'

'I don't want to touch it.' There were things you weren't supposed to know the feel of. The brown ring shone like a soldier's boots. It had little flecks of black in it that caught the light.

'Suit yourself,' Pa said, raising the cord to meet his own eye. 'I like to think he can still see me. See what I've become, thanks to him.'

'Who was he?'

'Thomas McDermott. Your grandpa.'

3 : 10

I have seen the burden God has laid on the human race.

Ecclesiastes

BOOK FOUR

BOOK FOUR

4 : 1

Ryan stayed out of the house the rest of that day. He played the game with Chunk, throwing the stick until his arm got tired, and then he took her a big bone from what was left of the hog. She couldn't believe her luck. She wanted to stay right there and enjoy her present, but he wrestled through her growls, pulling the leg-bone, and her with it, until she wasn't too far from the house. The coursers largely ignored her, their tails whipping in the speck-filled heat.

The men were everywhere – not in the way crumbers got everywhere if you kicked over a mound, but it was hard to go fifty paces in any direction without catching sight of one. Many were just wasting time, like him, ambling aimlessly about the place, and others busied themselves with the coursers, or their tack or collecting water – or smoking. There was a lot of smoking, another reason to steer clear of the house. The porch was like a cloud that couldn't bring itself to rain.

He offered to help Viv with the blightbird. She refused, as if his asking was some kind of insult, but he stayed to watch her for a while. He'd plucked his own share of chooks but a blightbird turned out to be a different proposition, with more feathers than a whole chook house. She had it strung up near the water pump. Beside her was a bucket of steaming water which, going by the dampness of the bird, she'd used for a good dunking. There was a separate bucket for the feathers, though with more of a breeze that might have been a challenge. She tore great handfuls of feathers from the body, but the wing feathers were big enough to need a more patient approach. Again he offered to help, and again she told him to go away. The tips of the wings were too tough for her slick hands, so she used her teeth to pull them out, one by one, and spat them straight into the bucket.

The bird looked much less impressive without its feathers. It was too long and too thin, and it had a limp spring to it that was grotesque. The hanging stretched it, which didn't help one bit: the one leg it hung from was pulled straight, the other dangling towards the floor. Its beak dipped close to the dirt. As Viv did her final sweep she made a pantomime of the bird, shifting limbs this way and that in a mockery of how they once moved. He left her there feeling like he had stones in his stomach, grinding together with each step.

He didn't get very far before Lee found him.

'Your pa wants you inside. He's got something to say.'

'To me?' Ryan said.

'To everyone.'

As they headed back to the house, Ryan noticed that the man had a slight limp – it only became apparent after a while, after he got into his stride, or tried to.

'Shot just below the knee, if that's what you're wondering,' Lee said.

'It was.'

'You were staring.'

'Did it hurt?'

'I was drunk; a blessing and a curse. Helped with the pain, but I'd have noticed the stableman otherwise,' he said, grinning.

'Thieving coursers?' Ryan said. He stopped for the answer.

Lee scratched at his beard. 'Is that how low you think us?'

'What my pa is about to say, will that make me think much better?'

'Likely not. But we don't steal coursers.'

'Knox did – took that messenger's animal and now it's hitched with the rest of them.' Ryan stared up at Lee's face.

Lee stared right back. 'That's different.'

'How different?'

'Man was in no state to care for the courser.'

'Because Knox shot him.'

'Ah.' Lee held up a finger. 'That's the "different".'

'And that's better than stealing his courser?'

Lee's nod was emphatic. He started towards the house again as if the discussion had met its natural conclusion. Soon his limp got going, though it was more pronounced than before, like he was making a show of it. He also made a show of insisting Ryan go inside first. It was somewhat ruined by Lee's scratching of his beard.

'You go at that beard a lot,' Ryan said. 'Why not shave it?'

'Because then I look your age.'

The room was full of bearded men and Ryan looked at each anew, now seeing them as little more than boys with hair on their chins. He tried to picture them as hairless as himself, but their eyes were still weary and their cheeks gaunt. He turned to tell Lee of his doubts, but the man had taken a position near the stairs.

Ryan stayed by the door. More men were coming in. His pa had taken the head of the table, as usual, though this time he was standing up. The cord around his neck was plain to see, but Grandpa's eye was hidden by his shirt. Pa cleared his throat for quiet, not that there was much noise beyond creaking floorboard and the scratching of beards. Every time a hand went to a face Ryan wondered again at their folly in allowing such a troublesome thing to grow on their faces.

'You've rested?' Pa said to the room.

'Yeah,' they all said, though Ryan didn't believe it, not to look at them.

'You've eaten?'

'Yeah.'

'You're bored?'

There were one or two sniggers at that, and one or two sighs too.

'Some of you have been reading: letters to sweethearts and whatnot,' Pa said.

Ryan crossed his arms and glared at those he knew to be keen readers.

'Well, Knox and I have been doing the same: that messenger had orders as well as personals. There's a wagon westbound on the Wilson Trail. Missive says oats and furs.'

'What d'we want with oats and furs?' a man said.

'Fine question, Werth. Missive also says twenty young Northerners are accompanying those wagons.'

'Odd number,' Werth said.

'Too many for oats, I'd say. Worst, we come away fed and warm for the winter. Blood to ashes, we come away with a lot more than that.'

There was more talk, more questions, and a lot more idle speculation. Some of it Ryan was able to follow. After a time his legs started to ache from standing, so he sat with his back against the wall as they settled in for the discussion. There wasn't much objection to the idea of going after the wagons and taking whatever was in them. And pulling them? More shaggies and coursers that of course they wouldn't be *stealing*. Instead, the talk was about why twenty men, why the Wilson Trail, and even why there was a message at all. There was a general consensus that Wilson in particular was a trail that was getting busier, and another debate sprang up as to why. Both colours used it, which meant fighting, which meant it was worth fighting over. Best anyone knew, it went into a range of mountains. That was the word they used: *range*. Ryan assumed it meant *a lot*. He rolled the word around: a range of blightbirds. A range of chairs. A range of beards. He was fairly confident he had a handle on the word.

'Where does it go after the mountains?' Lee asked.

'Why does it need to go anywhere?' one man answered.

Were the armies mining in the mountain range? Trying to outflank each other? Lee was sure the trail went elsewhere, but others shook their heads. There was talk of maps and edges. If they were mining they would need wagons to bring back whatever they dug up, and that would mean more than twenty men.

Pa let them at it. He appeared to be listening to it all; his eyes were following the conversations, though Knox looked bored. He was playing idly with a little huntsman that had run a line down from the ceiling to the table. It climbed along his fingers until he turned over his hand and the huntsman's landscape became four fingers wide again. At first it seemed cruel, but this was an endless horizon the huntsman could opt out of at any time.

'If Wilson is so busy, we really want to get involved?' someone said.

Pa spoke up. 'We won't make a habit of it. Nothing to get us noticed.'

The conversation dragged on, as if the quiet of the last few days was the pumping of a water well and now it all came out. Separate conversations sparked up between twos and threes. Ryan couldn't keep up with the different voices so he stopped trying, but Pa let it go on – this was clearly the way of things.

Eventually Pa stood. 'We'll set out tomorrow,' he said. He made his way over to the door. 'Come and keep me company while I stretch my legs.'

Ryan's backside was numb beyond fidgeting. He took his pa's hand.

They walked side by side in the orchard. Pa picked fruit for them to eat as they went; the juice ran down Ryan's chin and when he wiped at it his hand came away sticky.

'Those boots of yours look familiar,' Pa said.

'You didn't leave any laces. Someone gave me these.'

'I believe I did. I wonder what she did with them.'

'Maybe she shared them out amongst all the men,' Ryan said.

Pa frowned. It made the black marks under his eyes deeper.

'That started before you were born. I'm sorry you had to see that.'

'Didn't see nothing – just heard it.'

'There was nowhere on that farm you couldn't,' Pa said. 'One reason I took my leave.'

'She said you couldn't stand my bawling.'

'One reason. I shot at a man once as he climbed out of my own bedroom window. Figured he had the right idea.'

'You left me behind too.'

'I had no father to speak of and I didn't like it either. But I saw that bump on your ma and I knew I'd be no good. No good for you, no good for your ma.'

'And now?' Ryan said.

'Neither of us got much of a choice.'

They passed the strung-up blightbird, its pale body like the moon between the trees. Viv and her bucket of feathers were gone. There was a patch of dried blood underneath. Its head hung so close it might have been drinking what was left.

'Never figured a Walkin' could be as idle as that girl,' Pa said. 'Or maybe she's just stubborn.'

'You're going tomorrow,' Ryan said.

'And you're coming with us.'

'When did you become an outlaw?'

'Is that what you think I am?' Pa said.

'It sounds better than "thief".'

'It does. It took me a few years' riding with different men; I wasn't always in charge. Have to learn this trade like any other. I thought about coming back to get you, but it's no life for a little 'un.'

Ryan tossed away the stone from the fruit.

'You look like her when you're thinking,' Pa said.

'So people say. Was Ma right about Grandpa? Did you burn him?'

'She missed her folks, but she liked it that way – she liked the hurt of it. She was difficult to understand. You don't have to come with me. I could leave you here with Viv. She might even find you helpful.'

'Where you're going, there aren't any houses?'

'That's right.'

'Then I'll come,' Ryan said.

All of a sudden he picked Ryan up, lifting him from under his arms. Their faces were inches apart.

'You're an odd—'

There was a bang that echoed through the leaves. And then there was pain.

4 : 2

Ryan was on his knees, covering his ears with his hands, but he couldn't shut out the ringing, a continuous noise, higher pitched than the whine of a speck and louder than a swarm of workers. He daren't take his hands away or his ears would burst. Slow drops of blood ran along his cheek and fell to the ground. Like the blightbird, it was close enough to lick. His mouth was open. He was screaming, but he couldn't hear himself.

Then the burning came. It started under his hand, like he was holding coals against his head. He shook his hand away and blood fanned from his fingers. It did nothing for the heat, which crept across his face until his lips felt like ash. Every breath sent new flames back towards his ear. No amount of tears could stop the burning in his eyes. They were charring, just like his grandpa's.

'Ryan!' The voice was small but it was something other than the ringing. He focused on that.

'Ryan.' A little louder.

He looked for the voice, but he couldn't see beyond his

263

tears. He blinked until he could make out the shape of his pa: a silhouette at the base of a tree.

'Stay down, son.'

Now the ringing was gone his pa's voice hurt all the same. It squeezed his teeth, as if the words were trying to push through. He gasped, hoping to let them out.

'Knox! Knox, get out here! It's *her*,' Pa shouted.

The men came out and for once Ryan was glad of their eerie silence.

'It's her,' his pa kept calling, and they ran past, keeping to the trees.

Knox stood in front of Ryan, bold as day and just as big. He carried Ryan back to the house, and from over his shoulder the shadows of men and trees blurred together.

'It was just a candied drop,' Ryan mumbled.

'Easy, now.' Knox sat him down on the table. His head was still hot, and slick with blood. Viv pushed Knox aside but she didn't touch Ryan, just got a good look.

'Water, then whiskey,' she said.

Then they were both gone: he could feel Knox's heavy steps on the stairs but he couldn't turn his head to see. He stared, numb, at the wall.

Something soft touched his face. It was a welcome kind of cold. He opened his eyes with a start to find he'd drifted off still sitting on the table. Viv was wiping his cheek, concentrating, her gaze not quite meeting his. The cloth was red between her fingers, and it stayed red when she squeezed it in the bucket.

'Stitches?' Knox said, his voice now rumbling from somewhere behind Ryan. The urge to turn and look at the man was there, but he couldn't. And it was a struggle to keep his eyes open.

'Too shallow. Too close to the bone,' Viv said.

'Will be some scar.'

'The ear?' Viv said.

'Nothing I could find.'

They were talking like he wasn't there, and without the energy to prove them wrong, it didn't much matter. Viv came closer. Her hair was loose and his breath played on the black strands like a breeze in the trees. There were shadows there too: men ducking in and out of sight, looking for what couldn't be found. He closed his eyes and counted to five, but when he opened them again the men were still there, shadows chasing shadows. He wanted to brush them away, but his hands were as good as tied to his lap. He tried to tell her and his lips flapped uselessly.

'I won't be able to do much with this,' Viv said. She wet the side of his head and the cool water made him moan. 'At least it's mostly still there.'

'He was lucky.'

'One way to look at it,' Viv said. 'Pass me the bottle.'

The bottle's heavy bottom grumbled across the table. The smell was sharp enough to cut away the days at Pa's house, leaving only the nights he'd slept near the crate of Ma's empties. That smell would build slowly as more bottles were abandoned by the door, until he felt drunk from breathing. It was difficult to wake up on those days. When the man took them away he would know another month had passed, and to keep out of the way, at least until he saw the man leave her room.

And then the smell would start to grow again.

'This will hurt,' Viv said, locking eyes with him to make sure he understood.

He gave a small nod.

She touched his ear and he felt like he was falling. He hit the table as everything went black.

He was lying on something soft: a pillow. He worked some life back into his mouth. This pillow was big; he traced a finger along its taut surface all the way to the edge and he could only just reach. Where his finger made a shallow valley the pillow quickly sprang back.

'You're awake, then,' Viv said from behind him somewhere.

He started to roll over and warning shots of pain stopped him; just having his ear close to the pillow was sending sparks across his eyes. With some effort he sat up. Viv was perched on the end of the bed. *A bed*: a wooden frame, four waist-high posts, one at each corner, and a mattress – no wonder it felt like lying on a cloud. All those years his ma had been sleeping like an angel.

'Your pa wanted you to sleep as long as possible,' Viv said. 'It's almost dawn. They're waiting for you.'

Ryan swung his legs free of the sheets. He stood, but his legs wouldn't take him.

'I told him you should stay.'

'I should go.'

'He said you aren't right for houses. No good comes of it.'

'No good.' Ryan touched his cheek, wincing at the feel of scabbed skin. When he pulled away his fingers they were dry.

'He said you aren't mine.' She was looking out of the window. The sky was still dark, but edged with paler shades. He felt like if he just tried, he could touch the dawn.

When he finally stood, the throbbing in his ear started, and it bore right through him, right through to the back of his mouth and down through his jaw. He squeezed that side of his face, hoping he could just pop it somehow and be rid of that over-full feeling. There was some relief in the different kind of burning from his fingernails scratching his jaw, but the throbbing was relentless.

'He said if it still hurts, drink.' She held out a bottle.

'This will make it go away?' he said, trying to twist his words into the least painful shapes.

'All kinds.'

He took the bottle, ignoring the smell and its memories, and filled his mouth. The drink was a burn, like his fingernails, but different; it felt clean as it scraped down his throat, leaving everything behind raw and new. He started coughing and the bottle slipped from his hand. Viv caught it, though some splashed onto the floor. It should have set the wood alight.

'It gets easier,' she said.

He took another slug, and another, and each time it

scoured away a little more of his insides so there was less to protest. When a quarter of the bottle was gone he couldn't feel his ear. Or his cheek. Or his hands. His knees wobbled as if he'd run miles from the bed to the window.

Viv steadied him. 'Slowly,' she said.

He gawped at her: *slowly* was all there was. One foot forward. He licked his dry lips. Next foot forward. It would take all day to reach the door. He could feel the drink sloshing from side to side, rolling around in his stomach. He burped hellfire.

'You go on now,' he said, taking deep breaths between each word. He motioned to the door with the bottle, still so far away.

He glared at her hand on his arm and shrugged free, teetering on a single foot – the most graceful movement he'd ever begun. He saw himself overbalance, inches at a time, until Viv caught him again. He patted her hand.

At the door to the other room he firmly planted his feet. 'No,' he said.

The room was empty. The pallets were roughly made. Viv would have done a better job.

'They're waiting,' Viv said as he pushed his way into the room, swinging his shoulders like he was wading across a river. With extreme care he placed the bottle on the floor. He slumped onto the nearest pallet and lifted the corner. He grunted at the bare floorboards. He tried another pallet. Both corners. He stroked the sheets smooth.

'Gone,' he said. Viv was standing in the doorway.

'Maybe someone packed them?'

'Lee?'

'Lee,' she said.

He smiled. On the stairs she went first, backwards. He didn't like that – she wasn't looking where she was going and she would fall and do whatever it was that made Walkin' stop. He tried to tell her this, all at once. She held his hands, though he kept the bottle.

Downstairs was too busy to look at: people moving too quickly, running indoors like fat-legged babies. He stared right at Viv, letting the shapes beyond rush around as she led him out onto the porch. The cold air hit him all over, like he'd walked into a wall, and his skin tingled. He swallowed another mouthful of drink. That was a better feeling.

The coursers weren't at the hitching posts, but they *were* lined up, as if that was the only way they came: in a set. Standing close together as they were, he could push one down and watch the rest tumble after. Except that the first was Knox's mountain of an animal. He shrank back from its huge nostrils, blacker than any rifle barrel. If a courser ever had fangs it was that one. He waved the bottle at it, warding off its malevolence.

His Michael was sensibly at the far end of the line. He was saddled and his coat glistened like it had been polished. Ryan stroked his muzzle delicately. He'd let other people look after Michael, and that thought brought him close to tears. He whispered apologies to the courser and hoped he was forgiven.

Beside the other coursers men were readying saddlebags, re-fastening straps and inspecting hooves.

'Where's my . . . ?'

It wasn't a specific thing he wanted; he was casting around for *all* of his belongings. They weren't by the pallet, and they weren't here either. His pistol. His Good Book. His blightbird claw. These memories he had taken from each place he was made to go.

'Where's—?'

'Here,' Lee said. He had Ryan's bag, which bulged in uneven, angular lines. Ryan took it gratefully. He loosened the strings and looked inside, but the jumble of items made him giddy. He closed the bag and swallowed hard.

'It's all there,' Lee said. 'You know how to—?'

Ryan held up a hand to cut him off. 'Don't,' he said.

'You take it easy today.' Lee patted Michael; he was talking to the courser as much as to Ryan.

Viv helped Ryan up into the saddle. He did his best not to spill any whiskey whilst making the sign of the cross. His best wasn't good enough. He almost slipped right over the other side, but Viv held on to his ankle.

'Stay there,' she said, waiting until his feet were firmly in the stirrups. He hugged Michael's big neck, trying to stroke the courser's hairy ears, but he was flicking them too quickly. He stamped the ground, and Ryan stopped.

Viv returned with several lengths of rope and started to tie his feet to the stirrups.

'Hey!'

'Hold still,' she said.

'I will not!'

'Then fall and break your neck.'

He stopped wriggling and she looped a rope around his waist and under the cantle. 'Give me your hand,' she said.

'I can do it,' he said, holding the reins aloft.

She pinched his leg and he dropped them. 'Your hand.' She tied the reins to his wrist.

'That was mean.'

'Pour some of that whiskey on your ear at night. And try not to get shot.'

'You too,' he said, though that didn't sound right.

His pa and Knox came to his end of the line. His pa wouldn't look at him, only at Viv.

'You tied him in?' Pa said.

'You want him to ride or not?' Viv said. 'It was your idea to fill him with whiskey.'

'I could leave him here.'

'Fine with me.'

'Everyone up,' Pa shouted.

The men mounted and waited for Pa and Knox, who led them towards the bluffs and the rough land below. The sun was high enough to paint the land yellow. Ryan was at the back and Michael easily caught onto the idea of just following the others. Chunk also understood the situation, and she'd even brought her own possessions, managing both the half-gnawed hog bone and a thin stick in her mouth. She kept pace with Michael, who was long used to her now.

He looked back and waved to Viv with his free hand. She was standing on the porch, her arms crossed. Her hair was tied back.

'You all right?' Lee said. He was riding next to Ryan, and the man who'd thrown sticks for Chunk was beyond him.

'I haven't left anyone behind before.'

4 : 3

The path down from the house was steeper than he recalled and he couldn't help but lean forward, so the rope around his waist didn't take long to start chafing. When Michael turned the sharp corners he gripped the rope and avoided looking at the ground below. They had to ride single file, and Lee insisted on being the last man – last except for Chunk. Ryan had corked the bottle of whiskey and settled it squarely on the saddle, then used the end of the rope to secure it upright, which felt like a particular kind of clever.

They made it down to the valley floor without incident. Chunk still had her stick and bone. He raised the bottle to the rising sun, checking how much was left, and then returned it to its place. The pace was sedate enough, but Michael's rolling gait jarred and between that and the whiskey tumbling in his belly, he got to thinking about rivers and ferries and Bryn.

'I've still got your book,' Ryan mumbled. He grinned at the memories of old lessons: reading by candlelight, riding until his thighs would take no more. 'Never, the sea.' His grin turned sour and he choked back the sobs.

'She'll be fine,' Lee said.

Ryan glanced back to the bluffs, now small with distance. 'I wasn't—'

'It's all right. Viv can take care of herself – always has, and will do long after we're gone.'

'We might start the Walk too,' Ryan said.

'Not me. Pa didn't come back and neither did Ma, though we waited. She'd insisted she had it in her – was counting on it: she had plenty of debts left.'

'And what about *her*?' Ryan said, pointing at his ear.

Lee spat, making good to clear his courser by some way. 'I doubt she has issue with Viv.'

'And me?'

'Couldn't say, though she wasn't aiming at you.'

'Then she doesn't have much of an aim.'

'That's not been my experience. But these things happen.'

'You know all about her?'

'We're all well acquainted with the Drowned Woman,' Lee said, though he'd say no more on the subject and when Ryan pressed, he kicked his courser on and returned to the rear. Michael appeared in no mood to go chasing after anyone, so Ryan settled in and tried to find the animal's rhythm for the sake of his own backside. But the harder he tried the worse it became.

The track they were on wasn't the Wilson Trail. Ryan and Knox had travelled on *this* track on their way to the house, and there was something reassuring about that: he wasn't tackling new ground. He waved a hand back and forward in recognition of this old friend, and then hiccoughed. The nearest men turned at this sound but offered no comment. He glared at each in turn. The hiccoughs persisted, and another swig from the bottle was no help.

He worked out that the way to tell the track from the not-track, all through its twists and turns and the wind that at times found strength enough to shift the dirt, was the lack of thorn bushes. He closed an eye to squint better; the ground rose slightly, and the way was pale, and lacking the blotches that covered the low hills. Beside them, mirroring the track, was a different kind of mark on the landscape. Much smaller than the thorn bushes, these dots were also more frequent. They were bits of blacktop: he knew that much – he hadn't realised there was so much of the stuff. It surfaced in fields as individual lumps, rarely bigger than his fist but still causing him to stumble – here it gathered in puddles as if trying to draw itself back to some former glory. It would have to deal with the thorn bushes first.

'Wouldn't want to walk through that, would we?' he told Michael, trying again for the courser's ears, but the rope dug into his gut when he leaned forward and he couldn't reach. He started heaving, and with no time to swallow it back he leaned to one side – not quick enough. The vomit caught the toe of his boot and left a streak along Michael's flank. The remainder hit the dirt with a meaty slap. He wiped his lips to stop them stinging. The taste was like the angry younger brother of whiskey, twisted by coming later and resentful of being the elder's shadow. He thumbed his teeth to be rid of it, not trusting another drink to be the answer.

His mouth might have tasted horrid but he felt better with an empty stomach. The sun was barely halfway across the sky and he was already starting to feel the pull of sleep. He should stay awake, he knew that, but there was no fighting it. He dozed off, only to be jolted awake as he leaned back too far, then dozed again, snatching minutes of sleep as the day wore on. The riders didn't stop, as far as he was aware. The pace stayed the same; the landscape stayed the same, but every time he woke, he would find the sun closer and closer to the horizon. Michael was stolid, dependable, never more than a few yards from the others.

When they finally stopped it was as dark as the clear sky was going to get. The moon was big enough to see their tired faces. They set themselves up a little way from the track, away from any blacktop. There was no effort to hide their little camp, not that there was anywhere to hide, unless you measured eighteen inches and had a liking for thorns.

'You need a hand?' Lee said. Everyone else had dismounted and was busying themselves with water and food and fire. Ryan's throat was too hoarse to reply. Lee passed him a waterskin, full of warm water with the aroma of old sweat – and it was glorious. He drank until his stomach would take no more, and then he just held a mouthful, enjoying the feel of it. Lee worked on the ropes, cussing more than once at Viv's knots, though they had kept Ryan safe.

Lee helped Ryan down from the saddle, but his knees buckled and he fell flat on his backside. Chunk dropped her bone and stick at his feet.

'Can she?' Ryan said, and Lee cupped his hands for Ryan to pour the water. Chunk lapped at it so fast barely a drop made it to the ground. He refilled Lee's hands twice more before she was satisfied.

Coursers were being similarly looked after, though they drank their water from bowls of some dull metal. One was good enough to tolerate Michael.

Finally the men gathered around a fire. Dry scrub was scrounged to add to the flames and someone had had the foresight to bring a few hefty logs. Ryan didn't envy the courser that'd carried them the whole day. He sat down in the loose circle with Chunk on one side and a man busy working some sticks with a knife on the other. Chunk rested her head on his leg, similarly intrigued by this man, no doubt wondering if any of those sticks were for throwing. His hands were nimble, despite his squint and lack of front teeth. Ryan asked his name.

'These boys call me Porter, though that's not the name my ma gave me.'

'What name was that?'

'She wasn't around long enough to say.' Porter held the stick close to get a better look at the point he was making. Satisfied, he took a wider piece and started to bore a hole through it.

Ryan watched him work. The noise of the knife scraping at dried wood was surprisingly restful when accompanied by the crackle of the fire, but his ear started to ache. Just a little at first, making him blink when he hadn't meant to, and he tried to ignore it, to concentrate on the knife and its quick movement. It was no use: the ache spread from his ear until half his face was pounding. He pulled the cork from the whiskey and gingerly lifted the bottle over his head. His hand was shaking as he started to tip it.

'Whoa, whoa, what are you doing?' Porter said. He leaned forward, scattering his carefully cut sticks, and took hold of the bottle.

'Viv said to pour whiskey on it at night.'

'Crazy Walkin'.' Porter shook his head. 'Wait here.' He ambled off in a way that suggested he still had a courser between his legs and returned with two tiny glasses. He placed both on the ground. 'I say it ain't right straight from the bottle, so I carry these. You pour,' he said.

Ryan obliged.

'One for you, one for your ear, I reckon.'

Ryan raised the glass to his lips. The smell made his stomach cramp, but he'd take that over the throbbing shaking him. The glass held a good amount to swallow, like it was made with just that in mind.

Porter picked up the second glass and Ryan closed his eyes and locked his jaw, hoping the warmth trailing its way down his throat would be enough to cover the oncoming pain. He waited, but the pain didn't come. He opened one eye a fraction to see two empty glasses by his leg.

'That didn't hurt,' Ryan said.

'I should hope not.'

He raised a hand to his ear, and the shock of his touch almost toppled him. He swore blindly, loudly, and with no sense to the string of words. Porter was calm as a summer cloud. He tapped the glasses with his finger.

'My aim isn't as good as it used to be,' he said.

Ryan eyed him. 'We need a third glass.'

Porter agreed and fetched another. Ryan poured and tossed back the drink with force, to avoid the whiskey hitting his teeth and most of his tongue so the fire only kindled in his throat. Porter's aim must've improved because Ryan jerked to look at the man, feeling like he'd been slapped on his wound. Porter held up the empty glass in salute and Ryan closed his eyes as they started to water. The steady pounding hooves in his head stopped. Whiskey dripped onto his shoulder, though he couldn't feel it on his face.

'How is it?' Ryan said.

The old man leaned closer. 'You'll never be pretty again.'

'Is it bleeding?'

Porter shook his head.

'Is there pus?'

Porter raised his eyebrows, to aid a closer inspection.

'No pus.'

'Any hungry-brides?'

'Hungry-brides? Now where did you get an idea like that?'

'They feast on men – I've seen it,' Ryan said.

'When have you "seen it"?'

'Never you mind. I'll take your bell-igerence as a no.'

'You do that,' Porter said. He stacked the three empty glasses and went back to his whittling, entrancing Ryan once more with his measured, smooth movements, the sound of the knife taking its slivers.

Ryan belched hotly through his nose and hoped he wasn't getting the hiccoughs again.

More men joined them at the fire. Beyond were the coursers; with Michael somewhere amongst the shadows of long legs and swishing tails. Only Knox's courser stood out, an enormous silhouette; it snagged the eye in the manner that a gap of colour does, like a cave in a cliff, or a huntsman on a rock.

After a while Porter stood, holding his collection of worked sticks, and busied himself constructing something, his tongue poking out between pursed lips. He sighted down one stick like it was a rifle before finally placing it over the fire.

A spit. All that effort just for a cooking spit? Though he'd even fashioned a handle for the turning of whatever unfortunate was to be eaten. There was no applause; most of the men stared at the flames as if relieved Porter's brief interruption was over, but Porter accepted their silence as a suitable fanfare.

Another man, who had closely cropped hair and moved much like Porter, came to the fire holding the moon: an almost perfect slip of white that swung from his hand. Ryan blinked and licked his lips before slowly craning his neck skywards. He slapped his leg in relief to find the moon still in its lofty position and not on its way to the fire.

Pa stood and addressed the men. 'We eat blightbird tonight, thanks to Ryan.'

The men turned to him, their faces flat and not a single one grateful.

The bird was put on the spit in a way that made Ryan's stony seat uncomfortable. Its wings and legs were tied so they didn't droop into the flames. There wouldn't be enough meat for one, let alone all of them. The fire was scornfully quiet as the blightbird was turned and gradually browned. What little meat was passed to him was tough and flavourless.

He fingered the inside of his mouth, checking his cheeks and tongue and behind his teeth, all the while wondering if the whiskey had scorched away his ability to taste. Unsure, he opened his bag and found the candied drop. He shifted his back to the fire, careful Porter and the others weren't looking, and cradled the colourful drop in his lap. He picked off the dust and the fluff, then took a lick and waited. He smacked his lips, as if to wake or renew the once-active sense. He huffed, which only produced another whiskey-laced belch, and winced at the taste of *that*. There was only one more course of action: he hastily put the drop in his mouth and sucked.

The explosion of flavour was as vivid as the candied drop's colour. Whatever it was made of was now rushing from his head down to his toes, and remembering his hands on the way. He pulled up his sleeve and his veins were indeed the same kind of blue. But the drop was still heavy on his tongue. He spat it out and dabbed it with the hem of his shirt to dry it.

'What you got there?' Porter said, stretching up on his haunches like a ruft.

'Nothing.'

'Men don't cradle "nothing".'

'So you say.' Ryan held up his empty hands.

'I saw—'

'Porter, you're with me,' Lee said, nudging the older man with his boot.

'Naw, I took watch that last night on the trail.'

'Callum called for you specifically.'

'Of course he did; better eyes than a hungry blightbird.'

As far as Ryan could tell, Porter barely *had* eyes.

As the two men shuffled off into the shadows he settled down with his bag as a pillow. He decided to keep the drop in his pocket as a ready remedy for the taste of whiskey and the emptiness of blightbird meat.

As he was dozing off, Pa came to sit by him. 'Son.' He put a hand to Ryan's forehead.

Ryan struggled to keep his eyes open.

'Your ear is healing well.'

'No hungry-brides,' Ryan said.

'I heard she could shoot straight.' Pa patted his shoulder: good courser.

Ryan tried to say something, but he was too tired. Pa stood

and between almost closed eyes Ryan saw him walk back towards the fire. He was wearing someone else's boots: Pa had black boots, shined like Knox's, but these were brown. And he had a different hat – the shape was all wrong. Ryan fell asleep wondering if it really was Pa who'd talked about a woman's shooting and had hot hands.

4 : 4

Ryan's dreams smelled of whiskey and had a watery glaze that no amount of eye-rubbing would clear. He was walking through the camp, making an effort not to step on any of the prone shapes. He took them for the men, but he couldn't see their faces or hands or anything that looked like skin. The fire was very far away, on the horizon, the embers tickling the clouds. He laughed and reached out. His laughter brought fire from his belly and an explosion that shook the ground and whipped up dust. Then there were voices.

He kept wandering through the now moving blank figures who rushed to and fro, never touching him. With each step his grin grew wider until he could swallow the sky. The men – that was what he understood them to be – were shouting to each other. There were more bangs, smaller this time, like his ears popping, and he giggled. He made pistols with his hands and shot left and right in time with the noise. He didn't aim, and didn't need to. He preferred pistols: each round flew true. He rode the rounds like runaway coursers, his hat flailing and one hand on the pommel.

When the shot struck home there was a bloody dawn and he whooped, ready to fire another and another from his fingers. Someone stepped in front of him, large enough to block the stars, and when Ryan turned they were still there. He spun and fired, and fired and spun, and still there was no way out. He fell onto his backside and shrugged.

And then he was warm, and lying on something soft. It felt like Pa's bed. Someone was stroking his hair away from his face. Their fingertips made him shiver.

'No, Viv,' he mumbled, but she didn't stop. She opened his shirt and patted down his ribs and he shook his head, too tired to open his eyes. She made soft noises as she did his buttons up slowly, and it stung where she'd touched him. He rolled away from her and right onto the bottle, wedging it against his gut. That would be better: no need to taste it. He needed another bottle to press against his ear.

'No, Viv. I've done it already—'

Again she shushed him, but it was everyone else making the noise: their loud steps on the floorboards and the flat slaps of their rifles and the whines of the coursers. Why should he be quiet? He finally opened his eyes to tell her so; she was gone and there were only the sounds of men, the darkness and a sour taste in his mouth.

There was something on his bag, just inches from his nose. It was bright red and pulsed in the sunlight. Ryan didn't move: some huntsmen had red behinds and they were the dangerous ones – dangerous and angry. Without moving his head, he readied his hands underneath him. He counted to three silently and then pushed and he shot into the air, easily a foot, more like two, and he was up, one boot raised to plunge. A red candied drop stared back at him.

As far as he could tell, no one had noticed his foolishness. The fire was out and everyone was up and doing things, mainly with the coursers. His pa, Knox and a few others stood a little way off, to a man their hats in their hands. Pa was talking in a low voice.

Ryan pocketed the candied drop. He made sure he now had two, that the original hadn't somehow changed colour after he'd put it in his mouth. They both felt the same in shape and size. Two candied drops. Perhaps this next one would turn his veins to red. He gathered his bag, dusting it down just in case his sense of a huntsman wasn't entirely false.

Pa and the others were gathered around a man who was still lying on the ground. Maybe he'd had too much whiskey and wouldn't wake? Ryan rubbed at his eyes, knowing only too well what kind of deep and wicked sleep the drink could bring. But there was something in the air, beyond the sweat of unwashed shirts, courser droppings and wet ashes. He saw the blood before he saw where it came from: a small pool where no one was standing, near the sleeping man's head.

Ryan squeezed his way between two men, their pistol butts snagging on his shirt.

'You don't want to see this, boy,' one of them said.

'Let him be,' Pa said. 'She's already done her damage.'

With his pa's permission, Ryan got a good look at the

man. And then he looked back at his pa, just to be sure: the man lying there was wearing Pa's boots and shirt and hat. The fat handle of a knife stuck out from the top of Pa's black felt hat. A loud drip hit the dirt, like the man was a well that had been poorly tapped.

'You made him wear your clothes on purpose,' Ryan said.

'He was a good boy, did as he was told.'

'She killed him thinking it was you.'

'We need to bury him,' Pa said. He looked skywards; the blightbirds were already gathering.

'You're a coward!' Ryan said.

Pa grabbed him by the scruff of the neck. 'You think I don't know that?' Pa was so close that Ryan felt the words on his cheeks – he felt them against the scar she gave him. 'You think Jack there didn't know it?'

'Was he drunk or just sleeping when you laced the boots up?' Ryan said.

'Loyal. He was just loyal.'

'What if he comes back?' a man said quietly.

Ryan wriggled free of his pa's grip and straightened his shirt. 'He won't come back.'

'Boy's right,' Knox said. 'She made sure of that.'

Ryan watched them dig. They wouldn't let him help. It wasn't easy work; the ground was unforgiving, but the grave was chest-deep. The body was carried by six men. He recognised the man, of course, though he hadn't known his name. He was buried in Pa's boots and hat, with the knife still lodged solidly in his skull, deep enough to keep him from the Walk – perhaps one of those small mercies. The soil was shovelled back in without a word. Ryan leafed through the Good Book, hoping to find something worth saying, but he was too slow at his reading and when they were finished he had nothing.

'Best put that away,' Pa said, putting a hand on Ryan's shoulder. 'There was little in there for Jack when he was alive. Even less now.'

'I wish I knew it better.'

'Where did you get it?'

'A friend,' Ryan said.

'Let me see.'

Ryan was slow to hand him the book, remembering Knox's warning about Pa and the Good Book, but Pa was calm enough.

He looked over the cover, running his fingers over the battered lettering. 'Which friend gave this to you?'

'Just a friend.'

'Ryan.'

'He knew Ma, and let me stay with him for a while.'

Pa flicked through the pages. 'You're missing some,' he said. 'Pages have been cut from the spine. Exodus isn't the first book.'

'How do you know that?' Ryan said, peering at the gap.

'My ma made me read the Good Book, said it was something my pa would have wanted.'

'The whole thing?'

'The whole thing,' Pa said.

'Then you say something.' Ryan gestured to the now covered grave.

Pa stared at his feet for a moment.

Then he said, '"Follow me; and let the dead bury their dead."'

4 : 5

'You need some help?' Lee said.

Ryan had been trying to get on his courser for a good few minutes. Fortunately, Michael was a patient animal: he made his cross in the dirt and let Ryan struggle on. Chunk was getting impatient and making a nuisance of herself, darting between their legs like setting out was some great game. Ryan called to her, but it was Knox's hand that settled her down. He scratched behind her ear, and the thump of her tail made more than one man look up from his fastenings.

Lee gave him a leg-up. 'Want me to tie the ropes?'

'No ropes today. No whiskey today,' Ryan said.

'It's stopped hurting?'

'As good as.'

'That's something,' Lee said. He mounted, and they trotted some way to catch up with the rest of them.

Ryan gripped the reins. Michael's bouncing rhythm was raising something in his stomach that he had to fight to keep quiet. He sucked air in hard through his nose and out again, not daring to open his mouth; he didn't want to vomit again. Behind them they left three stains on the ground: blood, ashes and the grave.

The ride was as near silent as twelve men, one boy and fourteen coursers could be, so that the sound of someone spitting came as a shock. Ryan drifted on thoughts of soft beds and shade. At the time, he'd not appreciated the lazy afternoons in the orchard; they were little more than a day gone and already he missed them, more than he missed the chooks and the smell of their eggs in the pan, more than the reading lessons by candlelight. Perhaps that was what happened when you left a house full rather than empty: it pulled at you – there was something worth going back to. It wasn't an entirely good feeling.

The sun was long past its highest when his stomach started to twist and turn. Taking out the candied drops, he weighed them in the palm of his hand. Should he eat them in the order they were given, or go at them in turns, keeping both the same size until they were no more than coloured stars? He was wary of the red drop: her favourite colour. There was no doubt it was a present, just like the blue she'd given him in person, but he couldn't shake the impression it was like a huntsman's warning: do not eat me. He put the blue drop carefully on his tongue, worried his teeth might chip its perfect shape. The rush was no less powerful because he knew it was coming. He counted a slow twenty and then took out the drop, wiped it and put it back in his pocket. It felt half the size of the red one. He'd have to ration them.

The track began to wind through gorges and narrow valleys. Ryan was glad for a change from the wide and empty horizon; the others kept looking one way and then the other and up at the cliff walls, their eyes straining against the sun and the shadows. Hoofbeats were the only sound in the tight space, rumbling off the stones. Each man kept his spittle to himself as he shielded his eyes with a hand. Ryan wondered what they were looking for, and got so far as to open his mouth to break the silence, but then he remembered her wrinkled face gazing down at him and the way her face wobbled when she shook her head. It wouldn't be her face they'd see this time but the two black eyes of her pistols or the mouth of a rifle. She must have had *some* score to settle with his pa to go to all this trouble. He pulled his hat down further over his good ear.

Most of the gorges were striped black and pale yellow: the blacktop ran along one side, and it wasn't just a scattering of rocky pieces now. They kept to the cleared ground and left the blacktop to its ghosts of older times. There was never a situation where the way was so narrow that there was only blacktop, but there was no doubt they would all rather ride round than on it.

Just as they were entering one such striped part of the track there was the sound of rocks falling – Ryan heard them before seeing the puffs of dust bouncing down the high walls and to a man they had their pistols drawn and were staring up at the ragged top of the bluffs. The rocks ricocheted like a full-blown shoot-out. The fall took its time settling. No one moved. The quiet that followed was complete, even the coursers seeming to understand its importance. Eventually there was a hushed but animated discussion about proceeding. Plenty of men argued against, but Pa's decision to go through was final.

'On your head be it,' a man said.

Pa took off his hat and was the first into the gorge.

When they emerged without incident or sighting he glared at those who had doubted him – but he kept his hat tied to his saddle. They had the sense to look contrite, though many glanced back nonetheless.

It was late afternoon when the building came into view. They crested the top of a rise Ryan hadn't even noticed they'd been climbing and there it was below. It was old, blacktop-old, and just as abandoned, that much was obvious, even from a distance. It had the hollowness of a blightbird skull; there was a depth to the blackness of the two big windows on the top floor, like empty eye sockets. The blightbirds circling high above did little to help its appeal.

There was some caution in their approach. Pa sent two men ahead and waited a good mile or so distant. Ryan had a fine view of them dismounting and heading inside. He watched the coursers: if there was trouble, it would show there first, but they were idly nuzzling the ground. Those near him sat rigid in their saddles, and many rested a hand on a pistol, much good it would do. Porter had his tongue out again. Ryan couldn't see Lee – he must have been one of the riders. He had the feeling that this wasn't the first time his pa had used the old building, and that it wasn't always empty. When the men came into view again, unhurried, Pa waved them forward.

The closer they were, the less the building looked like a skull, which was something. It was all straight lines, empty windows and a flat roof: a squat, ugly place. They had to cross the blacktop, and he let Michael pick the way. The courser did so with no complaint, but it made Ryan's hair stand up on his arms: like it was a barrier to forgotten days that shouldn't be crossed. The men began to wither and age around him: their skin dried, bunching around their cheeks and nose like the blightbird's claw. They were old Walkin', maybe the first there ever was, in this crumbling place. Ryan shook his head and screwed his eyes tight. When he looked again the vision had gone. He picked up the bottle of whiskey still lodged against his saddle. He checked it to make sure the cork was there, that he hadn't taken a drink without remembering.

'We shouldn't be here,' Ryan said.

Porter turned in his saddle. 'These old ruins used to give me the jitters too.'

'What stopped it?'

'I got just as old,' he said, smiling.

They tethered the coursers behind the building, as best out of sight from the track as they could, but the land had flattened again and Ryan felt more exposed than he had in the gorges, or even in their camp the night before. It was like the building drew attention to them. He looked to the horizon in every direction until he started to feel dizzy.

'Ease up,' Porter said. 'Let your pa do the worrying.'

Out front, the men gathered in small knots of twos and threes. They were looking down at something. Nobody had gone inside yet, and Ryan wasn't going to be the first. He clutched his bag in one hand and the bottle in the other, wishing he had a third hand for his pistol. His hands as pistols: the image felt familiar, but he couldn't say from when. This was a strange place, it made him think strange things. He joined the group with Lee in it. Knox and Pa were talking, a little way off from the rest. Pa didn't look happy.

Lee moved aside. 'Got your water-skin?'

Ryan held up the bottle. The men chuckled.

'Don't go watering that down,' Lee said. 'Take mine.'

They were standing around a hole in the ground. One man was lowering a length of rope down into the darkness. A foot, maybe two, was visible and then it was gone. He kept paying it out until there was little rope left. He swung the bit of rope he held around, which was met with tuts and calls for him to hurry up. Scowling, he pulled up the rope and the top of a water-skin appeared out of the hole. The man knelt down and carefully drew it out. The sides of the water-skin were drenched.

He drank. 'Sweet as honey,' he said.

'That'll be the longtail piss,' a man said, but it didn't stop him lowering his own skin next. The whole process took some time, and the rope was surprisingly long.

'It's a deep well,' Ryan said.

'Not well – it's a cistern. It saves the rain,' Lee said.

'It rains here?'

'Once or twice. And yes, it is deep; whoever built these had a mighty thirst.'

When it was Ryan's turn, Lee waited with him whilst the others wandered off. He tied the rope to the water-skin with more knots than was needed, but then, it wasn't his. He felt it touch the water: the weight on the rope changing slightly. He dragged it around like he'd seen the others do and felt it grow heavier. When he pulled it up to drink from, he understood what the man had meant – it did taste different to Viv's well. He wouldn't have used the word "sweet". He gagged, spilling the first mouthful out onto the ground.

'Best we can do out here,' Lee said as he stoppered the water-skin.

Ryan resolved to drink only when he was close to the end, and out of whiskey.

They were the last still at the cisterns. Everyone else was inside. Men leaned out of the upper windows – if they could be called that without glass or shutters. Seeing people there didn't make him feel better about the building: they were out of place. Their voices jarred in the empty spaces, though they must have been rooms once. The bottom floor was a single cavernous room with nothing but dusty corners and huntsman webs along the ceiling, and even these were obviously not in use: their single strands were limp, moved by the coming and going of men. For all the talk of longtails there were no droppings and the walls were free of burrows. If this wasn't a place for men, it wasn't a place for animals either.

In the corner there was a set of stone stairs, each step wedged into the wall, though some were at odd angles like they had been jammed in there by an enormous child. He trod carefully on these, but they felt as secure as the rest. He had the sensation of floating, with nothing between him and the vacant room, his feet level with a man's head.

Upstairs, men were sitting against the walls. Some were playing cards while others were already sleeping. It was just as bare as the room below. One man leaned out each of the windows: they took turns and there was always someone at the window and someone at the bottom of the stairs. And that someone had to be awake.

As the sun began to set, the shadows in the room grew large. Porter, having been relieved of his duty on the stairs, sat beside Ryan and produced a single glass. Ryan shook his head.

'She might be crazy but that Walkin' was right – it needs bathing,' Porter said.

'It doesn't hurt so much.'

'Doesn't matter.' He pointed at the glass and Ryan poured. It smelled worse than ever.

Porter dabbed the whiskey on and Ryan sucked air through his teeth, but he didn't cry out – the room was too quiet for that. Porter steadied him until satisfied the job was done.

'You're not picking at that scab on your cheek?' he said.

'No.'

'Better man than me.' He put the glass down. 'You get some rest. I'll bring you something to eat when it's ready.'

Ryan made a pillow of his bag again, shifting until he was fairly sure he was lying on the Good Book. Missing its first pages. Beginning with Exodus. Ryan couldn't remember his first years, so maybe the first weren't so important.

He ran a finger along the stone floor in front of his face. There was dust and something else: little flecks of stone, like crumbs from a biscuit. But it was definitely stone. How could something like that last? It should have been ground down by the years and by the boots of passing men – but here it was. He blew on his finger, hoping what he'd scraped off would settle somewhere. The flick of cards and the mumbles of winners and losers lulled him to sleep.

4 : 6

There were no whiskey-dreams, no candied drop and no food from Porter. He was shaken awake by Lee. Everyone else was outside. The only sign they'd been there at all were boot-prints in the dust, but even these had an ancient look to them.

Lee helped him mount without mentioning the ropes. Ryan didn't keep the bottle to hand, instead placing it in his bag and putting his trust in the cork. They crossed over the blacktop. Ryan didn't look back at the building. They hadn't been riding long before Porter leaned over and passed him a battered tin can holding a few strips of dried meat and cold beans that had a firm skin. Porter waved away his thanks and he devoured the food. It might not have made his blood change colour or fly faster through his veins, but there was a satisfying heaviness to it. He licked his fingers clean.

There was more chatter between the riders today. Ryan didn't catch most of it as it was being spoken closely between small groups, the occasional 'liar!' or 'blood and ashes!' carried on the breeze, accompanied by laughter. When they entered a canyon there was still a hush to them, though gazes only drifted upwards and pistols stayed in their holsters. How quickly they forgot burying man and knife – perhaps they had to.

Pa wouldn't forget, Ryan was clear on that. He wore another man's hat now.

They left the track a little after midday. It had been steadily rising for some way and instead of following it to the top, Pa led them off to skirt the close horizon. The pace slowed as coursers picked their way between thorn bushes and other scrub. The ground was rarely even, and Ryan found his legs working harder as Michael crossed dips and rises. They went in silence once more, but it had a different air to it: focused rather than shaken.

When by chance he drew close to Porter he whispered, 'Wilson?'

Porter gestured to beyond the crest of the hill.

It took the rest of the day to cover a mile or two of the long ridge, which extended in both directions as far as he could see. The top rose and fell, and at times he could almost see beyond. He fought the urge to stand in the stirrups; he wouldn't be the one to give them away if anybody was watching. There was little on the ridge beyond the scrub, but they did pass what looked like an abandoned wagon, its wheels and canvas gone, leaving just the flat bed and broken frame. Many of the men spat as they rode by, as if warding off a bad omen.

They stopped before dark. Ryan patted Michael's neck –

he'd done well on the tough ground and Ryan didn't doubt he could have gone on, just as steady by moonlight, but was happy not to test that faith. When Ryan got down from the saddle, he moved like he was making his way through cold water. There'd be call for more than one of Porter's glasses this night.

Pa and Knox made their way cautiously to the top of the ridge. It was strange to see the large man move in such a manner: first bent at the waist, and then fully on his belly. The rest of them sat in a close huddle. A man produced a satchel full of fruit from Viv's orchard. There were groans at that, though they ate them all. Despite his best efforts, Ryan covered his chin in the sticky juice and no amount of wiping would get rid of the feeling. He went to clean up from his water-skin, but Lee stopped him.

'Don't know how long we'll be here,' he said.

Ryan scratched his chin. 'May as well have a beard.'

It didn't take long for night to set in, and the cold.

Ryan tried to work some life back into his arms. Leaning for so long on his elbows had turned them white and itchy. The Wilson Trail spread out below him. The area had been cleared of scrub. It was definitely bigger than the track they'd been taking, but there was no blacktop running alongside. Maybe there was no need to go west in those days. There were plenty of people heading that way now, and most of them wearing a uniform. Groups, some big, some small, some so enormous there was no way to count, if numbers even went that high. They left Ryan scratching his head and wondering, if so many were here, on Wilson, then who was at home? Whole towns had to be empty of men. Whole *counties*.

'Where are they all going?' he said.

Pa grunted.

Ryan took that as his pa not knowing, or not caring, and looking down on the blocks of colour made up of so many men it did start to feel like a question that might not have an answer. There were soldiers, there was a war; they'd have to move somewhere at some time. They couldn't just sit around and wait, and neither could Pa's group – not for ever.

He glanced back at what couldn't really be called a camp: coursers tethered close together and men scattered amongst the bushes, playing cards or sleeping through the heat of the day. There was no sleeping at night for all the teeth chattering. Pa said no fire – at first that had sounded like a good idea, but as Ryan watched the columns move along Wilson he couldn't imagine them ever going in anything except one direction, as sure as rifle-shot. The image of men spilling off the track and up the ridge just didn't fit, not with what he'd seen for the last few days.

There was a new group of soldiers every three hours or so. Ryan had his watch in hand, so he knew when to look where Wilson turned a corner near the horizon. He'd wager which colour the soldiers would be – his pa wasn't interested, but sometimes there was another man watching too and they'd bet coins they didn't have. Or he'd wager against himself. He won more often than not. Red, blue, red, blue. He was caught out by two reds in a row, but that had only happened once, maybe twice.

'Why don't they stop and fight?' Ryan said. He only spoke when the trail was empty, or near as, though he didn't think his voice would travel the many miles to a disappearing group of reds, and he was even more sure they wouldn't turn back.

'Maybe the war is over,' Pa said.

'Wouldn't we know?'

Pa shrugged.

'Maybe it's not worth it?' Ryan said. 'But it's worth it for us?'

'They have bigger plans than I do,' Pa said.

The only wagons they'd seen had been with the large groups.

Ryan dozed the rest of the day.

'Up!'

The call came as Ryan watched a stick tumble end-over-end through the air. They'd been waiting so long that when it was time, there was a slowness to it: his pa making his way down the scree, arms out for balance; the stick soaring, just a line in the sky like a blightbird, forgotten by Chunk. Men got to their feet awkwardly, with stiff knees and bent backs. When the stick hit the ground he started running towards Michael. The courser's ears were up.

There was no one to help him into the saddle. The others were already mounted, rifles in hand, and steering their coursers towards the crest of the ridge. It wasn't pretty, but he did the best he could and Michael was once again patient. He urged the courser on. Something knocked against the back of his knee. He flicked the reins and risked a glance. There was a rifle strapped to his saddlebags.

'Aim for the uniforms,' Lee shouted from the top. 'And I know, you don't like these.' He raised his own rifle and whooped, and then was gone.

Ryan kicked Michael, who responded likely out of surprise more than anything. When he made the top it was at a half-gallop and the courser's breathing was almost as loud as its hooves.

The world was vast at that moment.

He made noises like the rest of them – he couldn't help it. Each breath was too much and he needed to be rid of it.

There was a small knot of blue below, almost level on the trail, a wagon and a coach. The men around him were giants charging down bright-lies. He snatched the rifle and shouted for Michael to go faster.

The wagon and coach were shedding blue bodies and picking up speed. Those bodies were aiming rifles at Pa and the front riders. Pops sounded, like green pine burning, over the pounding of hooves. A courser went down, its legs twisted and buckled, too quick for Ryan to see the rider. Those at the front veered towards the coach.

There were more rifle shots – Ryan expected another

courser to lose its grace, but none did – it was the soldiers' turn to fall. He could see faces and hands and rifles being shakily reloaded, and then he was past.

He was hurtling for the back of the coach. There were mounted soldiers there, though not many. The driver of the coach pressed whatever poor beasts were pulling those heavy wooden wheels, but must have realised the folly as they turned to see the men bearing down on them. Ryan put his rifle against his shoulder. He couldn't keep it still enough to be sure of his aim – there were plenty of men *not* wearing uniforms in front of him.

Those closest exchanged powder with the soldiers, with no effect that Ryan could see. But they were gaining on the coach. Pistols were drawn. Ryan still had his rifle shot – just the one, that's all he had to count. He waited until he was certain. *A blightbird in flight.* He fired and a soldier on a courser turned as if he'd been called from inside the wagon and then dropped from the saddle.

Pa and some of the others were level now. Ryan kicked again, but Michael was doing his best. He drew his ma's old pistol. They had the coach covered on both sides. Pa and another man jumped from their coursers, hitting the panelled sides and finding enough purchase to hold on. They opened the coach doors at the same time.

And then they were falling.

Two shots. Two smoking pistols. Two wrinkled hands.

4 : 7

She jumped from the coach on Pa's side. Ryan raised his pistol, but others were quicker, snapping off shots before she hit the ground. Some might have even found the target. She rolled in the dirt like a felled courser, and then Ryan was beyond all three bodies. He pulled up on the reins but Michael took some slowing. Half or so of the men did likewise. The rest took the coach, and then the wagon. Everybody was slowing down. Ryan's heart was still galloping. He turned Michael and saw her standing there.

She had managed to keep hold of her pistols, but she wasn't aiming them at the men. One was half raised at Pa and she was walking towards him, none the worse for her tumble. Ryan and Knox were among the first to reach her.

'Put it down,' Knox said.

'Ha!' She glanced at them over her shoulder and brought her other pistol up.

Ryan pulled the trigger. He had one eye closed against the sun. The pistol felt too small, like trying to topple a tree with a knife, and for once he wished for a rifle. Her long coat swayed a little. She shook her head.

More men joined them, dismounting. Pa's shirt was stained red.

'Look,' she said, kneeling down beside him. She yanked his head upright. 'Look at your son's indifference. Where are his tears, Callum?'

'This why you've been hounding us for all these years?' Knox said.

'This, and only this,' she said.

Pa whispered something.

She leaned in closer. Pa was whispering again, but he looked right at Ryan. She shot him in the temple and let his head fall.

'The boy. Give me the boy,' she said.

The sound of feet shuffling in the dirt filled the air. A way beyond her the soldiers stood on the trail, their confusion obvious.

'What's in the coach?' Knox said.

'Not what, who. And look for yourself. The boy.'

Knox headed to the coach, leaving a score of pistols staring at each other. Ryan edged back from this woman who had given him candied drops and killed his father.

When Knox returned he was shaking his head.

'What are they?' Ryan said.

'Just people.'

'From where?'

'Beyond the mountains, so they tell me,' she said. 'Do what you want, but give me the boy.'

'Why should we?' Knox said.

'Because if you don't, I'll start shooting until I take him. How many of you want to die?'

'He's one of us,' Knox said.

'Is he?'

'You'd never make it.'

'If you trust your aim,' she said.

Ryan was still inching away, but then the men parted as if the Walkin' were Moses, their faces set in flat lines, one or two muttering.

'"You know how to shoot?"' Ryan mumbled.

'Everything else is yours. I just want the boy.'

'If you tell me why,' Knox said.

'Because he's my grandson.'

4 : 8

All eyes were on him – judging, as if he had a choice in the matter. He could call her a liar, but he couldn't do it with conviction. His ma hadn't talked about her parents much. Whenever he'd asked she had crossed her arms and looked anywhere except at him. Ma came back, and here was a Walkin' claiming to be *her* ma. No, there'd be no conviction in calling this Walkin' a liar.

The men were still staring. He spat and hitched up his trousers, as they would have done.

The Walkin' came towards him. He could tell nothing from her wrinkled face, but she took each step with her pistol raised until it came to rest squarely on his forehead. He couldn't move his legs – not to run, or even to fall away from the heavy barrel. At the edge of his vision the men were fidgeting. Few of them were watching.

'You know what you did to my girl: is that why you're not scared?' she said.

'What could be worse than this place?'

'You're too young to think like that!' she shouted. The pistol was shaking in her hand.

'You shot Pa for what he did. And now you'll shoot me.' She cocked the pistol. 'But you don't care.'

'Ma didn't care. She wanted gone for good,' Ryan said.

For a long moment the Walkin' stared at him, and he stared right back. She put down her gun. 'Get your things,' she said.

Ryan checked his bag and then went to mount Michael, but Knox caught the reins. 'Stays with us,' he said.

'But—'

'Fine,' the Walkin' said.

'He's my courser!'

'He won't come where we're going.'

'He's mine.' Ryan stroked the courser's cheek and scratched just above his nose as he liked. But Michael kept an eye on her, and his ears were flat to his skull. It was the same with all the coursers: they'd take chasing coaches on rough ground and rifles and pistols firing over a Walkin' any day.

Chunk was no different and it made him sick to the stomach. She stood by Knox, growling. She had almost got used to Viv, and Viv had brought food. This Walkin' brought nothing. Chunk was shaking a little under the tension. She didn't notice his hand.

'I'll see to her,' Knox said.

Ryan swallowed. 'I know,' he managed. He'd seen them

314

grow close over the days: a kind of respect Chunk didn't have for him. 'You carried her when she was shot.'

'I did.'

'You'll look after her.'

'I will,' Knox said.

Ryan knelt and turned the ruft's muzzle towards him, but she was still looking at the Walkin'. 'You bit me. I didn't shoot you. A lot's happened since then and there's nothing owed between us. But I'll miss you, Chunk.'

Ryan walked away from the men. Tears were forming, but he wouldn't let them see and wouldn't wipe his eyes neither. He walked away, though not towards his grandma. Two men had jumped for the coach.

It wasn't far to Lee's body. He'd rolled from the trail and into the scrub, finishing up lying awkwardly with his arms pinned beneath him. The Walkin' had done a better job on Lee: there wasn't so much blood, just a mark on his chest. He didn't look anything like Bryn – his cheeks were firm lines and his nose straight – but that's what came to Ryan: that he'd seen this before. A body in the scrub, a body in the long grass, a body on the bed. It was good he was leaving Knox and the men behind; this kind of thing followed him wherever he went. He knelt and closed Lee's eyes.

'He needs to be buried,' Ryan said as he walked back to his grandma. 'He said he wasn't coming back.'

'It'll get done,' Knox said.

Ryan reached down and snapped the leather cord free

from his pa's neck. He held it up to his grandma. The eye was swaying.

'You should have this,' he said.

She led him off the trail and into the scrubland.

They walked the whole day. She appeared to know where she was going. He shivered the whole night through and in the morning he said, 'Will you kill me today, Grandma?'

'Not today,' she said.

When the heat got too much and he stumbled one time too many, she stopped. They found shade beneath a short set of bluffs. He set his bag down and took out the bottle. His ear was aching again, not the sharp stinging he was used to, but dull.

'Can you?' he said.

She eyed the bottle. 'Can I what?' Somehow the folds of her face made it look like she was frowning even when she was talking.

'Pour a little on my ear.'

'And why would you want to do that?' she said.

'It hurts.'

She sighed.

'It was *you* who did it.'

She snatched the bottle and uncorked it. 'Still looks angry,' she said. 'They should have cut it off.'

The ache faded and he lay down. When he closed his eyes he saw a deep, pulsing red. Sweat lined his forehead, but it didn't take him long to fall asleep.

He woke up next to a dead under-mutton and a knife. Neither looked real in the moonlight.

'You know what to do with that?' she said.

'As long as you can make a fire.'

She tossed a little flint bundle next to the knife and settled in to watch him work.

It wasn't difficult to find tinder; in fact, everything other than the rocks was willing to burn. He gutted the under-mutton, skinned it and prised out the lead shot.

'Next time hit it in the head,' he said.

She grunted.

He didn't bother with a full spit, though Porter wouldn't be impressed. He just stuck the under-mutton on a sharpened stick and waited for the fire to burn down to embers. He stared at the flames.

'Pa said he burned your husband. He kept that eye around his neck every day.'

'Your pa's dead. And don't go getting any ideas: they say I can't be burned like other Walkin'.'

'That true?' Ryan said.

'"They" say a lot of things.'

'But someone tried? To burn you, I mean.'

'No,' she said.

'No one has before, and no one has since you started the Walk?'

'No.'

'Then it's true in a way,' he said.

Her face pulled into a horrid shape, like canyons sliding into each other. She was smiling.

'The Drowned Woman, that's what they call you, isn't it?'

'Among other names,' she said.

'And what's your real name, Grandma?'

'I haven't used that in a long time.'

'I'd like to.'

'Your fire is ready,' she said.

The embers didn't last long, so he ate the meat bloody. When he was done he kicked dirt over the fire and they started walking again.

'Where are we going?' he said, stifling a yawn.

'Somewhere I should have gone a long time ago.'

'Where's that?'

She kept going. He had to hurry to keep up. His feet were starting to get sore.

'I'm always following someone else,' he said to her back.

'Those people give you shelter? Food?'

'Most.'

'Then stop whining,' she said. She motioned to the open scrub. 'Be my guest.'

'You don't mean that. You were ready to kill those men just to get me, and then you couldn't bring yourself to pull the trigger on me.'

She turned and stuck a finger in his face. 'Don't think that means so much. I had years of tracking your pa to get used to the idea of ending him. I had a long way to travel – I've seen the sea. Might not take so long with you.'

'All right, *Grand*ma.'

'And don't call me that.'

'Then what should I call you?' he said.

'Nothing. Call me nothing.'

They carried on until dawn and they found shade again. She managed the whiskey, noting there wasn't much left. Ryan inspected the bottle himself and found her right. He vowed to curse Porter with every step that his ear pained him. He slept through the day. There was no under-mutton that night and when his stomach grumbled he sucked on a candied drop. He didn't need to hoard them any more – she had fistfuls. She wouldn't say where she got them, or why, and when he asked she produced them, and even in the moonlight their colours made him smile.

The nights slipped by at the same slow pace as the landscape. He had blisters at every stage: raw skin, small mounds, bloated hills and empty bags. He popped the first one himself, gaining an unnameable pleasure from doing so, but the rest he left alone. They gave him a different kind of pain to his ear, and there was something to be said for their being at the opposite end of his body. Every morning, before going to sleep, he asked her if she would kill him today. Her answer was always the same.

Once he woke to find her going through his things. He opened his mouth to shout at her, then he shut it again. She reached into his bag and brought out his pistol, cradling it in her hands like it might spill. She opened the chamber, and then put it down with great care. The watch and the claw were treated with the same reverence. She raised her eyebrows at the Good Book, and her face pulled in such a way he could almost see the woman she must have been before – and the resemblance to his mother. It was in the eyes and the nose, mostly. She didn't open the book. She didn't open the letters either, just inspected the back of each one.

'They all have something missing,' she said, looking over at him.

He sat up. 'What do you mean?'

'One round left, one book torn out, two letters not here.' She picked up the claw. 'A whole bird.'

'The watch works.'

'A messenger's watch without a messenger.'

'How did you know?' he said.

'I've seen plenty of watches—'

'About the letters. You said two were missing.'

She started putting his things back into the bag. 'His name was George. He didn't like me looking through his bag either, but he decided he'd like a shot in the gut even less – just like your friends back there.'

'They weren't my friends.'

'No, I suppose not.' She dropped the bag at his feet.

The town grew slowly on the horizon. She said it was called Leigh Creek. In the darkness it felt so close, but miles of gently sloping scrub lay before him. At least it was sloping downwards.

She didn't stop. They had been walking for most of the night and there was a weariness settling into his bones. She must have felt it too – after all, she still had bones under all those wrinkles. And she didn't sleep, didn't eat, or drink. He wiped the sweat from his brow and tried not to dwell on the strangeness of Walkin', of his grandma.

The heat gathered in hazes, in every direction except the way they had come. He turned his head too quickly and a dizziness took him. He squatted down, head between his knees and his eyes screwed shut, and took deep breaths. His ear was being difficult, and like most trouble, it was threatening to spread – he could feel it starting in his jaw.

He uncorked the bottle and the fumes conjured dark memories of knives, his pa's boots and burying a man. They would do a good job for Lee; they didn't need Pa for that. It might be better without any words from the Good Book.

'Want me to?' she said.

'I'll manage.' He cupped a hand, ready to rub the foul-smelling stuff into his skin for the little relief it gave. But the bottle was empty. He brought it to his eye, confused as to where the whiskey had gone, and then dropped it. His eye was streaming and stinging and he started cursing.

She laughed. Her wobbling face was echoed in the glass fragments, their edges cutting her cheeks and eyes and nose to pieces.

'Don't you laugh at me, you wet bag o' bones.'

She laughed all the harder.

He picked up the neck of the bottle, which ended in daggers, and squinted at her.

'Don't get sore,' she said. 'You're not the first man to look to the bottom of a bottle and come off worse.'

'"Man"? I thought you wanted the *boy*?' he said.

'Little difference, far as I can tell.'

'Does it take two lives to find such wisdom?' he sneered.

'You know it's not the number, but what you live through.'

He stabbed the bottle into the dirt. She offered him a hand up but he ignored it.

'You need sleep,' she said.

He walked past, one determined step after another towards Leigh Creek, and away from her.

The noise came first: a kind of roar that he took to be the head of the creek, where something small met a larger version of itself and was less than happy about it. But she didn't like it either. She changed course, angling away from where he judged the noise came from. They had picked up a clear trail into the town for the last mile or so, which made the going easier. The flat, wide grooves caused by many wagons were a welcome sight. Now she wanted to dive back into the scrub and punish his blisters.

'I need to refill my water-skin,' he said.

'Crowds are no good.'

The sound almost doubled, bouncing off the scattered buildings on the edge of the town. A crowd large enough to make that kind of noise was large enough to get lost in.

'I need whiskey too. My ear hurts something awful.'

She sighed with her shoulders.

'Whiskey, one meal, and then we leave,' she said. 'It's beyond me why they get so excited. It's only the races.'

4 : 9

The races had brought the whole town out, or so it looked to Ryan. Men, women and children were all packed along the fence that surrounded a large cleared track. Some of the smaller boys and girls rode their fathers' shoulders, sucking at toffee sticks or candied drops, enough for an extra row of teeth. Their sticky fingers made Ryan rub his own hands together.

The crowd was solid around the fence but he caught glimpses of men on coursers, their hats tied on tight. The coursers had numbers painted on their rumps, like they were chapter or verse. Either a race had finished or was yet to start; no one was in much of a hurry. A few paces or so back the crowd thinned enough to walk through. Here were the children who had spilled treats on best dresses and their scolding mothers, together with those hunting for a better view, walking on tiptoes, and men in clear need of a piss. The children grew wide-eyed at the sight of the Drowned Woman, staring openly at her, and then at him. She held him by the arm as they made their way, her grip none too gentle. One man, his mind and walk preoccupied with the pressing of water, bumped into her, but his curse died on his lips and he all but ran in the opposite direction.

Ryan stood straighter, puffing out his chest. He wished he had a holster for his pistol. He tried to shrug his way free of her, to walk her equal, but he might as well have pushed over one of the two-storey buildings that overlooked the track. Men in suits and women with laced dresses stood on balconies, every one with a handkerchief to their face. The air was admittedly heavy with the sweetness of sweat and the wallowing aroma of courser shit. It was the smell of things, just on a grander scale. While the stench didn't bother him, he did find it difficult to know where to look. The crowd milled in a dazzling array of arms and legs and different-coloured hair, and it made him feel tired. The pounding of his ear wasn't getting any better.

At least they had some room. Grandma was given a wide berth. Perhaps there weren't many Walkin' in Leigh Creek? Or they didn't, as a rule, attend the races? All the faces he saw – before looking started to hurt his head – and none of them lacked for life.

'Not many of your kind here,' Ryan said.

'No.'

'These people are scared of you.'

'Not all Walkin' look like me, and not all of them openly carry pistols,' she said.

'Is it like this in every town?'

'Lots of towns out there, and each one is different. But mostly people are scared.'

They passed a line of men waiting outside one of the smaller buildings. They didn't look too comfortable. Ryan planted his feet as firmly as he could. 'I need to piss,' he said.

She weighed this up, glancing at the line and then back at him.

'Then piss. Nothing I haven't seen.'

'But all these people—'

'You're making this difficult,' she said.

'I *need* to go.'

She marched him to the back of the line, huffing and tutting at its slow progression, and glaring whenever a man made the mistake of catching her eye. When they finally reached the front, there was a large open doorway. Inside it looked like a lot of outhouses had been confiscated from homes and then lined up together to form a square. He stopped at the door.

'You can't come in,' he said.

'Nonsense.' She tried to pull him forward.

Ryan went as limp as he could. 'This is boys only.'

'He's right,' the man behind said. 'There's women's privies on the far side of the eating-house.'

She turned and jammed a pistol in the man's gut.

'Does it look like I need to piss?' she said.

The man opened his mouth and was cut off by the click of the hammer. Ryan would have liked to hear his quip about the Drowned Woman having plenty of water to pass.

327

'I'll be here,' she said to Ryan. 'Do *not* keep me waiting.'

The next outhouse free happened to be near one of the corners. The urge to look back at her made the hair on his neck stand up, but he knew she was watching. He closed the outhouse door.

There was a ripe blend of piss and shit. A swarm of specks were either angry or excited by his arrival, and he flailed wildly at them. 'Please, please, please,' he whispered.

He turned slowly and found a gap at the top of the rear wall, as he'd hoped: a gap that was supposed to let the smell out. A gap he could fit through.

The wooden bench was slick with the obvious. How a man could miss a hole that big was beyond his reckoning. He slipped, but managed to catch himself and pulled himself up. There was some space between the outhouse and the building and he fell into it.

'What the—?' someone in another outhouse said.

Ryan stayed on the ground. He'd expected a floor, and instead it was dirt beneath him: dirt that felt like it had been raining. He quickly turned his face away. He might have tasted it, but it was difficult to tell.

Using the wall to push himself upright, he saw daylight at either end and headed towards the furthest from him – and from *her*. He spilled out into the light, coughing and spluttering.

'And now you smell.'

He squinted against the sun. At least she wasn't laughing.

He tried to brush off the muck from his trousers and that just spread it around.

She grabbed his arm again.

'Help!' It just came out. He was as shocked as her. 'Help! Someone help me,' he screamed.

She took hold of his shirt and yanked him up onto his toes. 'You really want to do this?' she said.

'Help! I don't know this person.' That turned one or two heads.

'You want to get someone shot?'

'Help – please help me!'

'The kind of person who helps a stranger?'

'You wouldn't have to shoot them,' he said. He looked into her eyes – as wooden and dry as the one on the cord: Grandpa's eye. She would kill as many as she had to, and he didn't understand why.

A small group of men were starting towards him. They weren't even carrying pistols.

He hugged her and she let go of his shirt and patted him on the head.

The closest man scratched his beard, and then he and his friends moved off.

Back with the crowds they found a shack hawking liquor. Bodies were four-deep in front of the counter. Those working it were on some kind of raised platform, being head and shoulders above the rest, and frantic. As his grandma moved among the men, a number of them suddenly weren't so thirsty. Ryan followed in her wake.

One of the younger tenders was wiping the bar with a cloth.

'What'll it be?' he said.

'Whiskey,' Grandma said.

He looked up from his cleaning. His mouth dropped open and stayed there. An older man with a stained apron eased him aside.

'We don't serve many of your kind.'

'Don't or *won't*?'

He raised his hands. 'No need for that. Whiskey, you said?' He brought out a small glass from beneath the counter.

'The bottle.'

'We don't do bottles.'

Grandma pulled out a pistol. The heavy clunk it made on the bar cut through all manner of conversations. Those nearby shuffled backwards.

'The bottle.'

'We don't sell them that way. I wouldn't know how much to charge, even.' The man kept rubbing his hands on his apron.

'You know how much you charge for a glass.'

The man nodded, though it wasn't a question.

'And I'm sure you know, to the exact number, how many glasses you get out of the bottle?'

A lot of heads turned to the tender.

'I could make a good guess.'

'Could you,' Grandma said flatly.

He named a price. She paid it. And then she passed the bottle to Ryan.

'Hey!' the tender said, but they were already moving away. He didn't come after them.

Ryan uncorked the bottle. The smell singed his nostrils. He took a slug and felt its warmth seep through him. She let him wander without her guiding hand. There was an understanding that she was watching, and he wouldn't get away if he tried. If he noticed a gap between the press of bodies or a spot to slip behind a building, the feel of his damp trousers against his thighs was a reminder that he had little hope. She would find him, as she had found his pa.

He turned his attention to the task of forgetting. After three gulps he forgot the burning on the side of his head. Another two and there was only the fence and the coursers beyond. He worked his way through the crowd, leaned on one of the posts and raised his bottle to salute the nearest rider. Number one. Or seven. The number stretched and squirmed as the animal sauntered this way and that. Ryan jeered and booed, making his dissatisfaction clear; why weren't they racing?

Those around him started clapping and he clapped too. The coursers were lining up now, not far from him, and the applause became silence. His breathing was too loud – he would spook the coursers. He put a finger to his lips and showed the man next to him. But the man was too intent on the line of racers. Ryan felt a hand on his shoulder. Only one hand could be that cold in the heat of the day.

A shot was fired and then they were off. The thunder of the coursers made his bones shake. They were gone in a matter of moments, leaving his heart beating in time with their gallop. He was cheering with the rest of the crowd. He had to squint to follow the riders' progress as they became small and appeared to slow down, then they came past once more, now following one after the other. He'd galloped on a courser before – he knew what it was like to feel the powerful animal underneath and the rush of wind against his face – but not with people watching. He cheered them until his throat was hoarse. He struggled to count the times they went by – and then it stopped. The winner was pulling up to a walk and raising his hands in triumph. People ducked beneath the fence and rushed to join him and Ryan made to go too, to congratulate the man who looked like a giant with his hat tied around his neck, but the hand stopped him.

'There's been a shadow over me, all my years. A different person sometimes, but always someone,' he said.

'You need to eat,' she said.

By now there was a large crowd around the winner. The other riders had to pull to the side to avoid them. Ryan got a good look at their faces, at their sallow disappointment. He followed her to the eating-house.

It was a two-storey building with a wide front. When they entered, a man carrying more bags than any man would need brushed past them. His family came down the stairs not long after. The mother took one look at Grandma and hurried after her husband. The little girl was less afraid; she stared at him blankly. She had pretty curls. He went to tell her so, but she was gone. He blinked. He was standing alone in the entrance-way.

'You need a bath,' his grandma said, leading him past the stairs and down a corridor.

The room was big, with eight bathtubs sitting empty. A girl was pouring water into a ninth, the closest. She dipped a hand in, testing the water, and seemed satisfied.

Grandma coughed and the girl stared at them both, no doubt wondering which was the least likely occupant of a bathing room in an eating-house. He didn't know himself.

'It's for you?' the girl said to the Walkin', figuring age important enough to defy all logic.

'Just get out,' Grandma said.

The girl didn't need telling twice.

'You could be nicer to people,' Ryan said when they were alone.

'I could.'

He left his clothes in a heap and stepped tentatively into the hot water.

'Hurry up,' she said.

'I'm just getting used to it.'

She pulled up a stool and took a hold of a bar of soap.

'Lean forward.'

'Why?'

'Just do it!'

She scrubbed at his back something vicious and he wriggled to be clear of her hard hands, but she followed.

'Your ma squirmed just the same. Helped her none too.'

'You're enjoying this,' Ryan said, throwing his shoulders from side to side. There was no escape, until he thought it through and simply sat back in the bath.

She moved her hand quick enough, and dropped the soap in his lap. She tipped his head to one side.

'Your ear's looking better; won't be the end of you at any rate,' she said.

'I'll scratch it from the list of things trying to kill me.'

She knelt by the bath so her eyes were level with his. 'That a long list?'

'Long enough.'

'I'll get you some clothes.'

Ryan glanced across at the empty baths. 'Could you leave the door open? Just a little?'

Grandma was sitting at a table for two, looking at him. He scratched at his shirt and joined her.

'Whoever this shirt belonged to, he slept with woollies, or danced with them maybe,' Ryan said.

'He had that look to him.'

There was a plate of food on the table: meat in a gravy, potatoes, something green – more than Ryan could ever eat. He felt sick with hunger. He barely had his backside on the seat before he had the fork halfway to his mouth. The food was almost hot, and tasted glorious.

Between mouthfuls he said, 'You scare people.' He didn't just mean the bath girl. The people at the other tables were glancing her way, some clearly rushing their meals.

'Not much I can do about that.' Her side of the table was bare.

'Maybe if you weren't so mean,' he said.

She laughed, and that really upset a couple two tables over. They left in such a hurry the woman forgot her bag. It had shiny handles but wasn't a sensible size – she'd fit little more than the Good Book in there. He had his own bag in his lap; that way he wouldn't leave it behind.

'Are we going to live in Leigh Creek?' he said.

'Would you like that?'

'I like the races.'

'No,' she said, 'Leigh Creek is no place for us.'

He finished chewing. 'Where is?'

'You'll see. It's not far.'

'You keep saying that.'

'It keeps being true,' she said.

'My feet hurt.'

He ate until he thought he might burst. He licked the gravy from the plate, though there were still some greens left, which tumbled to the floor. Best place for them. He'd also cut off the bits of fat; Chunk would like them. He glanced around for the ruft, then he put the plate back on the table.

'What did he say?'

'Who?' she said.

'Pa. What did he say?'

'He said, "It was the boy".'

'What was?'

'You tell me,' she said.

'And then you shot him so he wouldn't come back.'

'The world is a better place without him.'

'That's what she wanted, I think. A better place,' he said.

'Your ma?'

'She begged me.'

'Begged you to do *what*?'

'I still have candied drops in my bag. I'd like a candied drop.' He reached into his bag, first finding the Good Book and the letters, and then Ma's pistol. The handle felt cool against his palms.

'She couldn't do it,' he said. 'She'd ruined her hands the first time.'

'So you helped her?'

'That's what she wanted.'

She was looking right at him. Waiting. This is what *she* wanted.

He raised the pistol, but the barrel clipped the edge of the table. He pulled the trigger in a hurry and the plate shattered. In the middle of the jagged pieces, the round was embedded in the table.

She didn't smile, or laugh, or shout at him.

'When I found her like that, her wrists a mess, I cursed my slow feet and wished a courser would take me. She might have done the cutting, but there were others to blame. Callum. You.'

She drew her pistol.

'You going to kill me today, Grandma?'

'I wanted to hear you say it.'
'You just had to ask,' Ryan said.
'She was my little girl.'
'Higher, Grandma.'

4 : 10

With their own hands compassionate women
have cooked their own children,
who became their food
when my people were destroyed.

Lamentations

EPILOGUE

The mountains looked dark, both when he saw them from afar and when he was walking among them, but really, it was the trees. Their dark needles – not leaves, she corrected him – were so small but so many. They were like hairs on his head: alone, barely visible, in great numbers, a covering. He liked the feel of them, rubbing needles between his fingers. Those he crushed made a heavy, damp smell that stayed under his nails for a good many hours. He raised a hand to his nose often. He even tried to lick his fingers and this gave him nothing. He sighed.

'Are you coming?' she said.

'What's the rush?'

He breathed in and held the air for minutes. He plugged the hole in his chest with a hand and breathed out through his nose, making the most of the feeling.

'I see why they choose to live here.'

'I don't,' she said.

'You'd choose the scrubland over this? The dust and grit?'

'I like to see my horizons.'

This he could understand. Even on the cleared stone path the trees dominated every direction. Looking up, there was only a strip of blue sky. The clouds crept up on you. He re-joined the path, marvelling again at its clean, pale edge. The pine needles must have slipped straight off the smooth surface, though he hadn't seen it actually happen. The tree roots avoided it too, and many could be seen turning back on themselves. Whatever stone the path was made of, it was seamless, as if it was one piece that stretched for miles. He didn't think that possible. On their first day on the path he kept an eye out for a joint. By day three he gave up.

'What do you think it's made of?' he said.

'Why would I know what it's made of?'

'But you're sure it leads to Black Mountain?'

'No.'

'Then where *does* it lead?'

'You ask too many questions.'

'And you answer too few.'

When he had opened his eyes in the dark eating-house he said, 'Why the meal?' He blinked to let his eyes adjust and get rid of the feeling they were covered in sand. But the feeling wouldn't go. They were sitting alone.

She had her arms crossed. 'I know what it's like to start the Walk on an empty stomach,' she said.

He looked down at his stained shirt. There was a round from her pistol inside him. He stretched and when he raised his arms it snagged. He had poked around since then, but couldn't find it. She refused to help.

At nightfall on the fifth day there was someone on the path. They both stopped, startled. It was as if the parting rays of the sun had deposited this person on the rise ahead.

Grandma had a pistol in her hand.

'That's your answer to everything,' he said. She didn't put it away, even when they drew close.

'Hello, Ryan. Hello, Sarah.'

He looked at this woman wreathed in moonlight, wondering if he knew her.

'Lydia?' Grandma said.

The woman smiled. 'You remember.'

She had skin the colour of running water.

'Thomas said it would be you. He said you would deny us.'

'He was wrong.' Lydia came forward and brushed her hand against Ryan's cheek. 'After all these years, is this how you wanted it to end, Sarah?'

Grandma looked at him. 'No. But what could I do?'

'Nothing.'

'I tried.'

'You did,' Lydia said.

'I was too late.'

'You were.' Lydia turned to her. 'Was vengeance worth it?'

'In a way.'

'But you let Ryan begin the Walk.'

'He's all I have left,' Grandma said.

'You didn't forgive, but I know how sorry you are – it's all over you.'

'For everything.'

'Then find rest here.' Lydia stepped aside.

They walked up the rise. Below, a huge valley stretched out where stars had fallen to the ground.

Grandma held out her hand. He took it.

The End.